THE
LASCAUX PRIZE
2015

THE
LASCAUX PRIZE
2015

edited by
Camille Griep
Stephen Parrish
Wendy Russ

ISBN 10: 0-9851666-4-9
ISBN 13: 978-0-9851666-4-9

Cover design by Wendy Russ.
Watercolors by Albrecht Dürer: "Das große Rasenstück" (1503) and "Hirschkäfer" (1505).

Lascaux Books
www.lascauxbooks.com

Contents

2015 Short Story Winner
The Imminence of Flight, by *Chris Connolly* 1

2015 Short Story Finalists
Cancer (& Other Unforgivable Curses),
by *Michelle Collins Anderson* 19
Campaigning, by *Janna Brooke Cohen* 43
Linda Peterson Sounds Like a Reasonable Name,
by *Jennifer Dupree* 56
Rebirth of the Big Top, by *Jen Fawkes* 68
Satan Takes 12 Steps, by *Perry Glasser* 83
Her Mother's Ghost, by *Lesley Howard* 96
Thy Neighbor as Thyself, by *Judith Lavinsky* 121
Broken. Everything. by *R. Daniel Lester* 148
Cigarettes and Birdhouses, by *Jenna Loceff* 157
Crazy Talk, by *Louise Marburg* 160
The Amazing Adventures of Hannah O'Hare,
by *Karen McIntyre* 176
Gathering Moss, by *Jason Pollard* 192
Noblesse Oblige, by *Karen Recht* 201
The Edible and the Beauteous and the Dead,
by *Anneliese Schultz* 214
We're Standing on a Shallow Sea, by *Sheila Thorne* 224
The Cartographers, by *Alexander Weinstein* 241

2015 Poetry Winner
    Sefeed, by *Mathew Javidi* 257

2015 Poetry Finalists
    User, by *Heather Altfeld* 259
    God Bless, by *C. Wade Bentley* 262
    Manifest, by *Kierstin Bridger* 263
    Viewing *Guernica* in Madrid, by *Susan Cohen* 265
    My Father Asks for One Last Thing, by *James Crews* 267
    Hermes in Hades, by *Elizabeth Crowell* 269
    Chetwynd Morning, by *Jesse Mavro Diamond* 271
    What I Mean by Beauty, by *Doris Ferleger* 273
    Line of Scrimmage, by *Alexis Finc* 275
    They call all experience of the senses mystic,
    when the experience is considered, by *Kim Garcia* 277
    one sentence on the old house, by *Megan Gilmore* 279
    Karaoke Night at the Asylum, by *Jennifer Givhan* 280
    Boarding Up, by *Alex Greenberg* 282
    Crisis Hotline, by *Christina Hammerton* 283
    The Maximum Effective Range, by *Matt Hohner* 285
    Living Room, by *Andrea Hollander* 287
    You Are Not Here, by *David Jauss* 289
    The Drift, by *Abriana Jetté* 291
    The Traveling Voice, by *Jeffrey Kingman* 293
    By the River Bank's Edge, by *Carol Munn* 295
    The Night Before, by *Barry North* 297
    Living Too Long, by *David Sloan* 299
    Each Photograph That You Take of Me,
    by *Colby Cedar Smith* 301
    The Dreams of Daughters,
    by *Elizabeth Harmon Threatt* 303

Editor's Choice Awards:

Fiction

Superman, by *Emile DeWeaver*..305
Down in the Station, by *Seth Sawyers*..............................308

Poetry

Dark Rum & Tonic, by *Molly Fisk*.....................................316
How to Pay Respects to a Serial Killer,
by *Robert S. King*..318

Essays

Sunday, by *Lee Martin*..320
Things I Did Not Learn From Dead White
Male Authors, by *Jennifer Zobair* 323

Contributors.. 331

for Philip Levine, poet, 1928-2015

Some things
you know all your life. They are so simple and true
they must be said without elegance, meter and rhyme,
they must be laid on the table beside the salt shaker,
the glass of water, the absence of light gathering
in the shadows of picture frames, they must be
naked and alone, they must stand for themselves.

—*The Simple Truth*, Kopf, 1994

Introduction

Few people are aware of the effort that goes into selecting contest winners and finalists or deciding what does and doesn't make it into an anthology. The process is anything but casual. From the contestant's perspective, she submits a story, poem, or essay, it appears in a book. She has little idea how much the judges have talked about her behind her back. To the writers appearing in this volume: your ears should most certainly be burning.

We read hundreds of shorts stories and thousands of poems for the *2015 Lascaux Prize Anthology*. At times the experience was admittedly tedious. Then something would come along that made us sit upright. We discussed these. We debated them. Ultimately we agreed on the pieces that would go into the book, and on those that would win the $1000 prizes. It was an exhausting job, but we weren't complaining. There was fulfillment to be had at the end: telling hardworking poets and writers their work paid off, they came out on top.

To the readers who have found their way here: read slowly. We chose the enclosed stories, poems, and essays not for their quick entertainment value, rather for the demands they make, the engagement required to appreciate them. The writer-reader relationship is a two-way street. Our purpose is the same as every editor's: to find quality writing, to acknowledge it, to bring it to light.

Camille Griep
Stephen Parrish
Wendy Russ

The Imminence of Flight

by Chris Connolly

From the kitchen, where we've been talking about Greece and sunshine for the past hour, searching for flights and browsing indulgently through photos of villas and hotels, we hear the boy's return. We listen to the rattle and clunk of the turning lock, the unlubricated screech of the front door and the dull thud of schoolbag on carpet, followed by his adolescent clomping through the house like some sort of pre-neolithic, booted simian.

I have been missing this simple thing, this dependable confluence of sounds. Now that I am around to hear it, it becomes more intriguing each time; I am beginning to get a sense of the things I don't know exist, that do.

"Hi, Sweetheart," his mother calls.

She is cradling a giant mug of coffee in both hands, as if for warmth, sitting beside me at the table, our upcoming holiday plans immediately relegated by the boy's return, overridden by maternal concerns. Mark is just fifteen and, naturally, the sun around which his mother orbits. In this respect I am like the moon.

I watch June as she watches the empty doorway of the kitchen, waiting. The look I see is one of patience, devotion, and vague concern, the concerned aspect falling away once Mark wanders in and a visual assessment of his well-being can be made. She smiles then and nods almost imperceptibly, as if part of her was expecting a limb to be missing, or his face to have changed. He makes no eye contact as he moves purposefully towards a cupboard and reaches inside.

"How was school?" she asks.

"Fine," he manages, but barely, the utterance just enough past guttural to be considered a word. "Any mass shootings?" I say, and my question-cum-joke goes either ignored or unnoticed by Mark, receiving only the faintest of eye-rolls from his mother.

This type of humour is of a kind which, until recently, would have produced a guffaw from the boy. Or at least a faux-exasperated eye-roll like his mother's. But even my best material these days seems to go unacknowledged. Lately my relationship with Mark, which has always been congenial and pally, and often delightfully conspiratorial, has seemed strained—somehow lessened or fractured or dulled. I sense a brooding behind his eyes when he looks at me, or when he deliberately doesn't.

"You're thinking too much, getting hung up on things," his mother says when I mention this in the intimate darkness of our bedroom, the location of our most serious and confiding moments. (It amazes me, this very particular blackness, its allowance of an openness not quite possible by light, eye to eye.) And she is probably right. Currently I have too much time on my hands, and far more of this time than I would like—or than I've been told is healthy—is spent considering things which shouldn't be considered so intensely, such as my step-son's take-it-or-leave-it attitude regarding Yours Truly this past while, and how long it might last or what it might mean. I think of other things too, like global social unrest and climate change and general extinction. I try not to take it personally.

"He's just at that age," his mother says, and I try to remember how it felt to be fifteen. But I find my recollections involve only people or places, and not any corresponding emotions. My memories all seem to be nouns, when what I need are adjectives. If this has always been the case I am only noticing it now.

But the simple sound of June's voice is always soothing, and as a result I am not yet at the stage of losing sleep. In truth I have lately been sleeping soundly and easily, which is surprising given the typically inactive nature of my days—and the more active nature of my anxieties—since I stopped going to work.

My job merits only the barest of descriptions. Enough to say that it provides satisfactory and reliably incremental remuneration, but little in the way of emotional or moral nourishment. Whether I am simply bored with my work or searching for the aforementioned nourishment is a good question. In any case, I have neither escaped the former nor achieved the latter, though it is still early days and I have high hopes, vague as they are. And I have time, too. My job is there when I choose to go back, they tell me. The term used was "non-specific temporary sabbatical," which is fine with me. I'll be missed, they insist, but they'll manage. Of this I have no doubt.

The boy hunches himself over a bowl of cereal, his entire body involved in the act of devouring it as quickly and completely as possible. His mother and I watch him eat. It is an impressive thing to witness, culminating in a two-handed raising of the bowl almost above his head, the dregs poured straight down his throat in one last go. It reminds me of a bird feeding its chick, or a priest drinking from a chalice. The act is both animal and holy.

"Make sure you get all of it," I say, and he grunts as he swallows.

*

A man with a clipboard and an agreeable face tries to sign me up to a new electricity provider. Standing at the threshold of my house in my dressing-gown, listening to his spiel (nodding where appropriate, looking interested and occasionally raising an eyebrow) I am conscious of the fact that we are both wasting each other's time, but that he doesn't yet understand this. The man becomes more enthusiastic the longer I let him continue. I don't do so to be cruel but because these late-morning hours—when June is at work and Mark in school— are dull and empty times. The complete stillness of the house is something I remain unaccustomed to, and it is strangely difficult to relax within. Sitting alone sometimes in this stillness I feel like I am outside my own body, like I am watching a tiny and compressed version of myself from a position in the sky or in space, flattened to a mere dot on the landscape.

It strikes me that in allowing the man to go on I am behaving like one of those poor souls with nothing better to do. When finally he finishes and I tell him that I'm sorry, but I don't live in this house or know anything of the homeowner's electricity needs, he looks confused for a moment, and then disappointed. That light in his eyes visibly dims: Why would I let him go on like that?

I apologise again, and I mean it. Why I told him I wasn't the homeowner is another good question.

I have started telling little lies. Mostly the kind of lies which have no real effect on anything, and serve no real purpose. This is something I didn't do before, and it is now something I don't set out to do but find myself doing nonetheless. Not all that often, but sometimes. There is no advance warning. And it is another of the things I have lately been wondering about: What might it mean?

*

This trip to Greece is June's idea, of course.

I was expecting a more jaded response to news of my non-specific temporary sabbatical, but "Perfect" was the first thing she said to me, with no hint of sarcasm. For some time now I have been supplying worthy and bottomless excuses with regards to a holiday. The idea of it—of flying, of heat, of new surroundings, of enforced relaxation—produces an ominous sensation in me that is as strong as it is baseless. But I now have no excuses left, and am attempting a positive outlook: June is all excitement, and for that alone it is worth it.

Mark is due to stay with his father—his biological one—while we're away. I have an absurd recurring vision of father and son spending two weeks' worth of evenings reclining in fireside armchairs, engaged in heated philosophical debate, sharing their deepest feelings and moral centres, smoking cigars and sipping expensive brandy like two old men. I am aware that this vision is obviously wide of the mark (and even more baseless than my trip-related disquiet) but still it is there in my mind with all the other things, drifting around like malevolent icebergs.

Henry is, probably, the type of man I would end up watching sports or drinking a beer with if it wasn't for our shared situation. As it is we act meek and apologetic, and are almost spookily accommodating of each other. We have an unspoken understanding about things—about the boy, and about what's best for him when it comes to us. There is such a genuine lack of animosity that it is June who seems most uncomfortable on those occasions we are all in the same room, when really it should be me or he that feels awkward and threatened; after all, our many similarities are not necessarily simple or coincidental ones. As parents—and husbands—I suspect we have a lot in common.

What these similarities might or might not mean is a question I am familiar with, but thinking about it is not the answer.

*

At the supermarket I see a young mother gently weeping in the cereal aisle. Her baby watches her curiously, possibly stumped by this reversal of roles, or possibly too young—and too overloaded by the screaming rainbows of packaging and general sensory excess—to even understand. I look at her for just a second. A stranger's sadness could mean anything. Maybe the father has left them, or died; or maybe she is simply having one of those days, and cereal reminds her of the unfairness of the world, and of motherhood. I turn and walk the other way, leaving her to it.

I spend much longer than I need to in the baked goods section. I stand staring at a wall of bread, basking in the smell. If oxygen smelled like this it would be okay with me. I stay standing there, closing my eyes until I sense someone nearby and, upon opening them again, see a security guard watching me. I smile guiltily and move on.

There are eighteen different types of mustard here, an entire aisle of vari-plyed and bewildering toilet-paper, enough cheese to pave a street; there are deals and discounts and quagmires of nutritional information. Maybe the sheer range of choice is the cause of the woman's tears—I could understand that. Food shopping is one of the tasks I have volunteered for, now that I have time on my hands. June appreciates the sentiment, but we are both silently aware of my lack of supermarket aptitude. I don't know how she navigates it all so easily. "Just stick to the list," she says, but there is nothing simple about this place.

June works four mornings a week. After she finishes each day, and before the boy arrives home from school, she has a little window of time that I never thought to ask about before. She shops, she tidies, she reads; she gets nails done, meets friends for lunch, goes to yoga, has a nap. Now that I am home during this window I find myself eagerly awaiting a detailed recounting of what, on any given day, she has been doing. She humours my odd enthusiasm with confused eyes.

I am fascinated by these new things I am learning, this new time I am discovering, this new universe I didn't know existed. It is thrilling and monotonous at the same time.

And I find myself fascinated, too, by the boy's homecoming each day, those sounds he makes, the same sounds being made in countless other homes at almost exactly the same time—yet still original somehow, hums and echoes solely his own. But I worry I am intruding on something, that maybe this particular time of the day—which until a month or so ago I was absent from—is a sacred stint of bonding between mother and son, one now somehow altered by the mere fact of my presence. Perhaps this has something to do with the boy's gloominess, or perhaps not.

At the checkout I see the woman with the baby again. There are ancient people here, hunched and hawk-eyed, shrunken; there are bored employees filling bags and mopping spills; there are barcode scanners beeping and light so unnatural it attacks the eyes.

No one else is crying.

*

The air in our kitchen is dense with scents of breakfast. In my dressing-gown I feel underdressed. June watches Mark ingest several slices of toast with a minimum of chewing. I watch mother and son and feel both comforted and anxious. Lately, as I watch over them at breakfast, or while I drive the boy to school, or as I search for the correct type of detergent or yoghurt in the supermarket, a thought has been infiltrating my thinking: What if they both died? What then?

It goes without saying that the answer is not even approachable, not something I could even begin to imagine. But the question itself is the problem: Why would I think such a thing?

My head is in my hands, fingers applying pressure to my lidded eyeballs. I hear a desperate sigh that could only be the result of—or precursor to—some terrible psychic catastrophe, and when I look up I see two sets of eyes staring back at me, and realise the sigh was my own.

"Are you okay?" says June.

The boy, with a piece of toast frozen now midway between plate and palate, looks at me with a kind of disbelief. Or suspicion. Or maybe just curiosity. His face has become difficult to read.

"I'm fine," I say, displaying my artificial smile, attempting an airy and light-filled nonchalance.

"Just sleepy," I say, though I am wide awake.

*

Cars are places to find things out, to discuss and divulge, to share. There is no escape route, no television to distract or bedroom door to hide behind: We must engage.

"Any lady friends on the scene?"

His response is more a brief rumble of vocal cords which implies the negative, or the *none-of-your-business.*

"Huh?" he says.

These short lifts to school, or to friends' houses, or to other adolescent engagements, have traditionally been opportunities for me to connect with the boy, to subtly inquire about new goings-on in his hectic life, or about particularities of the modern teenage zeitgeist. Opportunities for him to tell me things he might not tell in the presence of his mother, and opportunities for me to dispense advice—solicited or not—on a vast array of topics (from girls, to smoking, to European history) which may or may not be of any use to him, but which at least make me feel more active as a parent, and make him feel (I hope) as important to me as he truly is.

Because I worry that Mark, as he continues his voyage towards adulthood, will begin to question my legitimacy: as parent, as husband of his mother. I worry that he might look at me some day and think: *Who is this man, and what is he doing in my life?* I worry that his mother might do the same.

I am paranoid, I know, but these are the things I think about. The icebergs.

He fiddles with the radio dials, flicking through a hundred stations before settling on one and turning the volume up several notches too loud. I take it he is not amenable to further discourse. From the speakers comes a man's strained, breaking voice, full of very weighty, undoubtedly contrived emotion.

Though it pains me to conform to the cliché, I find most modern music indecipherable and devoid of any real meaning. Whatever happened to *real* music? The Stones, The Beatles, The Clash...

When did it all go wrong?

*

June arrives home. I am recumbent, stagnant on the sofa. I listen to the noise. The rattle and clunk, the screech, the setting-down of handbag on table, the contented sigh. Hers are delicate sounds, the breeze to the boy's squall.

My day so far has consisted of little more than a lethargic (and unsuccessful) crossword attempt. The final clue eludes me.

"Busy day I see," she says, not unkindly, and joins me on the sofa.

"Tumultuous," I say, and I am only half joking.

We lie there together in warm silence for several minutes. Her breaths become deep and relaxed, and my own breathing syncs to hers. There is a weightless comfort in these minutes unlike any other.

June, eventually, raises herself from the sofa, kissing me lightly on the top of my head. "Augur," she shouts over her shoulder as she makes her way to the bathroom. "To divine or predict. Six across, five letters."

My eyes fall to the coffee table where the newspaper is spread, butchered by pencil lead.

"Ah," I say.

Beside the crossword lies her phone. Without thinking I find myself picking up the device and scrolling through call histories and text messages.

I feign a sort of indifference to myself, as if I am just passing time, as if I might as easily be flicking through a magazine about gardening, or motor boats. I have never done this before—it has never occurred to me. I don't know why I am doing it now, or what my doing it signifies. I stop myself.

What am I doing?

*

When he was just a little younger, Mark would arrive home from visits to Henry with excited tales of what they did and where they went, brimming always with new wondrous factoids about the world, the universe, people: birds are dinosaurs; two thirds of people have never seen snow; dung beetles navigate by the Milky Way; humans are 1cm taller in the morning than in the evening. Each new fact punctuated by a triumphant: "Did you know that?"

"Surely not," I would say each time, and he would beam and say, "Yep."

Henry is a good man, a good father, responsible but fun, and as disjointed family units go the boy has a solid and loving set-up, from all angles. We are highly functional, as a sum if not individually.

But now the boy stays largely silent about his bi-monthly weekends and once-weekly evenings with his father. In truth he says little at all about anything anymore—to me, at least. I am lately resigned to finding things out via his mother. Things about school, about Henry, about the universe.

"He's just at that age," she keeps saying. And if June isn't worried, that should be enough. But my thinking has become somehow deeper and more sensitive this past while. The inner workings of my mind are at times frenzied and inescapable, and at other times insurmountably inert. Each insignificant occurrence seems important. Omens abound. Every nothing seems like something.

"How are you feeling," she keeps saying too, and it is another good question; the simplest are always the hardest, and can only be avoided so long. She says it cautiously, half-concerned and half-casual.

"Fine," I reply each time, hoping my eyes don't betray my smile. It feels alien, this new rictus of mine. It feels other. It brings to mind the kind of derelict expressions sometimes seen on the faces of luckless souls recovering from skiing accidents, or high-speed car-crashes.

Things have turned strange.

*

Sun will fix me. My anxieties will loosen in the heat. I will relax and have a wonderful time with my wife, whom I adore. Everything else will recede, and in this way I will recover my previous unburdened self.

This is the wisdom, and it makes sense.

June cajoles me when my inner reluctance about this holiday—about doing something rather than nothing—overwhelms my attempts at optimism. We replay the same little dialogues over and over.

Q. Can we afford it, now that my income has been temporarily sabbaticalised? Is the timing right?

Q. What about the boy, shouldn't he come too? Two weeks is a long time. He hasn't been himself lately.

Q. Do you still love me?

She rolls her eyes at this last question like it's the stupidest I've ever asked: Of course she does.

She is incredibly patient, and for that—along with everything else—I love her more than I can say.

*

We are idling at a red light. The erratic vibrations of the car (there is some new thing wrong with my engine) make the loose change in the cup-holder jangle and rattle. The sound is hypnotically irritating. The light seems to be stuck on red.

Apropos of nothing the boy turns to me and says: "Did you get fired?"

There is a note of defiance in his tone. His eyes search my face, as if the true answer is more likely to be found there than in any verbal reply. The boy is smart and gets only smarter; that he is not yet at the stage of knowing his own intelligence is sublimely endearing. This is the first time he has mentioned my employment situation in my presence. It is, in fact, the first direct question he has asked me in longer than I like to think about.

"No, of course not," I say, feigning minor shock at the notion, glad that he is at least making conversation, but saddened by the nature of it.

He shrugs and stares out his window. Surely he has asked his mother this same thing, and surely she has given him the same answer I am about to.

"I'm just taking a break. What's called a temporary sabbatical. My job is absolutely still my job."

I say this last bit a little too forcefully, or maybe not forcefully enough—it's difficult to know what tone I should aim for. I wonder what Henry might say if he were in this position (though I have a sense he never would be) and aim for that. This is something I do from time to time, when it comes to dealing with Mark. Partly because I think there should be consistency across the board when it comes to how the men in his life (his two dads, in essence) behave around and towards him; also partly because I know Henry is a good, practical person, and I imagine he more often than not gets this kind of thing right; and partly (possibly mostly, especially lately) because I often feel like I have no idea what it is that I'm doing, or what I'm supposed to do.

The light turns green, finally, and I stall the engine. In response to the unnecessary honking of a horn I emit a variety of curse words, and salute the honker with a ubiquitous digital gesture. It is a while since I have used my fingers in such a way.

We drive on in that particular kind of silence only a traffic-related over-reaction can produce. After a while I say: "You shouldn't ever curse. It makes people think less of you."

I hope this isn't really true; the boy says nothing.

*

I tell the doctor I feel like a new man. Yes, the medication seems to be doing the trick. No, I haven't noticed any side-effects. I tell him I am energised by my recent break from work, and am looking forward to getting right back to it after the holiday, which I am also tremendously excited about. I tell him (as I have told him each week for more than a month now) that the incident in work was just a blip, an aberration, some sort of cosmic righting of the scales. A mountain of a molehill—and doesn't everyone get overwhelmed sometimes? The word I use repeatedly is "emotional." Whether he believes me or not is hard to say, and probably it doesn't matter.

I tell him it has all been a blessing in disguise, this recent turbulence—just what the doctor ordered. I tell him about the previously unknown tranquility of an empty house. I tell him about the supermarket, the smell of baking bread. I describe to him as best I can the joy to be found in the sounds of a child returning home from school.

I don't mention the sense of doom I sometimes feel alone at home, or the neon confusion of the supermarket, or the crying. I don't mention the persistent invasiveness of certain

14

icy thoughts. The doctor looks at me for a long time—his gaze could mean anything. It is an impressive countenance, and I wonder how many years of practice went into getting it just right. It is a stare loaded with important information—but information which it simultaneously conceals. A stare that knows things its recipient does not.

The tablets remain in their packaging, in the glove-box of my car. *Stashed* is the correct word for them, though I can feel their presence, their weight, the same way the presence of an unasked question can sometimes be felt, or a long-held secret; the tablets will stay there until I start taking them, or until long after I don't. The doctor talks about stress, about triggers. "It sounds like things are improving," he says eventually. "But it's important to keep on top of these things. Important you stick with the medication, okay? Let's meet again on Tuesday."

I ask him about going back to work, and he stares at me again, then says something about carts before horses. I note that Tuesday is a mere four days from now, and that our previous appointments have all been spaced a full week apart. I don't know if this is some sort of scheduling anomaly, or if it implies something more. I don't ask; either way, I have decided this latest visit will be my last.

I leave his office and sit in my car in the near-darkness of a deserted underground car park. The concrete here, the almost-silence, the unfilled, flattened space: this is a desolate place, a new kind of lonely.

Later, June casually enquires about my day.

I hear the strange pitch of my voice as I tell her it went great.

"It went great," I say, a little too loudly.

I concentrate very hard on June's eyes as I tell her this. I'm searching for hints of either acceptance or doubt, and end up seeing both.

I tell her the tablets were just a temporary measure, and then I hug her—because I feel like it, and because she is looking at me too intensely. "I'm fine," I say again.

When the hug ends she holds my face in her hands.

I have never before noticed how much information there is in an eye, how much data; in a single unsure eyeball there is an entire world of meaning, of hidden doubt and suspicion, of fear and resignation and love. I am once again smiling like a fool, knowing even as I do that from June, from this one person in the world, my smiles can hide nothing.

*

There are passports to be located and dusty suitcases to be retrieved from the attic; there are tickets to be printed and appropriate holiday attire to be folded just so; there are spare keys to be given to neighbours and high-factor sunscreen to be stowed. There is great upheaval in our usually sedate household, the storm before the calm. I take precise and continuous instruction from June, who is a woman possessed. She seems to be in every room of the house at once.

The boy lounges on the sofa, immune to the chaos. Teenage boys are not well known for their organisational skills, and Mark is no exception, but on this occasion his bags have been packed for a full 24 hours. They sit patiently by the front door, like overnight queuers for a rock concert. I am glad of his gladness to be getting away for a while. His baggage is neat and self-contained.

June is in the process of fitting two suitcases worth of clothes into one, and it falls to me to drop the boy to Henry's. Once in the car a change comes over him. These last weeks (or is it months?) of moping, of silence, of unspoken weariness, are suddenly expunged. Replacing them is a buoyancy, an excitement manifesting itself physically as he bounces around on his seat, looking out his window, looking at me as I drive, looking at the road spread flat out ahead. He is talking too, and though what he says is of no importance (chatter about school, about Henry, about everything in general and nothing in particular) it feels to me like so much more.

This openness, this excitement: it is unexpected and surprises me, absent as it has been. And though I understand it is not really meant for me—that it is simply an overflow of his eagerness to get away, to be with his father—I can enjoy it nonetheless, and I do. All his young worries and unsureties have evaporated, and how easy it seems.

"We might rent a boat and go fishing," he tells me.

"That's really great," I say. "I'm glad."

And as I speak I realise I mean them, these five useless words, more than any others I have spoken in months.

I angle my face away from his.

*

We sit at the departure gate, waiting. There is a general air of nervousness here, travellers both tired and excited, suspicious fingers clutching handbag straps and luggage handles, passports and duty-free.

June's head rests on my shoulder. Her hair itches against my cheek.

Baggage should not be left unattended, says the omniscient intercom.

"Honey," she says, and there is a pause then, and by the way she says the word, and by the length of the pause, it is clear a serious question is coming: this is the universal precursor to solemn conversation.

As I wait for what comes next I look at the people here. With the great weights they carry, their docile resignation, they are like emerging refugees.

"Are you okay," she says, "*really*?"

With nothing to say I say nothing.

The boy, by now, will be knee-deep in whatever fun activity Henry has thought up for him. Paintballing or go-karting or fishing, or maybe something more outlandish, like the time they rode in a hot-air balloon. "It looks like a map," he said to us later, meaning the landscape, the earth, from above. "Like everything's been flattened."

The simplest questions are the hardest, and I have no good answer for June. She cannot see my face. My eyes are trained on information screens and airline personnel, searching for hints of the imminence of flight.

I have no good answer.

I have no good reason to feel anything but happy.

Ω

Cancer (& Other Unforgivable Curses)

by Michelle Collins Anderson

I got the note in Esmé's backpack this afternoon: her long black cape has become "a distraction to the class" and she is no longer welcome to wear it to school. There was no mention of the wand. It is difficult to be a wizard among "Muggles"—your average, run-of-the-mill human beings. Just as I am finding it difficult to be human when I would gladly summon magic or pray for miracles.

Justin is with the hospice nurse now. She is checking his vital signs, making notes, checking the log of medications—the amounts, the times given—that I keep so meticulously, my letters curling around the white spaces of the chart. Soon she will bathe him, a sponge bath that will clean away the perspiration but will not erase the yellow of his skin. She will let me do the shampooing and the shaving: I insist. Justin was not—is not—a vain man, but he did love his hair. It is thick and black and edged with gray; he liked to keep it just the slightest bit long, which gave him the rumpled professor look I love. He is an artist, a painter, but made his living as the creative director at a local ad agency—overseeing all the words and images that go into ads and commercials and websites. He is what they call a "creative guru," a "big idea" man: he sees forest, not trees; constellations rather than stars.

He was diagnosed just seven months ago. Pancreatic cancer. It was what my O.R. nurse friend Julie called a classic "peek-and-shriek:" the surgeons opened him up to see what was going on inside and promptly sewed him back together and sent him home to die. Julie doesn't mean to be macabre or insensitive. I think she simply forgets that most of us don't see this every day.

The sound Justin makes when he breathes now is a like a percolating coffee pot, the kind my parents had on the farm. Similarly, he is boiling hot and bringing things up to the top, like the foamy yellow-brown spittle that needs to be swabbed regularly from the insides of his mouth. Julie says that means we are getting toward the end.

Sometimes I hate Julie. That know-it-all bitch.

"Esmé," I call up the stairs.

"Yes, Mummy."

Esmé has the most adorable British accent—which I only mention because we are not British. We are Americans. Midwesterners. Missourians. We do not take tea and crumpets, although we do love our sweetened iced tea and just saying the word "crumpet" is somehow altogether satisfying. Perhaps it is the English in my blood, from my grandmother on my mother's side. Or maybe it is because I am a librarian who cannot help but delight in the way a word can feel in my mouth.

"May I speak with you for a moment?"

"Certainly," she says.

I hear the clomp of her black boots before I see her at the top of the staircase. She is a vision in her black skirt, white oxford shirt and tie—the latter two nearly obscured by the cape, which is tied in large, childish loops at her throat. Her magenta cat eye eyeglass frames—while not standard-issue black circles like Harry Potter's—nonetheless sport a scroll of masking tape at the bridge, like the young wizard's in Book One. Her glasses are not broken. She waves her wand at me. It is a replica of Harry's, which—I should not admit to knowing—is precisely eleven inches, made from holly and contains a single phoenix feather. Esme's is molded plastic—no feather—but quite realistic.

"Hi, Mum."

"Hi, darling. How was your Monday?"

"Oh," she pauses before making her way down. "Decidedly unmagical."

She is only eight, but her vocabulary is what the teachers label as "well above grade level," as are her reading and writing skills. I will credit J.K. Rowling where credit is due, despite my professional distaste for her excessive and unimaginative reliance on "l-y" adverbs. Esmé has read the entire Harry Potter series of seven books seven times through and is about to finish round eight. She started in kindergarten, when the heft of a Harry Potter book in her backpack could nearly tip her over.

"I'm sorry to hear that," I say. I raise an eyebrow. "Is there anything you'd like to tell me?"

Her small face is pensive, surrounded by a curly brown mane of hair—my hair—more Hermione Granger than Harry Potter, but she refuses to be swayed. It is Harry whom she loves; Harry she pretends to be.

"Not in particular."

"I've gotten a note that says your cape is a distraction."

Esmé sighs. "It's a *cloak*."

"Cloak, then. So?"

"Muggles," she says finally. "They've no imagination."

"Have you considered that perhaps you have a bit too much of one?"

Esmé treats me to her newly perfected pre-teen eye roll. "Mummy," she says, exasperated. "Listen to yourself. There's no such thing as too much imagination. You've said so yourself. Besides," she adds, almost as an afterthought, "I neutralized my spell on Rebecca as soon as Mrs. Warson asked me to."

"Spell?"

"I had to put a *Silencio* on her," Esme says. "She talks too much. Chatters away, really. I think even Mrs. Warson felt relieved someone had taken her in hand."

"But…?"

Esmé shrugs.

"Mrs. Reece?" The nurse is calling me. Back to my duties.

"We will talk more about this, Esmé," I say. "But no more cloak. No more wand. And for heaven's sake, you must stop cursing people."

"*Spells*, Mummy. They are spells," she says indignantly. "I would never put a curse on anyone. That would be *unforgivable.*"

*

Esmé is right, of course. I should know my wizarding lore from all the hours of Harry Potter I have read to her at bedtime. The young wizards at Hogwarts School of Witchcraft and Wizardry learn all sorts of spells—and how to use them responsibly. But the dark wizards—the Death Eaters—have no such scruples. They would not hesitate to employ one of the "Unforgivable Curses," of which there are three:

• The *Cruciatus* curse inflicts unbearable pain on its recipient. Much like, say, a very aggressive, untreatable form of cancer.

• The *Imperius* curse causes the victim to follow any and all commands of the curse caster. A victim of this curse expriences total release from responsibility for one's actions at the cost of free will. Such victimhood, in my current circumstances, has much more appeal than I care to admit.

• And the third, the *Avada Kedavra* curse, is also known as the "killing curse" because it causes instant, painless death in its intended victim.

Now that I ponder it, is that last curse truly so unforgivable? My last few weeks with Justin may have convinced me otherwise. Imagine: an incantation. A wave of a wand. And poof! No more pain.

But no more person, either.

That is the caveat to *Avada Kedavra:* there is no counterspell, no means of blocking it. It is irreversible. Irrevocable.

Forever.

*

It is time to begin our goodbyes, the nurse says. Robin. Her eyes are gray and wise. She eases the blanket back from Justin's feet and ankles to show me the violet mottling under the golden sheen of his jaundice. She mentions the percolating, too.

"But he is so warm," I say. "Not cold at all. His hands and feet."

"His heart is strong," she says. "But his lungs are filling up." For the first time I notice the worry lines in her face. She takes my hand and runs my fingertips along Justin's closed lids, fringed with long, dark eyelashes. Nothing happens.

"Just two days ago, he would blink or twitch when we did that. Remember?"

I nod.

"He is in a coma now," she says softly. "It's time to make some calls."

I hear part of me telling her I will do it. But part of me is somewhere else, hovering just beyond my body, her body and his. Watching. As if this were someone else's drama, someone else's life.

"Mrs. Reece?" She summons me back.

"Evelyn," I say, for the umpteenth time. The intimacy she has shared with my husband, with our family, makes formality seem ridiculous.

"Evelyn. One more thing: you need to tell Justin that it's okay for him to go."

"I know," I say simply. Yet I cannot imagine how I will do this.

"He can still hear you," she says. "Talk to him. And touch him."

"I will," I say. "I do."

*

"I do."

When I said those words at our wedding nearly thirteen years ago, I was crossing my fingers beneath my bouquet.

Justin and I met in St. Louis and decided to get married there in the lovely little Lutheran church where I had been baptized as a baby. My parents had lived in the city early in their marriage, before my dad gave in to his yearning for small town life. So although I wasn't a member at Hope—or anywhere else, to be honest—I liked having that small connection to the church. I was in my first year as a librarian in the downtown branch of the public library after receiving my master's;

Justin lived and worked in St. Louis, too. We both had friends there. A city wedding made more sense than having everyone traipse down to the tiny Ozarks town where I grew up and had only my mother and one ancient set of grandparents remaining, a place where we couldn't serve beer and wine at the reception or dance without the whiff of scandal.

What we had not counted on—with the caterer already booked, the flowers and tuxedos ordered, the dresses made—was the premarital counseling this conservative church would require. I discovered over the course of these sessions that I was required to "submit" to my new husband, to "obey" him, and would have to promise as much in my vows. I also learned that Justin was to be the "spiritual head of the family."

"Think of it like a mobile," Pastor Lucero said seriously, his dark mustache and beard giving him a look uncannily like Lucifer himself. "God is at the top, of course, with the father pie plate hanging beneath. Then the mother pie plate below him, and the children pie plates hanging under her. If the daddy pie plate pulls away from God, the entire family goes with him."

"But Justin doesn't even go to church," I said, practically smirking. "In fact, I am not sure he believes in God. How can he be the top pie plate?"

Justin kicked me gently in the shin.

"Just cross your fingers for the submission part," Justin said after we had escaped the oppressive heat of that tiny office into the cool spring evening. "We know what we believe. It's okay. Besides," he winked. "I love it when you're the boss."

So I did. Cross my fingers, I mean. But not for the rest of it: for richer, for poorer, in sickness and in health. 'Til death do us part.

And the whole time I thought I was getting away with something. Avoiding the hard part.

*

It is the next day, Tuesday, already. I awoke early to the irritated meowing of Justin's old cat, Van Gogh (giant orange tabby, one ear) coming from the kitchen. There I found the poor, cross old thing lying on the counter, writhing and flopping helplessly from side to side, wearing two pairs of handcuffs fashioned from the thick blue rubberbands that typically hold together bunches of broccoli or asparagus. Esmé appeared to be poking his face with a pair of tweezers.

"Esmé!"

She whirled around, dropping the tweezers in alarm. But then a cool look remade itself on her face and she retrieved the silver instrument with one hand, while trying to hold down Van Gogh with the other.

"What on earth are you doing?"

"I just need one long whisker for an elixir," she said, flipping the growling, hissing mound of fur onto its other side. I pitied him his de-clawed paws. "Hold still, Van Gogh!"

"*Elixir?* Esmé! Stop that right this minute!"

With a horrible *thunk,* Van Gogh rolled off the counter and onto the kitchen floor. Handcuffed cats do not, for the record, land on their feet.

"But it's for Daddy." Esmé jutted her chin out.

"Daddy has all the medicines he needs."

"Then why aren't they *working*?"

I found myself unable to explain how Justin's medications aren't for healing, but rather for amelioration, for relief. "Symptom management," the doctor called it. The cancer gets to do whatever it likes. Manage *this,* I thought, mentally flipping off that physician who had sat so casually in his neat white coat amid the beeping, blinking ICU monitors. I hustled Esmé upstairs to brush her teeth while I set a highly agitated Van Gogh free. The look he gave me over his shoulder as he walked away was one of utter and complete disgust. I envied him his freedom, his ability to disappear beneath a bed or in the back of a closet until it was safe or desirable to come out.

After the cat incident, I sent a cape-free Esmé off to school, but somewhat reluctantly. Is it better to hold on to some shred of normalcy—although how normal can it be to go to school with your dad dying in your front room?—or to shuck routine and just embrace this time for what it is: a vigil? I have decided this will be her last day, that having her out of the house today will enable me to make those phone calls. To get ready for the onslaught. Justin's parents, his brother, my mom. His boss, my boss. His friends, our friends. Neighbors. My best friend, Julie, whom I have already mentioned.

I do not hate her. She is not really a bitch.

But a know-it-all? Absolutely.

It occurs to me that this will be almost like having a wedding in reverse. All our loved ones gathering to witness a dissolution, a breaking of the earthly bonds. There will be tears, prayers and flowers. Organ music. Suits and dresses. Tons of food.

No dancing. Although I think Justin would encourage dancing.

They have all been with me throughout Justin's illness, of course. My mom and his parents and his brother have taken turns these last few weeks, ever since Justin was hospitalized after collapsing in the kitchen and we decided a few days later to bring him home on hospice. I just sent them away, actually, three days ago. I needed a break from all the bodies in the house, the morose faces, the helpless hands. The constant need to think about what people might want or need to eat, even as Justin stopped eating altogether. I needed some time alone with just him and Esmé.

Early last week he could still talk a little, although I could tell it exhausted him. He could still hold me when I climbed into the hospital bed we had ordered for him and set up in the living room along with the oxygen machine. It was—it is—his favorite room: shelves full of his art books and my substantial fiction collection (alphabetized, of course), walls hung with his paintings, the brick fireplace, our family photos, a comfy camelback couch, the floor-to-ceiling windows. He loved the light. In the evenings, he would light the dozen or more pillar candles of varying heights that decorate our mantel. There is something about candlelight, Justin said, that is kind to paintings and human faces. It was a ritual: he used a bottle of butane to fill the heavy silver lighter inscribed with his grandfather's initials, then carefully attended to each wick. This is where we read, together, after dinner and homework were through. Sometimes even Van Gogh deigned to join us.

Justin even managed, just a few short days ago, to lie waiting, patiently and expectantly, as Esmé cast a host of spells in her efforts to make him better or different or someone else entirely.

"Just call me Dumbledore," Justin said, reaching for her small, be-caped body.

"No, Daddy. You can't be Dumbledore. He is old and gray with a tremendously long beard," she said seriously. "And he dies in Book Six."

Justin and I tried not to look at each other.

"Lord Voldemort, then?"

"Too evil."

"Snape?"

"Well, you *do* have the same black hair. But he's creepy, Dad. Plus, he dies in Book Seven."

"Esmé!" My voice came out sharp, a warning.

"Well, he *does.*"

Justin seemed nonplussed. "Hagrid, then."

Esmé smiled, pleased. "A giant, Dad? Really?"

"A giant who loves animals, magical creatures and above all, Harry Potter." Justin squeezed her tight. "And who doesn't always know the right thing to say."

Here he looked at me. I shrugged. Me, either.

Now I check the oxygen tank and give Justin his litany of medications. Esmé calls them his "potions." Ativan for anxiety. The Atropine to dry up the goo in his lungs. The Roxanol for pain. Haldol for agitation. There are drops and pills I grind up and mix in a liquid that can be drawn into a tiny syringe, something I can slip between his teeth and cheek while I hold his chin to make sure it all goes down. I tell Justin everything I am doing, everything I will do.

I love you, Justin. But I would be lying if I said I'm not a little pissed off.

I reach for one of the special caps Robin has left me and take it out of its wrapper. It is a shower cap of sorts, which I microwave for a minute or two and then secure to Justin's head, tucking in all that unruly hair. I massage the cap and soon lather builds up, seeping from beneath the edge of the elastic band. Afterwards, I remove the cap, towel his hair and comb it. Not as good as a real shampoo, but it will do. Marvelous inventions they have for the infirm and dying these days. The shaving is a bit trickier—there is no microwavable substitute for shaving cream and straight edge. But I manage.

The phone rings. Justin's mom? Or mine? I am not quite ready for what I am supposed to say today.

But the number is local. The school.

"Mrs. Reece?"

"Yes?"

"This is Mrs. Warson from the elementary school. Esmé's teacher?"

"Of course. Is something wrong?"

"Well…" There is one of those silences. "I'm afraid Esmé is still wearing her cape today. And as I had mentioned in my note yesterday…"

"Yes, I got the note and spoke with Esmé about it. She understood that she was not to wear it to school anymore."

"I am afraid she hid it beneath her fleece jacket this morning. All balled up. She looked like a little hunchback. I am surprised you didn't notice."

Ouch: the inattentive mom zinger. So that's how she wants to play it. But I see your politically incorrect hunchback reference and raise you one "C" word.

"Well, we are both dealing with the small matter of her father's *cancer*," I say, allowing only the tiniest bit of snark to creep into my voice. "I'm sure you understand."

"Yes. Oh, yes, I'm so sorry. I hate to even bring this up at all."

"But?"

"It seems she has cast several spells on her classmates," says Mrs. Warson. "She silenced Rebecca yesterday and then this morning she put a freezing spell on Jorge."

"That's ridiculous."

"Well, I know it *sounds* ridiculous, but the fact is, Rebecca still will not say a word and Jorge has not moved from his chair. Not even for recess."

"What? Is this some kind of joke?"

"I wish it were, Mrs. Reece. But I honestly don't know what to do. The other children seem a bit afraid of Esmé."

"She is an eight-year-old girl. She barely weighs fifty pounds—"

"She is in the principal's office right now," Mrs. Warson interjects. "You should probably come and get her."

I start to say something extremely unkind. But what would that accomplish?

"*Expelliarmus*," I say instead. This is the most expedient way to disarm a witch.

"Excuse me?"

"I'll be there as soon as I can."

*

A knock on the door of our Dutch colonial, with its barn-shaped dusty blue second story atop the cool, gray-white limestone of the first. It is Margie. One half of Margie-and-Tom, our across-the-street neighbors. They have one son, Griffin, who is eleven. He and Esmé used to play together until fairly recently, when it became uncool for either of them to associate with the other gender.

"Hey, there," Margie's eyes are already welling up. "How is Justin?"

"Not too good," I say. Her tears seem to harden, rather than soften me. "Coma."

"Oh, Evelyn!" She throws her arms around me and I let her hold me, although I can't seem to hold her back. I am stiff, like a papoose strapped to a board. But unable to allow myself to be carried on someone's back. She wipes her eyes with the sleeve of her windbreaker. It is spring. The fact of it surprises me every time I step outside: all the bursting colors and un-furling green life everywhere. It hurts my eyes.

I lead her into the living room, show her how to shift Justin with pillows if he seems uncomfortable. Write down my cell phone number. Point out the hospice number, just in case. *Just in case.* Justin's case. A hopeless case.

"I'll be right back," I say. "Fifteen minutes."

"Take your time," she says. "Take all the time you need."

*

It would not matter if I had hours or days. Esmé does not want to talk.

In my rearview mirror, I see her staring out of the window, avoiding my gaze. Her face is swollen and blotchy, although she was not crying when I picked her up. I told the principal I would be keeping Esmé home until things settled down.

"Of course," he said. "I'm sorry. But I understand completely. We all do."

I nodded, all the while herding Esmé out of his office and through the heavy steel double doors of the school. The playground smelled of sun-warmed earth and cedar mulch and was full of running, boisterous children. I am finding it difficult to remember what is normal, what kinds of things go on out here in the world.

"Esmé," I say. "Look at me."

She refuses. Her hands in her lap are balling and unballing her black cape. We drive in silence, with just the hum of the motor and the occasional bump from the street beneath. In the driveway, I turn off the engine and it makes a metallic pinging as it cools.

"Esmé," I finally say. "Daddy may not be with us much longer."

I turn to meet her eyes. They are hazel like Justin's. The color of surprise.

"Where is he going?"

It is a terrible thing to break down in front of your child. I remember my father crying exactly once: when his mother died. That scared me far more than my grandma's shrunken, lifeless body at the funeral. She didn't look like someone I knew. But my father crying? He looked the same, but I did not know that man at all.

Esmé has climbed into the front seat and hands me a paper napkin embossed with McDonald's arches. I swipe at the tears and snot coalescing at the bottom of my face.

"Daddy is dying, sweetheart."

"I know. But where will he go?"

"I don't know," I say. The yard is practically pulsing with purple crocuses, brilliant yellow jonquils, the bottlebrush blooms of lavender hyacinths.

"When Dumbledore died, Harry could still talk to him inside his head," Esmé says. She shoves open the car door.

"Maybe it will be like that," I say. But the door is slamming, and the only one I am left trying to convince is myself.

*

Inside the house, Margie tells me that everything is "perfectly fine." I never knew what an ironic world I lived in until Justin became so sick. Or perhaps it is just that one's definition of words such as "perfect" and "fine" change relevant to the circumstances in which one finds oneself. All of which is to say: if everything here is perfectly fine, I would hate to see the alternative.

I want to stop thinking so much. But my librarian self cannot help noticing how words can be so impotent and meaningless and yet, at the same time, positively loaded. I am horrified by how pedestrian, how unexalted my thoughts are at a time like this. I don't know *how* to think anymore, how to be in my own skin. But then, I suppose, this is my first dying husband. I should cut myself some slack. Everything is *perfectly fine.*

Margie promises to send over chicken soup. I say thank you.

It is too much trouble to tell her about our freezer, already filled to bursting with donated casseroles assembled from chicken, Campbell's Cream of Mushroom soup and crushed stale potato chips. If I felt like eating—which I don't—I might die of a heart attack or an artery-clog-induced stroke. Who knew food could be so beige? Esmé and I eat one-dish meals around Justin's bed: popcorn or a bowl of ice cream or cold cereal. Still beige, but so much yummier somehow. It feels like we are camping out, like this is just temporary. That we will return to regular programming soon.

"We're thinking about you," Margie says at the door. She hesitates a second and grasps one of my hands in hers. "We're praying for you all, Evelyn."

I know she is putting herself out there to say this. We are the non-churchgoers on the block. The Sunday layabouts. The agnostics. The daddy pie plate has swung wide and taken us far from the fold.

"Thank you, Margie," I say. "It means a lot."

*

Robin is here already. The day has disappeared, shadows falling. She was coming every few days, but told me yesterday that she will come every day now until the end.

"I didn't expect to find you and Esmé alone," she says pointedly but gently.

Esmé likes Robin. She shows her lots of little tricks to help make her father more comfortable. Like dipping the small, stiff swabs in water before use so that they are softer inside his

34

mouth. Or putting Vaseline around the rims of both nostrils where the oxygen tubes chafe. A bit of lip balm on his cracked, flaking mouth.

"I had some things come up," I say. I laugh at how preposterous that sounds. As if anything could trump the drama in my living room. *Things have come up.* A comeuppance? "But I'll call while you're here."

"Atta girl."

*

"Nancy," I say, when Justin's mom picks up. They are in Indianapolis, only five hours away, but our connection sounds as distant as another universe.

"Oh, God. Evelyn." She puts a hand over the phone. "Paul? Paul! It's Evelyn."

"Is everything okay?" A twinge of hope yet in her voice, but mostly fear.

"Yes," I say. "I mean, no. He's alive, but the nurse says it won't be long now."

"We'll get right in the car," says Paul, his gruff voice extra loud on the extension.

"No, no need of that," I say. I am not ready. Give me just one more night, I think. Please. "Just pack and get things in order. Tomorrow will be perfectly fine."

Perfectly fine. Did I really just say that?

"We never should have left." Nancy is sobbing. "Are you sure, Evelyn?"

"Yes, I'm sure." No, I am not. But I push on, asking them to call Justin's brother, Jake. Before we hang up, they assure me that they love us all so very much.

"Me, too," I say.

After I hang up, my hand rests heavily on the handset. It is so exhausting to talk. Punching in numbers, connecting with someone I love—who loves Justin, too—to talk about *disconnecting* from this life, this person we all care about. I lie down, paralyzed.

Is there any place lonelier than a double bed you used to share with someone? I realize I have not slept here in weeks. That, in fact, I have not slept here since Justin fell. I have slept, of course. But not much—and mostly on the living room couch.

Even though I knew in the back of my mind that there would be a last time we slept together, I thought I would recognize it happening in the moment. A flashing neon sign or a message in marquee lights, perhaps. Or at a minimum—and this sounds absurd—I imagined soft lights, gentle touches, Brahms in the background. Instead, I helped Justin up the stairs and he was so exhausted he just lay there while I undressed him and drew up his blankets. The whole thing made him so angry, so disgusted with himself—with his cancer—that he lashed out: "Don't touch me, goddamnit!" Then he turned his back to me—no good night kiss, nothing—and slept fitfully all night, facing the wall.

The next morning he fell in the kitchen and suddenly, we had already spent our last night in our bed. It was in the past. And we hadn't even known it was happening.

"Mrs. Reece?" Robin pokes her head in to let me know she is leaving.

"Evelyn," I reply, staring up at her from my prone position on the bed.

"How are the calls coming?"

"One down."

She frowns. "Can someone else help? Justin's time may be short."

36

"Short." I repeat the word without really assimilating its meaning. I have never associated this word with Justin before, either in height or temperament.

Justin is short on time. *A short-timer.*

"A few days at most," she says. "I'm sorry. You may have noticed, his breathing has gotten more shallow. There's no urine output, either."

She is right. It has been two days since I emptied the plastic pouch of dark gold liquid hanging from his bed. "His kidneys are shutting down," she says.

"My nurse friend Julie," I say. "She'll know what to tell everyone."

Robin smiles. "We nurses don't always know what to say," she says. "But we usually know what to do. Do you want me to call her for you?"

I hand her the phone. Robin's end of the conversation sounds more like a soothing flow of music than distinct words. She gives me the phone back. Nods.

"Hi, Jules," I say. "I am sorry. I couldn't seem to dial the damn phone."

"Oh, Evelyn. Oh, baby," she says. "I'm the one who's sorry. I should've called earlier. I'll tell them all to come tomorrow. And I'll be over first thing to check on you."

"You don't need to do that."

"Evelyn," she says firmly. "Let me help you. I can do this."

"Okay," I say, my throat closing over a painful sob. I am relieved. I do not hate her anymore for her competence. For understanding what all of this means.

"Hang in there, baby," she says. I flash on a poster I had at Esmé's age: the darling tabby kitten dangling from a branch, eyes desperate, claws dug in. *Hang on, baby. Friday's coming.*

Robin helps me up. "I'll let myself out. Wash your face, okay?"

"Yes," I say. "I will."

"Justin's stable right now," she says. "But there's a little girl down there who needs you."

*

From the top of the stairs I can see that the living room is dark, but for a small bedside lamp beside Justin. His face looks more relaxed than it has in days. The oxygen machine in the corner gives the house a womblike hum. Everything is so still.

But then a small movement catches my eye: there, in front of the fireplace with her small, cloaked back to me is Esmé. She is mumbling something, words that I cannot quite make out. I take another step closer, stealthily, not wanting to interrupt. I understand that she is summoning someone or something, perhaps; making some kind of magic for her father. It tears at my heart to see hope so naked, so earnestly and hopelessly employed. And yet I am transfixed by the scene, this simple, genuine act of faith in the very face of death. Envious, even.

Slowly, she brings her arms up from her sides. Her wand is in her right hand. She reaches for something on top of the mantel—a bottle?—and kneels down, pouring its contents onto the trio of decorative white birch logs in the fireplace grate.

"*Incendio!*" Esme says now, loudly.

Too late, I see the silver lighter in her left hand as she bends closer toward the grate, her wand raised high in her right. A tiny click.

"Esmé, no!"

Then there is a bright flash that knocks Esmé back onto her heels, her cape blown open, her arms flung up to her face. Flames flare briefly; a wispy black cloud rolls back into the room and dissipates. My mind panics—there is Esmé, Justin, the oxygen tank—and then I am taking the remaining stairs by threes until I am at Esmé's side.

She stares up at me, her mouth making silent O's, a fish gasping on a river bank. Her bangs are singed and her eyes open wide behind the smudged lenses of her glasses, wider than seems possible: I realize then that her eyebrows are gone, giving her a look of horrible, perpetual surprise. The flames in the fireplace have died away, leaving the birch logs smirched but whole. There is the smell of burnt hair. The oxygen machine hums on, oblivious. Justin, too, remains unmoved.

"Mama," she whispers, and for a moment, she is no longer British, no longer a wizard. I lift her into my arms, brush aside the sizzled hair at her forehead to reveal a black, lightning-shaped scar near the upper right hairline. I recognize this as the work of a Sharpie, not the result of the fire or a fall or other mishap. How magnificent, I think, to be so clearly marked by suffering. I am frightened that when Justin dies, people will look at me and be unable to see him, too; the ways he marked my life, the ways he changed me. Terrified that he will simply disappear.

I am already having difficulty picturing Justin anywhere but in a hospital bed, any way but jaundiced, wasted. Wordless. Already I can no longer recall exactly the way his eyes looked at me or the smile that always began a bit reluctantly on one side of his mouth—was it the left?—before taking over his entire face.

But there is Esmé, of course. She is right here. I clutch her to my chest and rock her.

*

After a bath in which I affirm that both eyebrows and a measure of pride are the only casualties of Esmé's wizardry-gone-

39

wild ("But Mummy, Harry conferences with other wizards in the fireplace flames all the time—for advice, you know?"), we join Justin in the living room once more while we eat a dinner of toasted frozen pancakes slathered with peanut butter. Esmé is in her footie pajamas and cape at the end of Justin's bed; I pull an armchair closer to the side and lower the metal rail so that I can touch them. I can make out the two flat shining buttons of Van Gogh's wary eyes in the dark beneath the couch.

Soon, Esmé will request Harry Potter and lose herself in Book Seven, the one where Harry dies but doesn't, talks to Dumbledore (his dead mentor who is still available for counsel), vanquishes Voldemort and lives happily ever after. Harry even marries and becomes a parent.

He has no idea what he is in for.

Esmé will eventually fall asleep, curling up around Justin's feet. I will mark her page, gently close her book, smooth her cape and cover her with a soft fleece blanket. I will give Justin his meds, hold his hand, and watch him breathe.

Rennervate, I will whisper.

Reparo, I will plead.

Please, God. Please.

But Justin will not wake up. Justin will not heal.

It's okay, I will say. It is okay for you to go.

They will be here soon, the others. The ones who love Justin, too. They will ring the doorbell and wait politely for me to open the door. Someone will knock. My father-in-law, Paul, perhaps. And then he will knock again, more loudly. They will look at each other and shrug before letting themselves in.

"Knock, knock. Hello? Evelyn? Esmé?"

They will look for us in the living room, moving quickly to Justin's bedside and the rumple of bedclothes and blankets, sheets, pillows and the clear plastic coils of oxygen tubing.

40

Sunlight will stream through the tall windows. The air will be faintly tinged with the scorch of human hair.

But we will not be there. They will not find us.

We will already be gone. We will have joined hands and said the right words, envisioned ourselves elsewhere. *Disapparated.* Disappeared. We will be flying like Harry Potter, through time and space. Into another universe.

When we land at last, we will tumble, laughing, across some strange terrain. Justin will rise slowly, dusting off his pressed white shirt cuffs, and run his fingers through his thick, tousled hair and grin at me. Esmé will adjust her taped magenta glasses and look around, wonderstruck.

Obliviate, I will say. And everything terrible, everything perfectly fucking fine will fall away, forgotten.

*

Later. Much later. My head jerks up from the side of Justin's bed, where I've fallen asleep, resting against his arm. The sky is streaked with light.

Someone is knocking.

Quickly now. Do not be afraid. Let me take your hand. Ready?

I love you.

Forgive me.

Avada Kedavra!

Silence.

Just the low drone of the oxygen machine and my words echoing off these high-ceilinged walls. Our living room. *The dying room.*

Esmé's eyes are open.

"Mummy." Her voice is a whisper, but it holds a reprimand. "You are just a Muggle."

She pulls herself up until she is seated once more at the foot of Justin's bed. I am still holding his hand. She reaches for his hand, too.

"I know," I say. "I'm sorry."

"It's okay."

We watch Justin's chest go up and then—after what seems a long while—down. His breath is barely audible, his pulse faint. We will keep watching and listening and holding on, spellbound. As long as it takes. Forever.

The knocking again; louder, more insistent.

"Someone is at the door," I say. "We better see who it is."

Ω

"Cancer (& Other Unforgivable Curses)" originally appeared in *Nimrod International Journal.*

Campaigning

by Janna Brooke Cohen

James is coming over tonight; our third date if you count the coffee he bought me after I found his lost cell phone at Starbucks. James has a strong jaw, a Master's degree and a brogue, so the stakes are high. I Googled a recipe, but it makes me nervous, because it calls for a double boiler, and I rarely see the need to boil food singly. I've enlisted my desk-mate, Jodi, for logistical and culinary support. One, tiny snag ... before we leave for lunch, I sort of steal her wallet, a cheap move, though not an easy one.

Some women sneak the free donuts at reception when they're stressed. I'm not a sweets person. I steal. I like to wait for the perfect moment, when the person is frantic and distraught about their missing item, and then I "find" it for them, and we bask together in the connection of relief and gratitude. Bear claws and Boston crème's don't have that kind of muscle.

Given: Jodi's the type who knows where her things are. Her desk drawers are business Marines. The insides are wiped clean, pens and pencils loaded flawlessly into right-sized compartments in one of those plastic thingies from the organization store; none of the gum wrappers, old listing pages, and crumbled receipts that clog mine.

Logical conclusion: When Jodi busts me, it goes without saying that she won't be able to live with herself unless she presses charges. How do I know? Every morning she reads me truisms from her Tony Robbins desk calendar: *If you can't, you must, and if you must, you can.*

"And if you could, then you shouldn't," I tease, "and if you shouldn't, then you would."

Martin Lipchitz, the unfortunate-looking, small-handed man who completely gets me and works in the catty-corner cubicle chimes in, "And how much wood would a woodchuck chuck, if a woodchuck could chuck wood?"

"Very funny, you guys," Jodi says, good-naturedly, but I can see that Lipchitz and I have hurt her feelings. "Tony Robbins is extremely successful and wise. Maybe if you two read his books, you might stop your complaining about not doing better at work." She has a point, and here's another: Jodi Schwartz is a woman who knows the whereabouts of her wallet.

*

Before lunch, Jodi has a phone altercation with her brand-new husband, Craig. "No, honey," she pleads. "We have to return the bedding before thirty days." She writes Craig's name on a sticky note while she listens to his response, dotting the "i" with a daisy. "Yeah, but it's day twenty-eight, babe, and then it'll be—" Craig interrupts, and Jodi listens patiently, determined to excel at marriage. "Craig ... Craig-Honey, *I'll* do it when I get home ... I'm just saying, watch the game, just don't forget to record *Dancing with the Stars* ... Okay ... I'll try to find you some ... I love you."

When it comes time to pay for lunch, she'll realize she's missing her wallet. *You must have been distracted by Craig,* I'll say. And, when I find it for her, back at the office, she'll be so gleefully relieved and indebted that she'll kiss-off dragging protuberant bags of failed bedding to the Garden State Mall to help me figure out my dinner.

*

We walk six blocks from the office for the "good" salad bar. Jodi won't eat at the one on our block. "It's disgusting, the lady at the register is super rude, and they use *oil-packed* tuna," she says. "Don't get a lot of cucumbers," she advises. "They're heavy and they make the salad expensive."

Jodi begins with a preliminary, observational lap, peering through the translucent sneeze guards at the day's offerings, breaking her container into quadrants to include a balance of raw and cooked veggies, cold and hot proteins, and a side, *always a side,* of fat-free dressing. Without her tutelage, I'd collect salad ingredients willy-nilly and inevitably run out of room before getting through half of the bar.

I have to ask, "If there's no fat, what are the ingredients in the blue cheese dressing?"

"I don't know. Who cares?" she says. "The point is that it's fat-free."

She pauses at the tuna, not the tuna *salad,* but the chunks of taupe, unmixed tuna fish straight from the can, takes a closer look, to make sure it was packed in water, then spoons about three ounces onto the bed of spring mix she's prearranged into a supportive nest.

"Eve, do you watch *Dancing with the Stars*? That show is seriously great!"

"Nah. I don't have cable," I say.

The plan was to surprise James with a picnic and the Philharmonic in Central Park, but he has to work past eight. The new plan is to laud his heritage with a traditional Highland meal followed by a rented movie and earth-shattering sex, but I have no idea what Scots eat, and the only items in my fridge are half-and-half, wine, and assorted Chinese sauce packets. I search *food Scottish* on my phone and let it load.

Jodi plants multicolored cherry tomatoes and three cubes of feta (more worth it than mayonnaise, fat-wise) in a flower formation around the tuna fish. I follow suit and even mine looks superb. "*Everyone* has cable, Eve," she says while starting on a roasted beet-potato combo.

"Everyone but me," I say, aping her handling of the tongs.

"Well, anyway, *Dancing with the Stars* comes on network, and I'm just saying, you should try watching it sometime."

By the time we're done, my salad looks almost as good as Jodi's does, and I reconsider making her frantic for the walk back to the office, "Jode, you paid last time … let me get this."

"Oh, thanks," she says unsuspectingly, "that's so nice of you."

*

On the stroll back to work, we pass a couple of college kids distributing campaign flyers. I take one from each without stopping, but I am with Jodi, whose blond, newscaster bob, summer-wool shift, and loafers (with actual pennies inserted in the leather saddles above her metatarsals) are conservative enough to inspire a campaign of their own.

"Excuse me, may I ask you ladies a question? Do you vote in New York or New Jersey?"

I keep walking (sure to wave my flyers in acknowledgment), rushing to get back so I can find the wallet and eat my salad, though I already know I'll be hungry after and bat eyes at Lipchitz for a hunk of his invariable meatball sub.

Jodi bites, "New Jersey, actually." I stand aside while they chat for a minute, her head nodding in constant agreement, and then, still smiling, she strides toward me.

"Who are *you* voting for, Eve?" Jodi's worked across from me for almost a year, but our inchoate friendship still flaps around on wings of wilted romaine. I am the work-friend with whom she can do girl stuff, talk shop, and tell "Craig" stories over the occasional mani-pedi or salad lunch, but right now it's past one o'clock, and according to Yahoo, I need to figure out how to make forfar bridies and partan bree.

"I know you don't want to hear this, but I vote Republican, which everyone *really* would if they paid attention. So I might as well learn what the deal is, right?" I let it pass but she pushes it. "Right?"

"Oh, sorry," I say, "I thought you were being rhetorical."

Jodi reads her flyer while we walk, "Huh? No, *Republican*! Craig's one, so I am too. I'm guessing you're a *Democrat*," she says with more than a smidgeon of practiced tolerance.

"What makes you guess that?" I'm teasing a kitten with a feather, one who only wants to cuddle me and be my friend, and I hate myself for feeling superior, considering this particular kitten's wallet is an anvil at the bottom of my purse.

But then she pushes, "Oh, c'mon, *obviously* ... because you dress like one and stuff."

"How does a Democrat dress?"

"Ugh, you know what I mean." Jodi waves her hand up and down my outfit—an embroidered, Mexican blouse tucked into high-waist, men's slacks from the thrift shop, wedge-heeled espadrilles, and two fresh asters that I plucked from the Park Avenue median and pinned in a loose bun on the crown of my head—and I laugh, because I *do* know what she means. I got dressed this morning thinking: *Annie Hall* with a hint of *Night of the Iguana* and a touch of *Reds.* "You're so skinny and daring and fashiony. I could never pull off your crazy outfits...

But you *are* a Democrat, right? I know I'm right."

"I don't really follow politics." I keep trying to walk on, but Jodi, flyer in hand, won't budge.

"Well, Craig thinks," she says, "and I wholeheartedly agree," she puts her hand over her heart in a pledge-of-allegiance-to-Craig, "that it is our responsibility as citizens to know what is going on in the world. I mean, like, how can you *not* follow the news?"

I'm already at angles today, and she push, push, pushes. "Jodi, campaigning is not news. It is political posturing ... it's like, ephemeral bullshit. I mean, how can you stand to listen to them blustering on and on when they never really *fix* anything?"

"I just meant that..."

"And cable loops it twenty-four seven too. So depressing. And, with so many channels, how do you choose what to watch, and then you only learn from the channels you choose, so how do you know you're right? I mean, how do you know whether or not that guy on your flyer ... what's his name again?"

"Jack Hutchinson."

"Yeah, Jack Hutchinson. How do you know if he's the salt of the earth, or a complete monster, or a fucking nincompoop? And what channel are you supposed to watch to get the truth?"

Jodi looks like I whipped her with a hickory switch. I resume discomfited silence, painfully aware of the probability that she was only trying to sound important, and I've just bullied her backward, onto her tippy toes in the deep end.

I grab at the chance to veer. "Hey, Jode, ever heard of *haggis*?"

She waits a beat and then says, "If you don't follow politics, then why did you take the dang flyer?"

"I always take a flyer."

"What? Why?"

"I guess I just figure that giving out flyers is their job, and if I take the flyer, then they'll feel successful ... they'll feel the satisfaction of being good at something, y'know, that they've done their job well."

"Oooh-kaaay," Jodi mocks, but then capitulates, "well, I suppose that's very nice of you."

I grab at her olive branch. "So, what do you know about mutton?"

"It's not very genuine though, right? Like, you're not really being *yourself*, you're not *really* interested in what they're selling; so it's like, kinda fake, in a way."

"Well, sometimes you need to give someone else a turn to be *him*-self. I mean if everyone focused on his own needs all the time, the only person who would *ever* take Jack Hutchinson's flyer would be Jack Hutchinson. You should be more selfish sometimes, Jode," I say.

It makes me crazy how she skates atop life's grit. I want Jodi to vote how she chooses to vote, Craig-be-damned, and I want her to demand *Dancing with the Stars* in real time. Poor Jodi, who only wants to be my friend and for me to believe she is smart, when she is not smart at all, and for me to see her as stylish, when she has no originality. I want to be nice to her. So, I hold still as a lizard on a rock, sunning myself on one of

Jodi and Craig's seventeen nature channels, and when I do, she fucking pushes again.

"Well, to read this, Jack Hutchinson is a good American," she says, smoothing out a wrinkle in her shift as she finally catches up with me. "He wants to make the schools better, and like, Craig and I are going to be *trying* next year, after we get his bonus ... for like a baby ... and anyway, you have to campaign. How else will anyone know who you are and what you can do for our country?"

I should leave it be, but I don't. "A political campaign proves nothing, Jodi. It's just ... marketing."

"What?"

"Campaigning is just advertising a person. Like, *Compassionate Conservatism* and *Tippecanoe and Tyler Too* are no different from *A Diamond is Forever* and *Snap, Crackle and Pop...*" Jodi shrugs, fiddles with her wedding rings. "Look at Nike. To hear them tell it, Nikes literally transform you into an athlete when you wear them. I mean, I like Nikes, y'know, they're good sneakers, but they don't make me dunk like Jordan."

"Oh my *God*, Eve!" Jodi scoffs, exasperated, "Michael Jordan doesn't even play basketball anymore."

"So."

"So, Jack Hutchinson is *NOT* Nikes!"

"That's for sure," I mutter.

We walk in silence for a few seconds before she rallies, spying a pair of leopard flats in a boutique window, and my relief leads me to overcompensate, "Ooh, I love those, Jode. You could wear them with clam diggers and an Ann-Margret-y crop top," I say and start to pony down the sidewalk, double hopping from one foot to another, because aside from the twist, the pony is the dance that pairs best with leopard flats.

Jodi grins awkwardly. She has five hundred channels, but she hasn't seen *Bye-Bye Birdie*. Does no one ever pony on *Dancing with the Stars?*

Then Jodi stops short, pivots back toward the volunteers. "Hang on. I'm going to give them a donation," she says, plunging her hand into her bag. She feels around for the wallet she most certainly will not find, and a trap door opens beneath my stomach sending it free-falling into my feet. This is it. There will be no boyfriend for me—or work friend, or caddy-corner, doofus sidekick's meatball sandwich.

"Mea culpa, Jodi!" I shout, distracting her moving arm to stillness.

"Huh?" She's smiling fully now, shaking her head in that way she does when she's categorizing me as *weird*.

"I mean I feel bad. Sorry. I'm a bitch sometimes. Let *me* make the donation. I'll sleep better tonight, okay?" Jodi removes her hand from her bag to accept the twenty-dollar bill that I too quickly slap into her palm.

"Whatever, girlfriend," she says. She trots away to hand the volunteer the cash as I silently vow to be a better person, maybe do the therapy thing. Then she skips over and takes my elbow to hold me back from jaywalking and presses the crosswalk button.

*

Jodi hits the ladies room right out of the elevator. I have to wait a minute or two for Martin Lipchitz to take a phone call before digging out the wallet. Jodi reenters the office just as I yank the blue leather rectangle from my own bag.

"Eve, is that my ... What are you doing with my wallet?" She squinches up her button nose and furrows her brow, and it is hard to tell from her expression whether or not she's set to call the cops or give me advice about organizing my closet.

Her stare reddens my hand. "Why was my wallet in your pocketbook?"

I scroll the hundred perfect explanations that have worked for me for years. Jodi will buy into any one of them, but I feel the extra-thick shame creeping in early this time, and so fresh off the be-better vow I made at the crosswalk, I go with a risky version of the truth. "It's weird, I know, but, I wanted to buy you lunch, and I wanted to be sure you'd let me pay."

Jodi exhales. Taps her foot. Tilts her head to the side like a perplexed puppy. I hold her wallet out to her, but she doesn't take it. She leaves it to brand me as I begin to well up with defense (she doesn't know what I've been through, she with the mother who calls every morning at ten a.m. *just to check in*), which turns to pride (I'm a survivor and an original and an artist stuck selling real estate, and this is the spiritual price I pay), and morphs into hatred (fuck you Jodi, you and your wallet can kiss my ass). When I'm done seething, I look up to see that Jodi is tearing up and trembling but standing her ground.

"You think I don't know you steal things, Eve?"

I am also flushed, no, burning, yet, conversely shocked-frozen to my carpet square. Jodi shakes her head, maybe gathering her nerve, and then ... "I see you steal things all the time. You think you're so slick, but ... chips? Every time we go to lunch, you pay for the rest, but then you steal, like, a ninety-nine cent bag of Utz ... why do you do that?"

"Look, Jode, I think you're..."

"Shut up, Eve. I was being *rhetorical* ... Yeah, I looked it up, so, like, I know what it means now, because I try every day to learn new things and be a better person. And I have some more *rhetoric* for you, too." She says the word with such magnificent attitude that I can't help one corner of my mouth turning up, proud of her swagger, but she sees the smirk, misconstrues it—who wouldn't—and goes up in flames over it. "You think this is funny? This isn't funny, Eve. You are in a lot of trouble. I didn't say anything about your chips because I felt sorry for you, but this is my wallet we are talking about here."

I need to end this now before we attract any more attention and I lose my job. Time to stop cheering for Jodi and start wriggling free. "Look, I just wanted to pay for your lunch. The wallet is right here." I will myself to move and place the item on the corner of her desk. I ought to apologize, take responsibility, and promise her something, but instead, I hear this crap come out: "Nothing's missing, you know. You can't prove anything."

Lipchitz is off his call and raring to get in the mix. "What's all the hoo-hah girls?"

"Mind your business, Martin," says Jodi, and here, where she ought to let it die, take her wallet, call our boss, move her desk, write me off, whatever, she takes me again, by my elbow and yanks me to the ladies room. We are alone, but with the huge mirror, it feels like there are four of us: me, a pair of furious, sobbing Jodi's, and my reflection. Three against one.

Jodi sniffles, clears her throat. "You think I'm going to *tell* on you? I know about kleptomania. I know you can't help it."

"Look, I'm sorry, okay." I hand her a tissue. "I just have this date tonight, and I'm sort of freaking…"

"Oh, please. You like barely even know James. You do this with every guy who likes you." Now *I'm* treading water. "You don't even care about these guys. You only care about getting them to love you like poor Martin. He's been in love with you this whole time and gets all your weird jokes and he reads all the same smart books, and you don't even give him eye

53

contact unless you're making a joke on me. Tony Robbins says you should demand more from yourself than anyone else could ever expect, but you want everyone to live up to you. I feel so sorry for you. I talk to Craig about it all the time."

The mere mention of Craig sends me reeling toward apoplexy. I have such a speech prepared abut Jodi's *Craig*. Craig ... the stereotypical, sports-obsessed, ball-cap-turned-backwards, fantasy-football playing, frat-boy dipshit who wants Jodi to wander out into the night to exchange a dust ruffle, while he kicks back on their—no-doubt Pottery Barn—sofa to watch the Knicks, leaving her to play wife and mother and maid and house manager and chef...

Fucking Craig. Fucking James. Fucking Jodi. I am about to unleash the hounds on everyone, when I catch my reflection. There in the mirror stands Eve, the friend-ish, well-read, fashion-forward, two-bit chip-thief. One of the flowers has fallen from my hair. My outfit *is* a costume, trying as hard as I do to look better than I feel. My eyes are pink and puffy and filled with tears, and my mascara is streaked in charcoal half-moons down both of my cheeks.

"I'm not going to tell on you, Eve. I want to help you. You're ... like, my friend." My apologies are worthless. Half the time I don't even believe all the shit I end up saying. I reach out my arms, and Jodi comes in to join me for a trite ritual the normal me would righteously pan, but our protracted, sentimental girlfriend hug turns out to be magnificent, warm and safe, and we both mean it so much that when Jodi pulls back her arms I miss her. "We have to get back to work," she says, smiling like it's all over...

*

"I'm just saying Eve," she whispers after swallowing a mouthful of salad, "you should go out with Martin Lipchitz."

"Never going to happen."

"Whatever," she says, "your loss." Her blond bob bounces when she shrugs.

She does a little research and advises me to skip the haggis in favor of a nut, stone fruit and sheep's milk cheese platter and she prints out directions to the right shops in my neighborhood. She also prints me a recipe—annotates it in her tiny, typeset handwriting—with detailed instructions for how to make a dish called mince and tatties, that, as it turns out, is simply meat and potatoes.

Ω

"Campaigning" originally appeared in *Amarillo Bay*.

Linda Peterson Sounds Like a Reasonable Name

by Jennifer Dupree

We are on the way home from a Saturday afternoon family Halloween party and I am wearing my sexy witch costume which is basically a black leotard, tights, and a lot of eye makeup. I ditched the hat in the backseat with the girls. The leotard is riding up in both the front and the back and Lily, dressed as a black cat, has her face in my hat. Brit is fixing her pompadour. Ricky is singing some made-up Halloween song that is making Lily and Brit laugh.

Lily is four, Brit is eleven. They have spent the day eating candy corn, candy apples, mini Snickers bars, and pumpkin-flavored cupcakes at a party given by a school friend of Brit's. "I think the invitation was for you and Connie," I say to Ricky.

"Didn't you have a good time?" He smiles, wets his finger, tamps down his eyebrows.

I take his hand, rub the wet off against my hip. "Except for everyone asking about Connie."

He glances in the backseat. It's been eleven months and supposedly it was as friendly a split as divorces go but Brit's still sensitive about it. Or so Ricky says.

"I should call her," he says. "I told her we'd be home around four-thirty."

It is five o'clock and just starting to get dark. I tap the digital clock. "Does she start calling hospitals when you're five minutes late?"

Ricky digs his cell phone out of the pocket of his black jeans which, when he put on this afternoon, I told him I didn't even know people made anymore. He looked at me with his fallen-in little-boy face and said he thought they'd go with his vampire costume. I kissed him, said he looked fine, maybe a little eighties. I unzipped his zipper and slid my hand into the opening but he pulled away, said the kids were downstairs, waiting.

He hands me his cell phone. "Can you call and let her know we're on the way?"

I let the cell phone dangle in his palm, midair. I look in the back seat and Brit has her hand on her stomach and her eyes closed.

"Are you feeling all right, sweetie?" I ask, all maternal. I glance at Ricky to see if he notices but he's back to watching the road.

Lily says, "Are we still having pizza for dinner?"

"After we drop Brit off."

"Can't she spend the night with us?"

Brit rolls her head side to side and moans.

"Maybe we should get her some ginger ale," I say to Ricky. Connie is the kind to be quick to pick up the phone and blame me for her kid pigging out and then throwing up all night. "There's a Seven-Eleven up the street."

"She's fine," Ricky says. He has put the phone between his legs. "Connie practically has a pharmacy at the house."

"She's amazing," I say.

Ricky smiles.

The night we sent Brit home with temporary tattoos, Connie called Ricky and told him I made her kid into a street walker. She's a little extreme, I told Ricky. He said he liked my casual parenting style. Then I heard him call Connie back and tell her to try a little rubbing alcohol.

He told me they broke up because the love "just wasn't there anymore." He said he liked my "passion for life." Sometimes I catch him touching the spot where his wedding ring locked in on his finger for twelve years.

Both kids have closed their eyes now and I have my hand way up on Ricky's thigh. He squeezes my hand, then returns it to my lap. "They're asleep," I say.

"We should be careful," he says.

"Slow and steady," I say. If he notices my sarcasm, he doesn't acknowledge it. He nods, taps the steering wheel in time to "Born to Run."

"Is Connie a Springsteen fan?"

"Who isn't?"

"People who aren't goody-two-shoes," I say.

All of a sudden the car in front of us veers hells bells off the road. One second it's in front of us, the next second it's made a hard right into the woods.

"Holy shit," Ricky says.

"Holy shit," I say as Ricky pulls the car to the soft shoulder. "What are you doing?"

The car is way off into the woods, so far all I can see are the taillights. Ricky opens his door.

"What are you doing?" I ask again.

He tosses me his cell phone. "Call nine-one-one," he says as he runs down the embankment toward the car. His vampire cape flaps behind him.

"Do you have training for this?" I yell after him.

There's a lot I don't know about Ricky. We met when I was pumping gas into my nineteen-eighty Dodge pickup and he hollered across and asked if I got good gas mileage. Lily was in the backseat with a paper crown on her head and I stood so that I was blocking the window and told him I didn't know much about cars. On our first date he showed me how to change a tire so I guess he's handy.

I turn around and tap Brit's knee through her gray wool skirt. She's supposed to be a fifties secretary but she looks a little dowdy if you ask me. "Does your dad know CPR?"

She hops her knee and I try not to think she did it to get my hand off her. "I'm going to see if he needs help." She has her seatbelt unbuckled.

"You are not," I say. I tell the nine-one-one operator that we're on our way from Portland to Windham but I can't think of anything else. She asks the route number and I tell her I don't know.

"Three-oh-two." Brit rolls her eyes.

I lock the child safety locks so she can't get out. She shoots me a hateful look. "You'll just be in the way," I say.

"I have first aid training."

Ricky sells insurance. Health, life, car. And he's good at it. Sincere. Not willing to sell you stuff you don't need. Smooth with his hands, his voice. I put my head against the headrest and close my eyes.

Brit leans over and I can smell the waxy lipstick I let her borrow. "Shouldn't you go help, too?" She asks.

"I'm sure your father can handle it." I fish a pack of Bubbleiscious out of my purse and hand it over the backseat.

Lily takes the gum and unwraps a piece, then offers it to Brit who shakes her head. Lily shrugs, pops the piece in her mouth, unwraps another piece and pops that in, too. Mouth full of gum, she says, "Are those people dead?"

"Maybe," Brit says.

"No," I say. "And no more gum. The last thing I need is you choking." I expect Brit to repeat how she knows first aid but she just sits back, crosses her arms, and gives a little cat-smile. Just like her mother.

"I bet they're dead," Brit says.

Lily has her head in my witch hat again and she's crying.

"You'd better not spit your gum in my hat," I say. "No one is dead."

Brit says, "You don't know that. You've been sitting right here with us the whole time."

"Knock it off. Both of you." I shouldn't have had the two bloody Marys at the Halloween party but I figured Ricky was driving and I could just relax until it was time to read Lily her bedtime story. And maybe I could talk him into doing that, too.

Lily lifts her head, sucks in her bottom lip and stops crying.

"Thank you," I say. I turn around and smile at both of them, trying to soften the whole exchange. I don't want to be the kind of raving lunatic my mother could be when she was half in the bag. Not that I'm drunk, or even close. I'm just at the slightly dulled edge of sober, where things slip out of my mouth oh-so-much easier.

I watch the digital numbers on the clock slide by. Three minutes, four. "How long does it take to get an ambulance?"

Brit says, "My dad once saved a cat from a tree."

"What do you mean by saved? Cats go up in trees all the time, make their way down eventually."

"This cat didn't know how."

"Did it tell you that?"

Brit stares at me. "It was up there for four hours. Sometimes you just help because it's the right thing to do."

I feel tears sting my eyes and I roll down my window and pretend to listen. "I don't hear anyone screaming," I say.

Lily whimpers. Brit puts an arm around her and half-hugs her and the child-seat.

Finally, the ambulance wails to a stop behind us and I get out and point unnecessarily down the embankment. Ricky meets the paramedics halfway, talks in wide, swooping gestures as they move right past him. He looks ridiculous with the cape flapping out behind him. I stand there for a second thinking I'll gesture to him or something but he doesn't even glance at me.

Sometimes I find myself fantasizing that if I married Ricky, Connie would take Lily on the weekends she keeps Brit. It's already happened once. Two months after Ricky and I started dating, Connie took both girls to see Wicked down in Boston for Brit's eleventh birthday. They stayed at the Radisson. I don't know how she managed to get a four-year-old to sit through an entire Broadway musical but when I asked her if she used Benadryl she looked at me like I was a drug dealer on the schoolyard. For weeks after the adventure, Lily sang snippets of saccharine songs, told me how they ordered pizza from room service, drank cans of root beer from the mini bar, swam in the hotel pool and used two towels each when they took showers. In my mind, I always see Connie's name in lights just beneath Wicked.

"They've been down there a long time," Brit says.

I shrug.

"We should call my mother. She expected me home at four-thirty."

I pass my cell phone over the backseat. "Knock yourself out."

She dials her mother, ducks her head into the corner between the door and seat, murmurs about the couple, her father down there doing heroics. I don't actually hear her say the part about heroics but I imagine it and roll my eyes at Lily. She's busy pulling strings of gum out of her mouth. "Here," I say, handing her a tissue. She ignores me.

Brit tells her mother she loves her, then passes me the phone. "She's coming to pick me up."

"Why?"

Brit shrugs.

"Did you ask her to come pick you up?"

Another shrug, the bones in her shoulders nearly poking her ears.

"Don't just shrug when I ask you a question."

Brit points her chin toward the window. "Here they come."

The guys with the stretcher come up first, one with his gut peeking out from under his shirt, the other one sweating down his nose. Ricky trots behind them. He's still wearing the cape.

He gets in the car, settles the cape around him like he's some kind of hero and now I'm annoyed.

"You could lose the cape," I say.

"What happened?" Brit is leaning over, wrapping her arms around his neck.

"Maybe we should just get going," I say.

"Mom's coming," Brit says.

"Guy had a heart attack," Ricky says. "Wife smashed up against the dashboard pretty good. I don't think she was wearing a seatbelt."

Lily's eyes have gone wide. "Ricky," I say, squeezing his thigh. "Not in front of the girls."

He kisses Brit's arm which is still around his neck. "They can handle it."

"Maybe Brit can," I say.

He smiles, more at Brit than at me. "It's life, Jeanine." He puts the car in drive. "Call your mom and ask her to meet us at the hospital. You told her everything's okay, right?"

"I can't go to the hospital like this," I say.

"You look fine," he says.

"I'm not going like this."

"You can stay in the car with the girls, then. Connie shouldn't be more than twenty minutes."

Brit dials her mother again and mentions the cape her father is wearing.

I liked Ricky better in the beginning, when I didn't know how he could be so single-minded and self-righteous and I could fill in the blanks my own way. Before I came right out and asked him about his marriage, I liked to imagine Connie unplugging Sports Center and tossing the forty-seven inch TV onto the lawn. I pictured her with a closet full of Coach bags, a manicure every Thursday, and an aversion to blow jobs. But Ricky, in a fit of honesty, told me he would always consider her one of his best friends.

"How many best friends do you have?" I'd asked him.

"It's a shame you don't keep in touch with Lily's father," he said.

"I like my way better," I said.

"That's sad," he said. "Sometimes people just can't be married anymore."

"That sounds like a bullshit Hallmark card," I said.

"I like that you have so many opinions," he said.

"Does Connie not have *opinions*?"

Given his stance on not saying anything negative about his ex-wife, it was no surprise he didn't answer.

Across the hospital parking lot there's a small swing set lit like Christmas with parking-lot lights. As soon as Ricky shuts the engine, the girls set off for it. I stroll off after them and park it at the picnic table. Sitting, I try to discretely fix my leotard but it seems pretty well twisted. Connie will probably show up in skinny jeans and a sweater as white as her teeth. She'll fall all over herself telling Brit how much she missed her. One time I asked her if she enjoyed her alone time and she gave me a look like I'd just asked about the bodies in her basement. "I love being Brit's mom," she'd said.

"I could go for some alone time," I'd said.

"I'm lucky to have Ricky," she said.

"Right. Me too."

Brit is pushing Lily on the swings. Brit's skinny as a fawn. Glasses, overbite, smattering of pimples on her chin. "Unfortunate age," I said to Ricky the first time I met her and we'd watched her run up the walkway at Connie's. Ricky's old house was a two-story Colonial with a false brick front and huge rhododendron bushes out front. Connie collected lawn gnomes and they were all over the place—digging fake holes, picking imaginary flowers, bending over and kissing one another. I kind of liked the gnomes because other than that, the place had the personality of a paper bag.

"She looks a lot like Connie did at that age," Ricky had said.

I got the message that he wasn't up for talking bad about either his daughter or his ex-wife.

Connie's car is a Lexus, black, so clean it glimmers in the parking lot lights.

She gets out and eyes my leotard. "Night shift," I say.

Ricky comes out from the hospital like he's been watching for Connie's car. They greet each other with kiss-kiss. "A vampire?" She says, running the edge of his cape between her fingers.

He laughs. "I forgot I still had that on. Why didn't you girls tell me?"

Brit says, "I thought it looked cool. Like a superhero."

Connie smiles her veneered smile. "How are the Peterson's?"

"The Peterson's are fine," I say, linking my arm through Ricky's and leaning my head on his shoulder.

"They're not, actually." He doesn't exactly shrug me off but he moves forward and dislodges my head from his shoulder. "He's being taken into surgery and she's a mess."

"Poor things," Connie says. She's wearing a black leather coat that I would never have bought but now that I see it on her I want it.

"We don't even know them," I say. "They could murder small children during commercials."

Ricky and Connie stare at me.

The girls are standing one on either side of Connie touching the seams of her coat. I touch the diamond pattern of my fishnets. "I thought you said the daughter was coming? Is she here? Linda, was that her name?"

Ricky blinks, rubs his eyebrows. "Where'd you get Linda?"

I shrug. I made it up but Linda Peterson sounds like a reasonable name. All of a sudden there's a chill and I start to shiver like mad. "Is she here yet?"

Ricky and Connie shake their heads in unison.

"I need to get Lily home," I say. "It's getting late."

Connie looks at her tasteful white-leather and diamond watch. "It's six o'clock."

"We haven't had dinner."

"I'm not hungry," Lily says.

"You must have homework," I say. Even though it's Saturday night and she's in Pre-Kindergarten. I put my hand over her mouth to stop her from saying any more. Connie's eyes get all big and I think for a second she's going to say something about child abuse. I narrow my eyes at her and she looks away.

I squeeze Ricky's arm. "I want to get going."

He looks at me, then at Connie. "I can drive you home," Connie says.

Ricky smiles so wide I can see the crooked tooth in the way back. "That would be awesome," he says.

The kids race toward Connie's car. I stand there for another ten seconds to give Ricky a chance to change his mind. He touches the small of my back. "I'll call you later," he says.

"Great," Connie says.

Ricky laughs. "Both of you."

The whole thing creeps me out.

Connie's car is a silvery gray inside, leather, heated seats.

"It feels like we're in a spaceship," Lily says. She powers down the window, waves a hand out. "Helllloooo, world," she yells.

I close my eyes and lean my head back against the warm seat. "You and Ricky get along so well it's a wonder you aren't still together."

Connie laughs but it's a hard sound, more like a bark. "There's no sense in not being civil."

I'm happily lulled and not sure if she means them being civil to each other, or me being civil to either of them. The car is so smooth I can barely feel a bump in the road.

When she pulls up to my house, both girls clamor out of the backseat. Brit says, "I'm just going to walk Lily in, okay?"

Connie blows them kisses, her ivory hand coming just to her pink lips, then a flick and wave, sending invisible kisses off the tips of her French-manicured nails. She is still watching out the side window when I lean over and press my lips to the spot just below her diamond hoop earring. I feel the lotion-softness of her skin, taste the faint bitterness of her perfume, feel her fluttery heartbeat beneath my dry lips. "Thanks for the ride," I say, my mouth still against her neck, my warm breath carrying itself back into my face.

She turns her head and for one split second I think she's going to kiss me back. But her hand comes up in the slight space between us and her rings catch the light from the streetlamps. She will tell Ricky about the bubblegum smell of my breath, the over-slickness of my lips. She will wonder if I used the tip of my tongue to taste her perfume.

Brit is running back down the weedy lawn, opening her door, sliding into the backseat, breathless. I blink and smile and open my door and before I'm even all the way around the car, Connie is peeling off down the street, Brit waving with her arm out the window.

Ω

Rebirth of the Big Top

by Jen Fawkes

Miranda the Elephant Girl was the first of them. Trevor hired her to work concessions on Fridays and alternate Wednesdays. "I cannot cook, and I don't do windows," she'd joked in halting English. "Anything else, I'm your girl." Trevor guessed she was pushing forty. She wore a pair of cut-off dungarees and a half-shirt, making no attempt to hide her condition. From a distance, the skin of her arms, legs, and torso looked filthy, or like the spotted pelt of a jaguar. Close up, rough, gray scales leapt into focus. Trevor perched on the edge of his battered desk, watching her stare down the box fan that circulated stifling air through his office, words like *armored* and *stegosaurus* and *parched* scuttling through his brain. The skin of her back resembled a relief map of a locale he'd never imagined.

Gill Nathan's World Famous Carnival and Sideshow had been touring the southeast when an aneurism erupted in Gill Nathan's brain, killing him, stranding his employees outside Atlanta. Trapeze artists and lion tamers. Strongmen and acrobats. Bareback riders and clowns. A whole slew of human oddities.

"I cannot tell you how much appreciation I feel," Miranda said as Trevor showed her how to load and operate the popcorn popper, how to change the soda syrup and deal with the sticky drawer on the cash register. "Most of us have never known any other life. It would be nice if you could hire more of my colleagues."

But no one came to the drive-in. Trevor couldn't even afford the Elephant Girl. He wasn't sure why he'd hired her in the first place.

*

Cassie hadn't had the strength to see it through. Trevor had read as much in a note she'd affixed to the white door of the Frigidaire on a Monday morning in April. Joshua had just turned twelve. When Trevor touched the sleeping boy's shoulder, Josh's sunken blue eyes snapped open.

"She's gone?"

Trevor nodded.

Josh struggled to a seated position. "Where do you think she'll go?"

"California? It's where all the beautiful people end up."

That morning, Trevor quit his job in order to take over the boy's schooling. "Are you crazy?" Nick Peterson said. "You're the best we've got. You were born to do this."

Trevor had always had a knack for turning failing businesses around. When he was eight, the addition of fresh lime to his lemonade made his the busiest stand in a twelve-block radius. At ten, he'd suggested that his uncle Carl knock a hole in the south wall of his casual dining restaurant in order to install a drive-through window, and sales at Carl's Cozy Corner had tripled. And for his father, who hawked the pelts of small, defenseless creatures—sables, rabbits, minks—in the viscous atmosphere of north Georgia, Trevor's myriad suggestions—layaway, soft lighting, comfy chairs, cool drinks—added up to pure profit. As a consultant with the Atlanta firm of Dowd, Dowd, and Blessing, Trevor had traveled the country for ten years, studying business plans and cost analyses, telling people from all walks of life how better to run their businesses. On average, he increased profitability by an astounding fifty-seven percent—twice the percentage achieved by any other D, D, and B consultant.

"We could go under without you," Nick Peterson pleaded.

"Sorry," Trevor said. "My priority is the boy."

Cassie had been gone a month when Josh announced that he might like to see California. Trevor had just finished stirring pure Vermont maple syrup into Josh's oatmeal. When he lifted a napkin to wipe a glop from the boy's chin, an unexpected sob tore from Trevor, like pressurized molten matter escaping an active volcano.

"Shh," Josh said, placing a withered hand on his father's arm. "We're OK."

In terms of hair, Josh had only ever had a thin fringe hugging the outside of his enormous cranium. His body was the most brittle thing Trevor had ever touched. The wrinkling of his skin had started a couple of years earlier. Sometime in the next year, he would most likely suffer a fatal heart attack.

That afternoon, they studied geography. Trevor spread a map of the United States across the kitchen table, and he and Josh pushed Matchbox cars from state to state, memorizing capitals. Each state was a particular shade of blue; these tonal variations roiled over the map like ocean waves. Josh had spent his entire life in Georgia. Trevor decided what he and the boy should probably do was travel.

After the Elephant Girl, Trevor hired Neil, who'd accompanied Miranda to a Wednesday shift at the concession stand. The hirsute young man closely resembled post-transformation Lon Chaney Jr. in *The Wolf Man*.

"You do not mind if he just stands beside the counter, Mr. Trevor?" Miranda had said. "Neil has nowhere to go, and he is crazy for American movies."

Trevor, too, was crazy for American movies. He figured that this was why, after returning from his cross-country travels, he hadn't gone back to the consulting firm of Dowd, Dowd, and Blessing. Why instead he'd scraped together the remainder of his savings and purchased the Big Top Drive-In, an establishment on the brink of foreclosure and collapse twenty miles south of Atlanta. When he was a boy, his parents had often taken him to the Big Top; the cinematic outings had given his family a much-needed break, releasing the tension that forever charged the air of their home. Nights at the Big Top were organized by genre: Western Wednesdays, Noir Thursdays, Romance Saturdays. Trevor knew he'd seen *Arsenic and Old Lace* on a Tuesday, *Now, Voyager* on a Saturday, *Destry Rides Again* on a Wednesday. The taste of popcorn and fountain soda, the tinny sounds that burst from the metal speaker hung on the window of his father's Buick, the sticky sensation of bare thighs against leather, the sight of his mother resting her curly head on his father's shoulder—these were the bright spots of boyhood.

When Trevor took over the Big Top, he screened the films of his youth. He reintroduced genre nights. The public stayed away in droves.

"Perhaps you should try showing something modern, Mr. Trevor?" Miranda suggested after she'd been working at the deserted drive-in a couple of weeks. "Shirley MacLaine and Steve McQueen. *Bye Bye Birdie*. Warren Beatty. Then the people, they might come."

Trevor set Neil up in the booth, teaching him how to run the projector, how to spot the white circle that heralds the reel change, how to load the heavy spools of black film. "Where you from, Neil?" he asked.

"Upstate New York," the young man replied.

"Cold up that way."

"It's good for my condition. Better than this heat."

"What about Miranda?"

"Oh, this is the place for her. Swampy. Cold dries her out something terrible."

"You two together?"

Neil shrugged. "Sort of."

"Ever think about shaving?"

"Sure," Neil replied. "I used to. But it just keeps coming back."

*

Trevor had gotten his first tattoo in North Carolina. On the lower-right side of his back. "Cool," Joshua had said, running his fingers over the saran-covered Tar Heel State, shaded the same blue as its counterpart on their US capitals map. "I want one."

"You're too young."

Josh looked thirty years older than his father. The absurdity of Trevor's statement wavered between them.

"Come on, Dad. What are you afraid of?"

He feared the pain that streaked his son's face as Tiny, the tattoo artist, injected subcutaneous ink. The burly man had hesitated for several long seconds before agreeing to tattoo Josh. "You sure he's old enough?"

Trevor looked at Josh, who peeled off his striped shirt to reveal skeletal arms, a shriveled chest and back. The boy nodded enthusiastically. Trevor turned to Tiny and did the same.

Mingled with the discomfort on Josh's face was evidence of the boy's particular and serene strength—fortitude bred from a lifelong battle with agony. As they ambled back to the Mountaineer Motor Court, something swelled inside Trevor. He swung his son high in the air then hugged him to his chest. In cabin twelve, they stood with their backs to the mirror, shirtless, peering over their shoulders, studying their matching modifications.

"Cool," Josh said again, softly.

The plan was to hit every state in the nation, driving the Chevy up the east coast to Maine, making their way down to Alabama, then back up to Michigan, and so on. They'd set out in May. The weather was fine in Pennsylvania and New York, in Vermont and New Hampshire. They didn't spend long in each state, just time enough to see a couple of sights and add a tattoo to their burgeoning body maps. Trevor estimated that it would take three months to reach California.

"It's nothing like home," he told Josh. "The trees are different, and the flowers, and the animals. It's almost like another country."

"What do you think she's doing?"

Trevor couldn't imagine. When they'd met, Cassie had been an aesthetician with aspirations. She loved musicals— *The King and I* and *Kiss Me, Kate* and *Guys and Dolls*. She belted out numbers in the shower, and while washing dishes, and behind the wheel of the car. Occasionally, she would cradle Trevor's head in her lap, ruffling his thinning hair with her nervous fingers, singing softly, her eyelids low. She was too pretty for Trevor, who'd never been more than average-looking. If she hadn't gotten pregnant with Joshua, Trevor doubted she would have married him. He'd been working for Dowd, Dowd, and Blessing just over a year, building his unassailable reputation, when the boy was born.

"No," Cassie had said after Dr. Derringer sat them down, after he attempted to explain Josh's condition. "I don't believe you."

Their son was two. By the age of seven, he would appear to be fifty. It would be a miracle if he saw thirteen.

"That's not possible," Cassie had said, turning to Trevor. "Tell him Josh isn't sick. Tell him we can't watch him die. That we won't."

Dr. Derringer's office was flooded with afternoon light, but Trevor sensed a shadow creeping through. He thought of Max Schreck, of the eerie, jagged shade he'd cast on the walls in *Nosferatu*. The shadow of the vampire had heralded death; if it fell upon you, you were done for.

"Trevor," Cassie said, but Trevor was afraid to lift his eyes. He didn't want to look at his wife. He reached for her hand, which lay in his palm like something cold, scaly, inanimate. "Please," she'd said.

"Maybe she's working as an extra on a musical," Trevor said to Josh as they zoomed from Kentucky into Tennessee. "Maybe she'll get picked out of the crowd when the star breaks an ankle, and she'll take over the lead."

"Are you mad at her?"

"I don't know. Are you?"

Josh was eating animal crackers from one of those red circus train car boxes. He held up two elephants. Sitting on his knees, he walked them slowly across the dashboard of the Chevy, scooting closer and closer to Trevor. Just as the animals crested the rise over the instrument panel, Josh snatched them back and crammed them into his mouth. He pressed his heavy head into his father's upper arm.

"Yeah," he said when he'd finished chewing. "But I think I forgive her."

*

After Miranda and Neil came Julius, the Lobster Man, whose hands were shaped like two crustaceous claws. Conjoined twins Sheila and Shirley shared an enlarged heart. Duane had no arms, and Ruby, no legs. Gina the Giantess stood nearly seven feet tall. Bertram's parasitic twin dangled from his lower spine. Trevor gave each of his employees a shift a week in the concession stand or the ticket booth. Sometimes he paid them to pick up trash that nonexistent customers left in the lot. Even when they weren't working, his employees gravitated to the Big Top, where they hung around, chatting with one another, watching the movies Neil projected onto the screen. *Dr. Ehrlich's Magic Bullet. The Man Who Came to Dinner. Force of Evil.* One night, Trevor was awakened by a light scratching on his bedroom window. He rose and stumbled to the front door. His battered cottage stood on the back side of the drive-in and had been included in the asking price. On the tiny porch, he discovered Miranda, wearing her customary cutoffs and half-shirt.

"Why won't you show the modern films?" she asked. The scent of whiskey wafted from her curling lips. "Why do you insist on showing movies no one wants to see?"

"Does Neil know you're here?"

She shrugged. "Neil does not own me."

Trevor seized her scabrous arms near the shoulders. She smelled like the desert. Making love to the Elephant Girl was like going to bed with a belt sander. Marvelously painful.

Trevor wished that her warm, moist interior were as desiccated as her exterior, that her mouth and vagina would abrade him like the skin of her chest and legs. Cassie had been as pliable as room-temperature butter, and she'd smelled of new-mown hay. After Josh's diagnosis, she'd started slinking around Trevor, dim and silent as a shade. When the time came, she announced that she would school Josh at home. Trevor was both relieved and ashamed of his relief. "I know kids can be cruel," he said, "but the boy doesn't have long. Should we really isolate him further?" Cassie bared her teeth. She slapped her husband's face. She moved her things into Josh's room, sleeping in the extra twin bed. From then on, Trevor caught only glimpses of his wife. Impressions of her. She spent nearly every moment with their son, but Trevor knew nothing of what she taught him.

"I know how to make a business turn a profit," he said to Miranda as they lay sidewise across his rickety iron bed. "That's not what I'm after."

"What are you after?"

"I don't exactly know."

She placed a coarse palm against each of his cheeks. "You think you know pain," she said. "I see this. Something claws at your insides. But listen to me, Mr. Trevor. Pain is skin so dry it cracks when you smile. And you don't know shit about it."

The following evening, a small crowd of teenagers showed up at the Big Top around ten p.m. *Key Largo* had started at nine. They parked their cars in front of the screen but didn't remain in them. They got out and swarmed the concession stand. Bought popcorn and Sugar Babies, nachos and sodas from Miranda and Gina the Giantess. Rather than returning to their cars, the kids settled on the pavement. They sat munching and slurping, pushing hair out of their faces, watching Miranda and Gina talk with Sheila and Shirley and Julius, who carried legless Ruby in his arms. Just for fun, Bertram started juggling, and Duane ate popcorn with his feet. The teenagers applauded. They tossed coins, which clanked loudly against the concrete.

*

Trevor and Josh saw the Grand Canyon and Mount Rushmore. The World's Largest Ball of Twine and Little Bighorn Battlefield. They explored deserted mining camps and ghost towns of the Wild West. The geographic pictograms on their backs grew, filling out, moving toward completion. They ate at greasy spoons and bar-b-que restaurants, hot dogs stands and hamburger joints. They stayed in motor lodges, motor courts, motor inns. Even when he grew exhausted, which happened more and more often, Josh emitted a steady stream of commentary, speaking in a breathy rush, not only to Trevor but to anyone in earshot—vacationing families, truckers, melancholy drifters. Trevor had never seen the boy so animated. His conversations weren't the stilted exchanges one might expect between complete strangers and a kid who's spent his life in solitary. Josh was achingly genuine. He tore at Trevor's heart.

Occasionally, someone would ask, "Is that a kid or an old man?"

"He's my son," Trevor would reply.

"What's wrong with him?"

"Nothing," Trevor would say, or "I don't know what you mean."

"He has a degenerative condition," or "It's just that he's going to die soon."

As they cruised the Vegas Strip, sliding past the Tropicana and the Stardust and Circus Circus, Trevor snuck glances at the colored lights playing over his son's crumpled face. Josh kept coughing dangerously, but he was grinning like a mad-man. In Oregon, Trevor took him to a shaky, bandy-legged MD, who said the time had come to make the boy comfortable. Trevor had to practically force the pain pills down his son's throat. As they crossed the border into California, Trevor and Josh cheered, high-fived.

"How will we find her?" Josh asked at a diner outside Cupertino.

"I don't know," Trevor said, eating french fries the boy had drowned in ketchup. "I don't know if she's here."

Josh's wrinkled brow furrowed further. "Why did we come?"

"I thought you should see it," Trevor said, his hands rising from the Formica tabletop to carve a sphere in the air.

In Los Angeles, they visited Universal Studios and the back lots at MGM. They toured the La Brea Tar Pits. They took off their shoes, cuffed their trousers, and strolled along the beach. They scurried into the surf, dashing back as the tide chased them in. Trevor watched the sun's light diffusing softly, flowing around dunes and sea grass and side-stepping crabs, illuminating Josh with an impossible halo, one that made him look like a holy relic, a shriveled Buddha. Trevor couldn't stop crying. He wanted to take his son's hand and walk into the ocean, to keep walking, just the two of them, to tromp all over the sea floor, to find sunken ships stuffed with pirate booty, to commune with dolphins, tiger sharks, killer whales.

"Don't worry, Dad," Josh said. "I never believed it."

"What?"

"That I'd be OK."

"What else did she tell you?"

"That no one can hold a candle to Gene Kelly."

"What else?"

"She said you know how to bring things back to life."

"You believe that?"

Josh didn't respond. He slipped his cold hand into Trevor's.

They'd almost reached the Georgia border when Trevor tried to rouse his son and found that he was unable. He pulled off the road and parked on the shoulder. He studied Joshua, who lay across the front seat as though lost in slumber, his heavy head resting on Trevor's thigh. Trevor slid out from under the boy, stepped from the car. He staggered along the gravel edge of the highway, blinded. Pontiacs and Fords and Buicks whizzed past. Horns honked. The quality of the light knocked him off balance. The sun burned unbearably, like a thousand-watt bulb without a shade. Trevor shielded his eyes with both hands. He stumbled, falling to his knees. Motorists rolled down their windows and shouted.

"Watch it, buddy!"

"You trying to get yourself killed?"

An older couple pulled over. The man caught Trevor under the arms and eased him toward their convertible sedan. He opened the back door, sat Trevor down on cream-colored leather, handed him a clean, pressed handkerchief. Trevor mopped his brow and cheeks. The couple looked at him with concern. He told them about Josh. Everything. From the beginning. He started with the day his son was born, with the way the light in the maternity ward had coiled itself around the boy, illuminating his particular serenity. Even as an infant, Josh had rarely wept. There had been no fixing him, no way to understand his pain. Trevor envied Cassie her ability to deny. He wondered if, wherever she was, she sensed the shift in the natural order of things. If she noticed the way Joshua's passing had altered the sun.

"I wish you could have met him," he said to the couple. "I'm not sure how I'll go on."

He wrote to Cassie's parents. They flew in from Michigan, but there was no sign of Cassie. On the day of Josh's funeral, the US map etched across the boy's back was nearly complete. Trevor drove down to Florida and had the Sunshine State's blue shape added to his own map. On the way home, twenty miles south of Atlanta, he passed the decrepit remains of the Big Top Drive-In. He pulled over. He studied the sagging screen and the listing concession stand—landmarks that, like his son, had aged before their time. He thought of the bright spots of boyhood. Gary Cooper in *The Pride of the Yankees*. Margaret O'Brien in *Little Women*. Characters who'd faced death with a stoicism that had once struck him as pure fantasy. Trevor wanted to cry, but he was out of tears. He decided to buy the Big Top.

*

Less than a month after the first gawking crowd of teenagers showed up, the drive-in was crawling with customers. Not just high-school kids, but their parents and grandparents, their younger brothers and sisters. Whole families. Out-of-town guests. People came from Atlanta, then they started coming from Savannah, from Charleston. Neil projected movies onto the screen, but this wasn't what drew the crowds. Most nights, every parking spot was taken; those who couldn't get a spot parked in a nearby field and walked over. They milled between cars and around the periphery. Many brought blankets and picnic baskets. On a stage Trevor and Neil had erected in front of the screen, those employees who weren't busy serving popcorn, pouring sodas, or tearing tickets did what they did best. Put their perverted bodies on display. Showcased that which set them apart. Miranda roared and stomped her scaly feet. Ruby walked on her hands. Shirley and Sheila sang duets, songs straight from the heart. Bertram performed feats of magic, making his parasitic twin disappear and reappear. Customers thronged the stage and the concession stand. It was all the employees could do to keep up. Money started pouring in. Trevor kept only enough to maintain the facilities and equipment. The rest he divided evenly among his employees.

"Mr. Trevor," Miranda said as she mounted him in his rickety bed, as they bobbed together like buoys on the swelling surface of the sea, she sliding her abrasive skin across his, "how can we ever repay you?"

On a bright fall day, they stood together outside a silver trailer that housed an Atlanta tattoo parlor. "You do realize the pain will be only temporary?" Miranda said.

"Which is worse," Trevor said, "pain or humiliation?"

The Elephant Girl laughed. She shook her head. "I cannot say. These have been bound together since I was a child. What I find most unbearable is indifference."

Four six-hour sessions were required to coat Trevor's skin in tattoos that simulated Miranda's gray scales. He'd never planned to convert his business into a carnival sideshow, but the progression had been inevitable. This is what Trevor told the reporter from the *Atlanta Star* who came out to do a feature on the rebirth of the Big Top. After a photographer snapped photos of Trevor and his employees artfully arranged on the stage, Trevor and the reporter retired to Trevor's office. The man's tie fluttered in the box fan's sticky breeze.

"This place was dead," he said. "Like Lazarus."

Trevor shook his head. "Not dead," he said, "just sleeping."

Miranda and Trevor billed themselves as The Elephant Couple. Trevor relished taking the stage with her night after night, drinking from the sea of emotions that flowed from the audience to lap at his tattooed feet—delight and horror, pity and shame. When he turned to the screen, exposing his backside, and stood gazing up at twenty feet of Marlene Dietrich or Tyrone Power, a whispering rush sounded, a collective intake of breath followed by a weighty silence. As the crowd gaped at his geographical hieroglyphs, at the forty-eight continental United States spattered in varying shades of blue across prickling human flesh, he swiveled his head toward Miranda, who smiled, lowering her scaly lids. The Elephant Girl's belly swelled, its skin taut and crackling with life, and Trevor's fingers trembled, aching to stroke its splintered surface.

Ω

"Rebirth of the Big Top" originally appeared in *The Iowa Review*.

Satan Takes 12 Steps

by Perry Glasser

Satan comes to our Thursday night meeting. He sits in the back, close to the door. We all know what that's like. We have all been there. First-timer jitters. You sit. You smoke. You listen. Maybe you come back. Most don't.

But this is Satan. You have to wonder.

Two weeks go by. We figure we are okay. But then Satan shows up again. Don't ask me why Thursday; don't ask me why our meeting. No one gets turned away, right? But Satan says nothing. Just sits in the last seat in the fourth row from the back, the one closest to the wall. He smokes.

I let myself stare. It is a funny thing, but whenever Satan takes another cigarette from the pack he has on the metal fold-up beside his, the cigarette is a brand different from the last. You can tell by the color of the filters. It's not a cigarette case, just a pack like any other. But somehow, Satan's cigarettes are pre-packed variable. I figure, he has his pack special ordered. Maybe he is friends with people in the industry.

After the meeting, we break down the chairs, and then Marge and me go for coffee. Two blocks from the Hall, under

83

the el they serve the coffee in a small, steel pot. Real china. The cups are sometimes chipped, but they use saucers. It's a nice place.

Marge says, "What do you think, Louis?" She stirs three sugars, no milk, no cream, and hunkers way down in the booth. The rain outside seems greasy on the window.

I tell her I don't know. I am willing to wait and see.

Marge and I know each other what? five years? and we have been through some things. I have no secrets from Marge. She knows it all. I am pretty sure she has none from me, but if she did it would not bother me. If she wants a little bit private, that's her business. We are friends from the meetings. Three years ago, we fooled around a little, but that stopped. I think we both needed a friend more than we needed to fool around.

"I worry," she says. "Why is Satan at the meeting?"

I remind her that everyone has a reason, but no one needs to give one. When he is ready, the Devil will tell us why he attends our Thursday night 12-step meeting for degenerate gamblers.

She nods. "Eight to five he is up to no good."

"Could be," I say. "It is the Devil."

"That's right," Marge says. "He is the Devil."

We are not talking about some Charlie Manson look-alike. This is not Al Pacino as a lawyer. Make no mistake. Satan is near nine-foot. He wears a blue sweatsuit, but the guy's complexion is redder than the reddest Indian. He wears Nikes, cheap ones. His hands are big and, yeah, there is an aroma I never smell before but now it has been in my nose twice I know is brimstone. Rotten eggs. It's the sulfur. The guy at our meeting is Satan, all right. The Prince of Darkness. The Master of Lies is in an aisle seat at the VFW Hall on Thursdays at 7:00.

I ask, "You think we should ask him to come for coffee next time? Make him feel welcome? It might help him along."

"Get real."

*

The next week, Satan steps up. Third speaker, right after Allison the computer expert tells us she is working on her personal inventory. It's hard, Allison says. We all nod. It is hard.

Satan is too tall for the lectern, but he hunches down a little. His hands grip the wooden lip. We are a small group. We tried a microphone once, but nobody liked it.

"My name is Lucifer and I am..." He stops. We lean forward a little. You want to help. But he has to say the words. "My name is Lucifer and I have lost control of my life."

Close enough. We all say, "Hi, Lucifer."

People make fun of the name thing. It's easy to make fun of. But the first time you hear a group welcome you, it's something. After a while, you count on it.

"I don't know what to say," Satan says.

"Say what's in your heart," a guy named Earl says. Earl has been here a long time. A lot of us owe a lot to Earl. Anyone falls, you need a guy like Earl to make the catch. So it's good that Earl speaks. Me, I am wondering how many names Satan has and if we invite him for coffee, what will he want us to call him?

Marge is across the room. She looks at me. I shrug. Her arms cross on her chest.

"I never had control of my life."

His Satanic Majesty goes on in this way, telling us stuff. He's dodging, of course. Everyone had control of their lives, once. But no one catches him up on it. It's his first time. We listen. It's hard enough to get it right. You listen to help, not to judge. Everyone starts out with some control. No one is a vic-

85

tim from birth. Lucifer wants to say his life is not like that? Okay. You listen.

But later I say to Marge, "I think he may have a point."

"What point?"

"Maybe the guy never had control. He does what he does because he is supposed to."

Marge isn't buying. "He's going to have a hell of a time with turning his will and life over to a Higher Power," she says.

I see what she means.

"You don't get it, do you?" she says. She is waiting for her coffee to cool.

I tell her I get it.

"No you don't. The joke. 'Hell of a time'?"

She is right. I did not get it. "I got it," I say, and to keep my eyes from hers I signal the waitress. The girl brings me a cruller.

"Everyone chooses," Marge says. "You lose control, you lose control. No shame in it if you know it and take the steps."

I say that's why he is here. I say you have to give the Devil the benefit of the doubt.

"You mean 'Give the Devil his due.'" Marge says.

Marge can really piss a person off.

*

Just one meeting more and Satan—Lucifer, Nick, Scratch, whatever—is telling us he has always acknowledged that God could restore him to sanity and that he has personally asked God to remove his defects of character and his shortcomings. A person could take six months, a year, a lifetime, easy, to accomplish all twelve steps, but Satan is moving along every week. "God will not restore my sanity," Satan says. "I asked. He refused."

That has to be tough. We murmur in sympathy. Some of us nod. Even Marge nods a little. One of the things you learn in Group is that when you don't know what to do, you nod. Affirmation is sometimes all a person needs to see.

I steal a look at old Earl. Earl is chewing his lip on the side where tobacco stains his white beard. Earl once explained to me that the line on football and sports is not about what someone thinks is the quality of the teams, but is about dividing the betting public—that is you and me—into two equal crowds. This is how bookmakers make money. They do not handicap teams; they gauge bettors. So Earl is one smart guy, and though I know for a fact Earl goes to church every Sunday, I am also sure it does Earl little good to think God turns down requests for help.

But you have to admit, Satan is in a unique situation. Every degenerate gambler knows that temptation is everywhere, but it is something to have before you Satan who puts temptation before you. I knew a guy once took a week's receipts out of his boss's unlocked cash box to bet on a sure thing in the 4th race at Hollywood Park. He liked the jockey. I figure, unless the jockey can put the horse on his shoulders and run, there is no sure thing at the ponies. This is why I like the puppies myself, the greyhounds. You can handicap animals when there is no doping and no human factor.

Satan says, "So if it comes to a Higher Power, I need to look to the group."

Comes to the 12-step program, Satan is on Step 13. This is what I say to Marge after the meeting. He's got us going and coming. He's way past where we are.

She lights her cigarette with the burning end of mine. "He skipped the inventory," she says. "That's Step Four. 'Make a searching and fearless inventory of ourselves.'" Marge is one for getting everything right.

"I don't know," I say. "You name it, Satan takes the blame. His inventory, that's public record."

Marge squints at me.

"Wars, pestilence..." As I tick things off on my fingers, I start to see Satan's problem. No wonder he is at the meeting. "Look," I say. "Anything bad ever happened, Satan takes the rap. You start with Eve. Satan really is out of control."

"That's why he was cast from Heaven."

"You've been reading up," I say.

Marge shrugs. She went to college and then some, I remember. She could have been a teacher. In fact, she was once. "Eve could have said, 'No.'"

"So that's Satan's fault?"

"What?"

"That Eve bit the apple."

"You figure it out. I can't." Marge adds an extra sugar to her coffee. "He's either out of control or over-controlled. I don't care which. But what worries me is he wants us to be his higher power."

"That's a problem?"

"Geez, Louis. Sometimes you have to deal with the elephant in the living room."

"I don't see it."

"You want to be Satan's higher power?"

"If that's what the guy needs."

She shakes her head. "You figure God won't mind if you forgive the Devil?"

*

The next week, Satan does not show. Neither does Marge.

This is not the first time Marge does not make it, but you can see why I worry a little.

Marge calls me on the weekend. Like I figured, she was with the Devil. "Just coffee," she says. "I swear."

"It's none of my business."

"Just coffee, Louis."

I listen a long time. I can her breathing above the hum. There is always a hum on the telephone. You have to listen to hear it. It never really goes away. To talk heart to heart, you have to not be afraid of silence. I wait long enough and Marge speaks.

"Okay, maybe it was more than coffee. But nothing to be ashamed of. I swear. Satan wanted to know what I thought if he humbly asked the Higher Power to remove his liabilities." This is Step 7.

"Satan wants to pray?"

"I asked him that. Satan doesn't pray. He goes straight to the top if he wants to be heard."

I wait.

"Louis, he said the group is his Higher Power and so he doesn't have to go to God anymore. That's allowed, you know. He said he'd ask the group."

I tell her I am not sure of any of this

"This is why I am talking to you, Louis. I am not sure of any of it either."

You have to make 12-Step programs okay for atheists. Everyone is welcome, right? It's not a problem. You make the higher power the group. It works pretty well for most people. But the Devil is no atheist and is not most people. For Satan, it's not a matter of faith.

I am not sure, either," I say. I reach for my cigarettes. My pack is empty. "You need to talk?" I ask. "Anything else you want to tell me?"

Again, I listen to the hum of the line until Marge says, "No."

"So you are all right with this?"

"I did not say that. Louis. What if we forgive the Devil? What happens to us?"

It's a puzzle, all right. A real mindbender. "Where did you have this conversation?" I ask Marge.

"Don't ask me that, Louis."

*

The next Thursday, Marge and Satan do show up. They come into the Hall separately. I do not know what it is, but I cannot shake the feeling that they arrived together. Marge looks like she always does. Your jeans. Your scrunchy for her ponytail. No make-up. Bag-eyes. It would be hard to guess that Marge used to be a Casino junkie. Casinos usually call for class. Marge's game was Keno, which is like Bingo, but much, much faster. As far as your chances of winning, you would do better to flush your money down a toilet and hope the toilet will gush oil.

Satan is wearing his usual—blue jumpsuit and the Nikes. I feel jealousy, and have no idea why I feel jealous.

A lot of people are talking this night. It's a funny thing. People sometimes speak just to speak, but this night everyone is tripping over themselves to report progress. Irene tells us she has apologized to her daughter, and it is hard not to cry when she tells us that her daughter allowed her to hold the grandkids, Benjamin and Polly. James tells us he has worked hard and long to make a list of the people he has harmed. He has each name on an index card and carries the pack snapped in a rubber band in his pocket. He is working on the will power to make amends. If he thinks of something he did not think of before, he writes it on a card or makes a new one. We all know James is a bookkeeper. He does not know if he will have the courage to do the next step, but we all tell him he will find a way and that makes him smile. When he sits down, Marge stands up. This is not that unusual, but it is nice to see. She is making a continual effort to take a personal inventory and tells us she was wrong. She does not say about what, but that is all right with most of us. It's progress. Other people talk. The front of the room looks like the line to OTB on Kentucky Derby Day. Everyone wants a shot at the lectern. People seem to be smoking less. We go through the coffee urn twice.

Satan gets up front.

"Hel-looo, Satan."

Satan wants to improve his conscious contact with the Higher Power, which is us. I am not sure of this plan. But the mood is upbeat. We are all high on caffeine. Everyone says *Sure, Go for it.*

What happens next is hard to describe. It's like we all have a dream on turbo power, but everyone's dream is different. Boom, boom, boom, stuff is coming in. You don't hear it; you don't see it. You just suddenly know all the things Satan wants you to know about yourself. I look at Earl, and he is laughing. A lot of the group sits perfectly still, palms on their knees, stunned. I am a little staggered myself, and see the moment I realized that effort did not guarantee reward. I was what, 12? No wonder I spent so long not caring. My mother was not a good woman. I like to think she tried her best, but it's time to realize, she was not a good woman. I have wanted to think that everything makes sense—it does not. So what?

I shake off the feeling. I see Marge is the only person crying.

"He is the Master of Lies," she says out loud, but no one pays attention to her.

Marge and Satan leave together. He has his arm around her shoulder, and she leans in like she has returned to where she belongs.

*

I skip the meetings for three weeks. *Who needs this?* I ask myself. I know I have a problem. *Deal with it,* I say. When did it become right to think a guy what has problems is more admirable for admitting he is not equal to his troubles?

But after a month, I am looking on the Internet at the results in Florida and Texas. It used to be everywhere, but the game is disappearing. Looking at results is harmless, right?

I look-up the results four days in a row, and so I know it is not my imagination that sees payoffs at the dog races are such you think maybe it is Christmas. Not a winner is paying under $12.00. Never mind your quinellas and perfectas. These are straight win bets. Anyone with a half brain can make a living at this. Long shots are running box-to-wire as regular as Amtrak. Trifecta's are all Uncle Sam payoffs—meaning they are so large they have to withhold taxes from the winnings. The seven-box comes in four times one matinee at Gulf Greyhound in Houston, which means big, big dollars because your outside lanes are tough, very tough scores. Down in Orlando, the same day, a sixteen race card sees fourteen winners out of the eight-box. If you don't know the pups, let me tell you that these outside-lane winners on a single card are less likely than the animals catching the electric bunny and inviting it to dine on steak and ice-cream.

I download a program from Daytona, print it, and like a swell I light a cigar to play the Wednesday night card. I spend a long day staring at the sheet and I pick five out of the first seven before I shut down the computer.

I remind myself: I am a degenerate gambler. For me, it is not about money. It is not about winning. It is not about fun.

It is about losing.

I figure I am overdue for a meeting.

*

Things have changed.

The VFW Hall on Thursday night has music. There are colored lights and a mirrored disco ball hanging from the ceiling. Laser lights slice the smoke. There are streamers drooping on the light fixtures. There is a Latin band. There are some chairs set up, all right, but they are against one wall and no one is in them. The place is elbow-to-elbow with people smoking and blabbing and shaking their behinds at the music.

I can't find Satan, but I do find Marge. She is wearing a black dress and showing a lot of shoulder. Simple black pumps, but heels high enough her posture has that come-hither look you have to love. I think she has lost weight. Fact is she looks cuter than the bee's knees.

"Louis," she says. "Good to see you." She kisses my cheek and her breast brushes my arm near my elbow.

"What happened?" I have to shout. When Marge leans close to hear me, I smell her perfume. Opium, I think. Something like that. It's heavy and musky.

She takes my hand to lead me outside where the music is muffled and we can talk. She offers me a cigarette, and out of the pack comes a Marlboro Light—my brand—but next to it I see an unfiltered Lucky Strike Green. That's a brand from World War II, for crying out loud. You can't buy them. No one sells them. But there one is in Marge's cigarette package, a 50-year old coffin nail looking fresh as tomorrow's butter. As I take the Marlboro, it starts to burn. No match. No lighter. Marge has learned a few tricks.

"I forgave myself, Louis. I've never felt so unburdened."

"I mean what happened to the meetings?"

Marge's tongue wets her lips and she looks past me over my shoulder out to the darkness. "If you don't want to gamble, Louis, don't. Anything you do to excess, take control. It's simple."

"Marge, you know that isn't how it works." She takes a cigarette of her own. "Satan taught you that," I say.

Marge laughs. "Satan? Don't go fundamentalist on me, Louis." Her lipstick smears the end of her cigarette.

The music inside is Disco Inferno. I know, that's too ridiculous, but I am telling you just how it happened. So I say to Marge, "Satan. He was coming to the meetings."

"The tall guy? I remember. I had a thing for him, but nothing came of it. I practically forgot. He stopped."

"He stopped."

"The same day you did. We haven't seen him since you've been gone. He left when you did. Where in hell have you been?"

*

Friday, I catch a plane to Orlando. You reserve online, they give you a bargain, and I catch a sale. Saturday night, I get to bet Aldo Star in the 4th.

That sweet hound comes around the last turn in second, swings wide, and passes the leader to win by a head and pay $28.40. I've got ten dollars on him, so we are talking about a $140 score. There is no way to figure such a dog. I just know he is due.

But do I go home?

There are always more races, always another card, another day, another track. I can see where this is going. It is not about winning. But what it is is sweet. I am responsible. I may be out of control, but I am running my race. Mine. Like the puppies. There could be worse things, no?

This is me, box-to-wire.

Ω

"Satan Takes 12 Steps" originally appeared in *B-FAR*, Volume 1.

Her Mother's Ghost

by Lesley Howard

Lodi turned off her cell phone and pulled the heavy damask curtains over the inn's windows before the obligatory first-night-in-a-hotel romp with her lover. He was her third paramour in as many years, and this vacation, in Seville, was her first in a half-decade.

"You know I'm fine with the in-the-dark routine but it'd also be OK if we didn't block out all the light." This lover was a PR executive ten years her junior. "You're perfect."

"That's a lie, but I appreciate your effort." Lodi knew she fell short of perfect, although if she'd favored her mother she would have been, at forty-three, still spectacular. Lodi did not share her mother's stature, coloring, or classic facial features. Plus an unfortunate birth mark marred the skin between her breasts. This imperfection had so galled her when younger she had insisted on darkened rooms during sex; three decades later she'd outgrown her self-consciousnesses but the behavior it had inspired remained, an immutable habit.

When they'd finished, her lover asked if she'd like to return to the tapas bar where they'd eaten dinner, for a nightcap.

"No thanks," she said. "I want to sleep."

He paused, seated on the mattress's edge. "You OK?"

"Just jet lag. You go." She rolled on her side, away from him, and closed her eyes. He left the room ten minutes later, after sloshing water under his armpits in the sink and splashing cologne on his neck to sweeten himself. Lodi chose not to comment. Let him find a woman his own age. It would facilitate the break-up she felt coming, the familiar chasm in her heart widening itself with increasing frequency the past month, even when he embraced her.

She walked barefooted to the bathroom. Aegean ocean blue tiles covered the floor and the walls to shoulder-height. The white towels were as luxurious as promised by Liz, her personal assistant. Liz had stayed here for her honeymoon.

Lodi brushed her teeth, washed her face, peed and used the bidet. She pulled clean undies and a nightshirt from her bag. She straightened the bed's lemon yellow blanket before sliding beneath it and tightening her sleep mask over her eyes.

An unanticipated side effect of Lodi's requirement of absolute darkness during sex was her need for it to fall asleep, after. And her complete comfort in it when she woke with insomnia, as she did two or three times a week. This in turn provided the foundation for much of her success as a screenwriter. In the dark, she imagined set details; while she gazed unseeing she reworked dialogue. She could be anyone in the dark. A warrior, a woman with a houseful of spirited children, a daughter grieving her father lost at sea. When asked about her writing process, her screenplays having been the basis for three of the top-grossing films in the past fifteen years, she answered honestly: "I spend a lot of time staring into space." She didn't mention the space had to be devoid of light. Or that she'd yet to meet a man who hadn't complained about the lack of illumination in her bedroom. That ultimate solitude, she secretly believed, also figured in her success. It did not escape her notice that her entire notion of her self hinged on the total darkness that also concealed her physical imperfection from the gaze of her lovers, most of whom were more than happy to leverage their influence on her behalf professionally. This aspect of the hours spent in the dark Lodi chose not to dwell on.

She exhaled and she spread-eagled her arms and legs across the entire bed before curling herself onto one side. She wanted to be blissfully asleep before her lover stumbled over the threshold.

Later, she would calculate the moment of her mother's departure from the world based on the hour and minutes frozen on the Audi's crushed dashboard, and decide that the ghost had probably been in her hotel room while she readied for bed. The air above the footboard had seemed oddly hazy, but she was tired. She compacted her earplugs, squeezed them in, turned off the bedside lamp.

Her lover's throaty snores filled the room as soon as she removed her earplugs early the next morning. She dressed silently, slid her slender traveler's purse from the back of the chair, and closed the door behind her, intent on starting her day with a solitary café au lait at the bistro Liz had raved about. She pressed the power button on her phone as she descended the inn's three flights of stairs. After searching searching searching the "new voice mail" message lit the screen when she was half a block from the bistro. She punched in all her relevant numbers and Liz's voice crackled. "Enrique called me, the cops came to your house last night. It's Vivian. Car accident last night. Unfortunately not a good outcome, fuck, babe, she died at the scene. Call me. I'm handling it but of course you'll want to be here."

Lodi swayed and sank to the curb. Husks of peanut shells and an upturned bottle cap lay in the gutter, both filled with fairy-sized portions of rainwater. A tendril of mist, cool and damp, curled around her ankle. Her vision blurred. It wasn't until an approaching cat retreated, hissing and hunch-backed, that she noticed the mist ribboning her ankle led to a distinct, albeit soft-edged and partially translucent, resemblance of her mother. The apparition spun in a slow circle, half of a stunned, partner-less *pas de deux*.

In life, Lodi knew her mother's habit of wearing her mass of curls loose and tousled had been born less of a desire to look bed-tumbled and sexy than of laziness. Her hair had haloed her face in age as in youth, and now in death, it seemed, it would remain undiminished, like seaweed floating in a photographer's color-drenched picture of an underwater tableau.

She flapped at the spirit, she shooed it away. The few people on the street took no notice. She assumed the ghost was invisible to them, despite its wild mane. She stood. The tendril of mist remained around her ankle. As she returned to the inn, her mother's tresses floated against Lodi's shoulder.

Of course. Even in death her mother's hair remained more interesting than Lodi's own thick straight mane. Which would need to be washed, she thought, before she climbed on the plane back to LA. As her mother's sole blood relative, she had no doubt she needed to cut short her trip: details would fall to her. But she was good with details. It was an inconvenience, not a loss, she said to herself, matching the words to her dull footfalls on the stairs up to the room.

Plus it provided perfect cover behind which to abandon this lover and then split from him. Preferably in a phone conversation. He needn't know her mother's death was causing only a logistical annoyance. Her lover, third child of four from

99

an apparently affectionate and boisterous family, would not understand this response; she could use her false grief as cover under which to end their affair. She returned to the room. "We're paid for through Saturday. You may as well enjoy it."

"What?"

"There's no point in both of us going home. Stay. Enjoy it."

"Lodi. Your mother died. I should go with you."

"I need to do this alone."

The severity of her tone silenced him, though his forlorn eyes deepened her chasm before she could fill it with practicalities real and imagined. The bereavement fare was quickly arranged and she left before lunch, proffering only her cheek to her soon-to-be-former lover before stepping into the cab for the airport.

*

Her mother used to conscript Lodi as flashlight-bearer on the days she went to the beach before sunrise. They left in the absence of predawn light, and Lodi would illuminate her mother as she arranged an easel and canvas. Vivian wanted to witness the totality of subtle shifts in color the light's progression would bring, mix her oils *en pleine aire.* As morning turned to hot noon and then cooled, every tube would be opened, depleted. "Nothing better than the light off the Pacific," she would crow to Lodi when they unpacked in the living room at day's end. Her mother's nose turned tender red on these days; Lodi's nutmeg brown.

Lodi was thirteen when Vivian ascended into an elite group of highly respected regional artists with an opening at Adamson-Duvannes Galleries, the first of many shows to come. Lodi's mother had taken her shopping at Gump's for complementary shift dresses. After they slipped into them, her mother showed her how to apply cocoa-brown eyeliner and then smudge it to create a delicate, near-seductive look.

When Lodi finished, her mother examined her at arm's length in their tiny linoleum-floored bathroom. "Good." She unscrewed the lid to her foundation with a steady hand. She leaned close to the mirror and dabbed it across her forehead with quick assurance.

Lodi watched her mother's transformation. Vivian sucked in her cheeks and brushed blush in the hollows. She applied mascara with a delicate touch. Always pretty, she became spectacular.

And then, for reasons Lodi still cannot recall, she asked her mother the one question she'd bottled up all her life, instinctively wary of the unspoken story. "Why, since you love the beach and light so much, haven't you ever gone home to Australia?"

Her mother straightened abruptly. "That's not home. The place your parents live isn't necessarily your home, baby. Remember that." She paused in opening a coral-rose lip liner and looked at Lodi. "Besides, my mum and dad were alcoholics. They sent me to a girl's boarding school in London when I was just a year older than you. Can you imagine?" Vivian's eyes flashed. "It was a miracle, given their boozing, that they managed the paperwork."

"Are they alive?"

"Hell no." Her mother road-blocked that avenue of inquiry and spun a tale that Lodi, the rest of her life, remembered more for the defensive tone in which her mother spoke than for the facts related. "I was a savvy love child but I kept you when I found out I was preggers," her mother had said. "I've never left you cold, hungry or homeless. That's more than you can say for a lot of the girls who turned up pregnant:

101

they got rid of their babies one way or another, before or after they were born." Vivian misted Natori onto her wrists.

"But you've never made me a family," Lodi muttered, her newly-adorned eyes brimming with tears.

"We are our family, Lodi." Vivian left the bathroom.

Lodi trailed her. "That's a joke! We don't even look like each other. We need a father to make us a family."

Her mother faced her then, her voice loud. "No, we don't need a father. That's just what some script writer for *The Cosby Show* wants you to think. In the real world, you take your family where you find it, how you find it." She was rummaging in her purse for the car keys, her fingers shaking. These words served as the refrain for the arguments that would fragment them until Lodi left for Mills College. Vivian lowered her tone. "Your father wasn't available to be part of our family. And there hasn't been anyone else."

"There's a different someone every weekend."

"There hasn't been anyone suitable."

"Suitable? Suitable! Since when is that part of the consideration? Nothing around here is suitable, or appropriate, or right or normal." The living room was lined four deep with years of rejected canvases, the dining room table chockablock with tubes of oil paint. The canvases would disappear in the next two months, sold as "early works;" the tubes of paint relocated to a studio donated by a benefactor.

"I've been looking," Vivian snapped. "I'm doing the best I can, Lodi. You can't blame a gal for trying." She unearthed the keys and sailed out the door.

"You're not a gal. You're my mother!" Lodi chased her into the twilight.

*

On the crowded airplane, Lodi squished into a seat between a tweed-jacketed man engrossed in *Anna Karenina* and a mother with an infant. She planted her headphones firmly atop her ears, selected her jazz playlist and made herself as small as possible. Enrique met her at the luggage carousel.

"I could have taken a taxi," she said.

"It is always better to have family under these circumstances," he replied.

"You're—"

"Technically, I'm not family. Technically."

Enrique, fifteen years Lodi's senior, lived in the modest guest house studio on her property. He'd been working on transforming her garden for five years when his wife had decided she preferred the company of women and he'd asked to stay for only a couple of weeks after his wife threw him out. Ultimately, they'd agreed that the arrangement suited them both longer-term. Though Lodi occasionally blushed if Enrique saw she had brought home a new lover shortly after breaking it off with an old one, that negligible decrease in privacy was well worth the benefit of having him nearby.

Now Enrique took her home, but she only dropped her luggage before subsequently driving herself to the morgue, insisting she wanted to go alone. Enrique must have ignored her words, however, and called Liz, because her assistant embraced her in the lobby after Lodi had confirmed the remains were, in fact, Vivian. "You OK?"

Lodi nodded, a surprising and alarmingly stereotypical lump forestalling speech and she was grateful for Enrique's intuition. She'd signed papers authorizing cremation, the extent of her mother's injuries foreclosing any other possibility.

"I'm so sorry." Liz's eyes welled with tears. "I know you guys were—" she struggled for words "—having a difficult time, but still. We only have one mother."

Lodi's lump grew and threatened to plummet into her chasm. Liz continued. "Were you able to return her phone call?"

"No," Lodi managed and swallowed hard, willed the lump away. "I didn't return her phone call."

Lodi glimpsed big-hearted grief crumpling Liz's features at this information but Liz swiftly regained her professional demeanor; Lodi had made it clear more than once that Liz was her assistant, not her friend. Though if she'd allowed herself to imagine those boundaries could be blurred, Liz would, Lodi thought, make an excellent friend.

Liz segued to logistics. "Did she have a will?"

Lodi assumed she would feel better after she washed her face and put on a fresh coat of lipstick. "I have no idea. I'm not even sure how to find out."

Liz's husband Rob worked in the trusts division of his law firm, and within the day had a colleague on retainer for Lodi. On Lodi's behalf, Liz declined half-a-dozen interview requests from art magazines. She also coordinated a memorial service, to be held five days later in the gallery of Vivian's dealer.

Liz accompanied Lodi to this service. They sat in the last row, Lodi's legs itching in the opaque black tights she'd bought solely for the occasion. She knew no-one, and the depth of her estrangement sent a side of her chasm, carefully-reinforced with back-to-back meetings for the past week, tumbling. She didn't remove her sunglasses and no-one recognized her, though that might have been true even without the glasses: who would imagine the petite brunette in the back was related to the lithe blonde smiling in the photograph at the front? Her mother could have been someone's beautiful grandmother. Though of course there would have been a carousel of Grampas.

How many of these men did you invite to your bedroom, mother? she asked in her head. The ghost appeared then, at the front, but Liz took Lodi's gasp for a sob and passed her a tissue pack without turning her head. Vivian's ghost circled above the crowd, at least a hundred people on folding chairs. Her wispy tendrils skimmed their heads. She floated toward Lodi and slid behind her chair.

As if now her mother's presence could provide the comfort it never had when she was alive. Lodi seethed. But the prickling of her legs eased and she focused, finally, on the eulogist.

He was describing Vivian's tremendous talent, the richness of her newest works. He said he had seen canvases that showed a blossoming of Vivian's artistic vision, and declared that those pieces be made available for a retrospective show. "Everyone deserves to see the journey of Vivian's art," he said, his voice shaking. He took a deep breath, and repeated, "Everyone," before being overwhelmed by tears. Lodi shifted in her seat. The gallery owner, who was filling the role of minister as well, ushered him from the podium. After settling the man, he invited everyone into a moment of silent remembrance of Vivian's "bright spirit."

The woman in front of Lodi and Liz leaned over to her companion a scant ten seconds into the minute and whispered loudly enough to be audible: "Wasn't that—"

"—yes, yes, he's the one. It's horrible," the man responded.

Lodi shot a questioning glance at Liz, but she shrugged, miming ignorance.

*

Lodi left the service immediately after the final reading, forcing Liz to quicken her stride. They emerged from the cool white of the gallery into the winter sunshine. The ghost had vanished. They had to wait for the valet to bring the car. Lodi, shivering, asked Liz, "What was he the 'one' of? What was so horrible for him?"

Liz bit her lip. "The gallery owner mentioned that your mom had recently split from a long-time companion. He wanted to know if you and the companion would want, you know, reserved 'family' seating. That must have been him."

"Long-time companion? My mother's steadiest companions were houseplants. Which she hired someone to water on a regular basis. She was probably cheating on him with half a dozen other guys."

"People change." Liz offered, mildly.

"Not that much," Lodi snapped. "Leopards, spots, etcetera." She fell silent as three flamboyantly dressed women joined them at the valet queue, somber-faced.

"Such a pity," the brunette murmured.

"She was coming into her own. Moving away from all that beachy bullshit. It sold, sure, but that was so much less than she could do." This from a woman surely in her seventies, white hair a wild poof around her face.

The third woman muttered, "She had to do the beach stuff. Can't be a capital-A artist while you're a single mother. She was ahead of her time."

The others murmured assent.

"Though her daughter doesn't seem to know that. Does anyone know if she even came to the service?"

Lodi felt Liz restrain herself.

"I didn't realize she had a daughter 'til last year," the original speaker said.

"I heard she wouldn't return Viv's calls," someone replied.

The valet pulled Lodi's car so close to the sidewalk that the tires blackened the curb. She tipped him and slammed her door, her face burning.

"I was going to call her back," Lodi muttered, accelerating into traffic.

Liz fumbled with her seatbelt. "I know you were." She cleared her throat. "Do you want company tonight? Rob and I have reservations for the new kebab grill."

Lodi shook her head. "I'm going to bed early. I'm not sleeping well."

*

The ghost remained invisible most of the time. But at night, when Lodi returned home, her lovely home that she'd scrimped and saved to buy, and then decorated in an austere interpretation of fifties style but with touches of pop art: then the ghost occasionally appeared. Vivian sometimes trailed her when she wandered through the garden to examine the poppies Enrique had planted. Vivian would hover above her in the foyer beside the clerestory as Lodi picked up the mail from the tiled floor. Vivian floated beside her in the sickly sweet glow of the oversized pink bubbling lava lamp, in the reflection from the pool's lights after Lodi had locked all the entrances, in the gleam of the microwave's digital clock at midnight when Lodi double-checked the French doors connecting the kitchen nook to the patio and the pool.

*

Three time-blurred weeks after Lodi's return from Seville, she and Liz cleaned out Vivian's studio while drinking a late-seventies merlot. Vivian's wine cellar had been an unexpected discovery in the house they'd already gutted of its possessions.

"How many brushes does a painter really need?" Lodi grumbled after opening yet another drawer full of identical brand-new sable-tipped ones. "This is ridiculous."

"It's a lot," Liz agreed. She was cataloging everything on her laptop's spreadsheet.

"It's too much," Lodi said. "We don't even know what's worth the effort to save." She verged perilously close to whining. "I'm going to hire an appraiser and be done with it."

"Even the finished canvases? Some of those are nice. Regardless of what she was like as a mother, this is good art. I think."

Lodi frowned and Liz added hastily, "At least, definitely worth having an art specialist appraise them."

A dozen panels had been stacked against the far wall. They had seemed, when Lodi first flipped through them, to be more of the same beach-and-ocean scenes her mother was famous for, though abstracted and on a larger scale. Liz had arrayed them in a row and now Lodi, thinned by the tedium of sorting and cataloging, saw the blues of the sky and sea merged at the horizon line. The colors were layered, with a menacing brown undertone of dried blood beneath them at first glance—an undertone that vanished if Lodi stood and gazed with unfocused eyes.

The sea's blues—topaz, cerulean, Prussian—seemed to writhe, suggesting teeming albeit unseen life. The sky, in contrast, remained flat, mute. No pelicans to provide a sense of distance or expanse; the scale would be created entirely by the viewer.

She tilted her head. Was it a trick of the light? Or had her mother, in fact, been descending toward deeper expressions of her subject in an artistic evolution? Were these intended as a sequence?

"You should keep one or two," Liz repeated.

Lodi moved toward the pictures but stopped short, immobilized. Liz gazed at her steadily. "You're too tired and you've had too much wine to think straight. Pick a couple of paintings and make an appointment with my hypnotist about your insomnia."

*

The Peking Palace Chinese Buffet and a Walgreen's sandwiched the hypnotist's office in a strip mall on the far edge of LA County. The hypnotist was shorter than Lodi—barely five foot six, she guessed—and his eyes, had she been looking for a lover, would have intrigued her. But she wasn't looking and he was all business. "Relax in the chair. So your body doesn't distract you." She shifted a green tasseled pillow beneath her lower back.

He dimmed the lights. In a near-monotone he led her through the same routine as her long-abandoned meditation CDs. "First think about your toes. Each one. And the soles of your feet." And so on up to the crown of her head. Then he led her into the past, which during that first and only session consisted of her early memories of her current home.

On her initial visit the house was in decay. Crumbs of concrete lay in the weeds brushing the foundation and splinters blossomed in treacherous clusters on the wooden portico. She'd bought it anyway, against her realtor's advice. The hypnotist prompted her, "Now it is the year before, and the summer sun is hot on your head as you walk outside."

Instead, she was, abruptly, on the floor of her new home, six months later, not a year earlier, after the floors had been sanded and sealed, their coolness bracing her buttocks and thighs. Edward. That had been the refinisher's name, Edward. Edward had laid her down, the knobs of her spine aligned with the whorls in the wood, lavishing attention across the span of her hips, using the same circular strokes with which he'd sanded the floor.

The hypnotist sighed. "You return to the office. The chair is warm, your neck is supported, you are aware of the cool breeze from the fan on your face." She opened her eyes and knew he'd seen passion flush her face.

"Sometimes we linger in our happy moments," the hypnotist said, standing and indicating she should follow suit. "But if you want answers you will have to push past those. Hypnosis is work."

*

The first and only time Lodi had worked for answers had been on her twenty-first birthday. She'd gone to the LA County courthouse and requested a copy of her birth certificate. Under "father's name" was an empty white rectangle; under "place of birth," *Phoenix, Arizona.*

"You told me I was born at the USC hospital," she exclaimed to her mother as soon as she walked in the door, home at her mother's request for a birthday celebration. She waved the copy of her birth certificate in the air before sliding it across the table where her mother sat with a half-empty bottle of wine.

Her mother picked up the paper and sighed. "What did you get this for? Are you applying for study abroad?"

"No, I'm not going anywhere."

"Then what did you need it for?" Vivian spilled wine on a proof of an art gallery catalog as she topped off her glass.

"I wanted to see who my father was."

Her mother leaned back against the dining chair's slats. "His name isn't on there."

"So I see."

"I could have told you that."

"I wouldn't have believed you."

Her mother shrugged. "Now you know."

"Are you going to tell me?"

"Don't be ridiculous."

"It's not ridiculous. I have a right to know."

"Your rights. All you college-educated young women going on about your rights. The world doesn't owe anyone anything and that goes double for a woman with a brain or a talent. You don't need him. Please! The search for the father is a cliché, a stereotype."

"I need to know. I want to know." Lodi remained standing.

"Whatever on earth for?"

"So I can understand myself, know myself."

"You don't need your father, or any man, to do those things." Her mother finished her glass of wine.

"Easy for you to say. You knew both your parents." Lodi hurled these words with as much contempt as she could muster.

Her mother just shook her head. "My parents did me more harm than good."

"How do you know what my father would have been or done for me?"

"You may think I'm a terrible mother but you'd think even less of me if I'd not shielded you from him." Her mother stood and stepped unsteadily away from the table. "Your gift is over there." She nodded at the sideboard. "I need to go lie down."

Lodi stayed in the house's silence for ten minutes after her mother's bedroom door had closed. She looked at the square, turquoise-papered gift without curiosity, and when she rose to go, she left it there.

111

Lodi bought lo mein from the Peking Palace and slurped the noodles straight from the carton, standing up in her kitchen. It was easier that way, no dirty dishes. She dumped the leftovers. More of those since breaking up with the PR exec.

Lodi took the trash to the outside bin. Enrique's light was on. Sometimes they played gin, and he smoked a cigarette while Lodi sipped spiced rum. Lodi gathered her bottle and a pair of cognac glasses and headed around the pool toward his door but froze when she saw Vivian's spirit.

"Mom!" Lodi whispered. "Get out of here."

Her mother stayed where she was, intertwined with the bougainvillea.

"If you would stop haunting me we would both be happier," Lodi muttered.

Her mother shrugged, a minimal gesture compared to the extravagant eye-rolls and full realignment of her upper torso that would have accompanied this body language in life.

In life. When they could have talked.

Lodi hadn't planned for their last conversation to be a last conversation. She'd confronted her mother with the fallout of her youth, gussied up in therapist language while they'd hiked along the beach near her mother's house, the same modest but extremely expensive bungalow Lodi had cleared out with Liz. It overlooked the Pacific. The tide was ebbing. Lodi was thirty-three. She began, "David—"

"Who's David?" her mother interrupted.

"My shrink."

"You're not falling for that psychobabble, are you?"

Lodi forced herself to ignore this and continued, skirting a tide pool of tiny, sharp-clawed crabs. "In my work with David

I've been reflecting on my childhood. I want to compare my memories with yours."

"No one remembers anything, dear." Her mother turned her back to the sea breeze and lit a cigarette. She drew a deep drag before facing forward again. The wind pushed her hair, blonde paling to white, off her face. "That's why eyewitnesses are a lawyer's worst friend and best enemy."

"I want to check some things with you. Things I think you'll remember."

"Shoot."

"Did you bring home a different man every weekend?"

Another woman might have blanched at Lodi's blunt opening, but Vivian didn't. "Probably not every weekend. Probably not always different. I had four or five lovers. I rotated them."

"Rotated, like tires?"

"Like one was good for dancing, another for gallery openings."

"Mix and match men?"

"Sounds bad when you say it."

"I think it was bad. For me."

Her mother's cigarette burned fast, the ash disappearing in the breeze as it formed. "Why?"

"Because I don't have real friendships. Because I don't have a companion in my life."

"You're only thirty-three."

"By the time you were thirty-three, I was ten years old, you'd won a local art competition and were painting almost full time. I'm someone's assistant."

"Not just someone's assistant. A powerful, influential Someone's assistant. A movie studio executive."

"Big deal."

"It is a big deal. You can leverage it."

"If I sleep around like you did, maybe."

Her mother shrugged. "Sex is just another way of making conversation, Lodi."

"That attitude is why I'm in therapy. It is not just another type of conversation."

"What would you call it?"

"An expression of love and spirituality."

Her mother rolled her eyes. "If that's what you think, you'll never have your so-called companion in life, nor will you have any friends. Girlfriends bond by comparing fuck notes." She flicked her cigarette butt into the ocean.

"That's not exactly nice."

"It's not politically correct. The ocean can handle a cigarette butt or two."

"No. What you said. Fuck notes?"

"Women pretend to care about each other, but all they really want is to know if your man is a better lay than theirs. Does he provide more? Etcetera."

"That's warped."

Her mother sighed. "Regardless, I bet if you'd enjoy sex without expecting love and spirituality, your life would change for the better. And if I were you I'd start with David the shrink."

"I used to lie in the dark and listen while you weren't expecting love and spirituality, Mom. I used to lie there and make up stories so I wouldn't cry."

"And those stories have stood you in good stead, haven't they? Don't you have a script or two you're shopping around?"

They'd not spoken of anything consequential the remainder of the afternoon. Like a recovering addict, the day after their squabble, Lodi had followed the alternative script she'd developed with David.

Rather than calling her mother to apologize, she'd wriggled a sundress over her head, forced her feet into sandals—it had been scorching July—and, sweat circling her temples, driven her Toyota two blocks to a local café for an iced mocha. There she'd met Aiden, and fallen deeply in love. He'd dumped her six weeks later; she'd bedded a producer two weeks after that and sold her first script to that same producer during a post-coital interlude.

Her swift seduction of the producer was a grudgingly-made bet with herself about the accuracy of her mother's advice: when a bed-based *conversation* didn't tangibly improve her professional or personal life, she'd call her mother, victorious.

But that first time she made this gamble with herself, and the subsequent times—with entertainment lawyers, several head script writers, three agents, five foreign rights negotiators—all those *conversations* had bettered Lodi's professional life. And so she'd never called her mother again.

Now, she settled herself in a deck chair and murmured to Vivian, "I guess if it weren't for you, I wouldn't be where I am, professionally."

"Lodi?" Enrique opened his door and peered out.

"Talking to myself," Lodi said.

He stood in the doorway, his furrowed brow contorting his face, showing his age. "Lodi."

"What?"

"Your mother is here."

She froze. "You can see her?" It came out a croak. She flushed.

"Si."

"No one else can," Lodi said. She sank against the chair. "I don't know why she's here."

"It's hard for them."

"Them?"

"Ghosts. Particularly ones visiting their children."

"How do you know?"

He paused at the doorsill like a cat. Her mother's ghost was weaving amongst the yuccas he had repotted last week. "She's been around for a while," Lodi said.

"She's very connected to you."

Lodi offered him one of the cognac glasses, three-quarters filled with the dark golden rum.

He joined her at the patio table and sipped it. "I see things other people can't, but I'm not psychic. I didn't train up in it. I like plants better."

"At least they stay where you put them," Lodi said.

"For the most part, yes." He took in more of the rum in one neat swallow. "Sometimes spirits talk to me. But there's a lot of static in the communication."

"Can you ask her why she's here?"

He gazed at Lodi thoughtfully, seemed to weigh her. "It might be ugly." He emphasized the last word.

"I work for MGM. If I had thin skin I would have bled to death years ago."

"Learning why your mother's haunting you is probably, all due respect, different than getting a script rejected."

"Maybe, maybe not. She was always a drama queen." Lodi laughed, tightly.

"It's been a long time since you talked to your mom, yes?"

"Ten years."

"Must have been a big fight. For love?"

"No."

"Money, then?"

"No."

Enrique tilted his head. "It is always either money or love."

"She wouldn't tell me who my father was. Then she told me to solve my problems by—" she edited herself mid-sentence "—myself."

"Ah. Love." Enrique folded his hands around his coffee mug. "Your father is lost?"

Lodi rubbed at the sticky brown halo her glass had left on the tabletop. Hot tears pricked her eyes. "Still is."

"You are looking?"

"Not anymore."

"When did you stop?"

"I was twenty-six." Lodi felt heat flush her face again.

"And your mother's advice about solving your problems by yourself didn't help?"

"I never found him, if that's what you mean."

"No. Did the advice from your mother help you?"

"With my career." Lodi bit off these words bitterly. A breeze skittered over her feet.

Enrique withdrew a pack of Marlboros from the breast pocket of his denim shirt. He offered one to Lodi before he lit one for himself. He didn't ask if it would bother her. He blew smoke in the direction of the ghost, who absorbed it without any noticeable change in opacity. He closed his eyes and he smoked the cigarette down to its filter, never removing it from his lips.

Enrique crushed the butt in the dregs of his coffee. "Your mother was ... unsatisfied," he said.

"So it would seem."

Enrique ignored her snide tone. "In many ways. Not just professionally. Personally."

"I know. I was there for the breakfasts with the men."

"Men didn't do it for her."

"She was gay?"

"No," he chuckled. "But…" He trailed off, and cocked his head, obviously listening. "Did she have to steal things? Food? Or other necessities?"

"Not that I know of."

A petal fell through her mother's ghost as Vivian left the bougainvillea to hover over the swimming pool.

"She stole something. Something important." He sighed. "Something that was being damaged. She took it, gave it a home, loved it. It's unclear. Did she adopt a lot of stray animals?"

"She could barely mother me, nevermind any animals."

"It's definitely a living creature," Enrique insisted. He closed his eyes again.

Vivian was floating closer to them, her form more translucent than Lodi had yet seen it. She moved toward Lodi.

Enrique's eyes opened wide and he stared at Lodi. "Are you adopted?"

Lodi's heart seized and froze against her ribs, but she said, "No."

"Do you have any, I don't know, scars?"

"No!"

"H'mmm." He lit another cigarette.

Lodi raised the collar of her jacket and tucked her chin into it. "I don't look like her, but I don't have any scars. Only a birthmark."

Enrique gazed at her. "What's it like?"

"It's a couple of inches long, some skin that's a little bit raised, and smooth."

Enrique looked away. "Like a scar?"

"She told me it was a birthmark." Lodi heard a little-girl's panic in her voice. Her fingertips slipped beneath her jacket, found her birthmark, touched it. How would she bear a scar that large and not remember the accident that put it there? Unless she was very young.

Her heart sank, her chasm deepened. *Phoenix, Arizona.*

"You think she stole *me*?"

Enrique's cigarette tip glowed blood red in the dark.

"Why didn't she tell me? Or leave me a letter?" Her voice cracked.

Enrique refilled each of their tumblers. "I'm guessing your mother planned to talk to you again." Another beat. "I see ghosts, sometimes they have to say something before they can leave." He smiled. "Your mother wants to speak to you."

Lodi looked at the table, then at the pool, where Vivian's ghost now slipped in and out of the water, droplets hovering on the mist of her hair, shimmering in the underwater lights. Objectively, it was a beautiful image, reminiscent of a Maxfield Parrish print.

Enrique's voice was soft. "I think she did the best she could, Lodi. She feels very sad."

Lodi fumbled with Enrique's cigarettes. He reclaimed the pack and handed her one, steadied the lighter's flame for her. Had her mother rescued her, rescued her from someone who had hurt her with a scarring force? Had Vivian suffered her own version of Lodi's chasm, one with an unknown depth? Lodi inhaled the cigarette's smoke to rescue herself from that imploding emptiness, its sides caving in, threatening living burial.

Vivian's ghost waned.

Enrique stood. The pool's surface danced with pale golden leaves. He crouched and gathered a dripping handful. Lodi touched again the hard smoothness of her scar. Dry. Warm. She was forgivably, imperfectly her mother's daughter. She would have to create herself anew, in the dark, alone. The leaves dried and faded to shimmering tokens in her hands.

Ω

Thy Neighbor as Thyself

by Judith Lavinsky

After a week of sleeping off the long drive down from Boulder, Ran made the mistake of getting an early start. Her mother used the opportunity to issue a reminder. "You better call Brother Gulley about that job. He said he'd be waiting to hear from you."

"I don't even know that it's a job I'd want," she said irritably, watching her coffee drip.

"If you're really going to stay in El Dorado, you'll need a job, and this is one you might actually be able to get." Faye snatched her school teacher's lunch, a pack of Fritos and a can of 7 Up, from the pantry.

The coffee hadn't finished dripping, but Ran took the pot and poured as much as was there into her cup. The stream of dripping coffee sizzled on the hot plate and filled the kitchen with a scorched smell. Faye wrinkled her nose. "That's what your father used to do." And then, at the door, "Be sure you call him up today. A teaching job for an artist is a scarce commodity in this town."

To escape the burned coffee smell, she followed her mother to the driveway and drank her first sip as Faye backed rapidly towards the street. Her mother's reminder irked her. She knew what was important without her prodding. As she laid out her paints and brushes, she considered calling Brother Gulley, but it seemed too early in the day to talk about a job she wouldn't even want. Facing the blank canvas, she loaded her brush, took a deep breath, and began. As the color spread across the surface, the painting slowly became real, and in a few minutes she had left her world of troubled joblessness far behind.

Her concentration lasted only long enough to map the surface of the canvas. "Is Miss Faye at home?" A woman with the accent of a local called to her from the end of the driveway. Taken by surprise, Ran turned to look. The white-haired woman in a flowered dress and slippers looked vaguely familiar.

"She isn't home. I'm her daughter, Randa. Ran."

The woman squinted and stepped closer. "I saw you in the carport and thought to myself, 'Faye must have company.' I thought I'd come and check because if she doesn't have company, somebody in the carport might mean trouble. We have Neighbor Watch here and sometimes I'm the only neighbor watching." The woman stopped for breath.

"It's very kind of you to keep an eye on things," Ran said. The neighbor woman didn't leave. Instead she waited patiently, squinting at the work in progress. Ran realized she had no idea who she was. "I'm sorry. I think I've forgotten your name."

"Oh, don't worry about it, sweetheart. Sometimes I'm forgetful, too."

The woman smiled and continued to stare, and Ran finally remembered southern manners. "Could I get you something? A glass of iced tea?" She tried to remember whether her mother had left a jug in the refrigerator.

"I love sweet tea. Sweet tea with extra sugar. I'll bet Faye's tea is just as sweet as she is."

Reluctantly Ran laid her brush aside and moved towards the door.

"Your mother likes it when I keep an eye on things. We had a sign put up at the corner, 'Neighborhood Watch,' but somebody stole it. Can you just believe that? I called the mayor's office, and he said he'd get another one put up, but that's the last of that. He's not much of a mayor, if you ask me. I'll bet your mama isn't going to vote for him again. Or for that Clinton fellow either. Some governor he is."

Hearing the woman's comments, Ran realized why she seemed familiar. After her father died last spring, the neighbor from across the street had made a few condolence calls that left Faye more annoyed than comforted. "She's just desperate for company," Faye had said. "Her son lives right here in town, but he doesn't pay her the slightest attention. Now she'll be here twice a day to visit and always talking politics, too."

"I'm sure she appreciates your keeping an eye on things, Mrs. Godwin." Ran reached for her brush again. The neighbor woman had evidently forgotten about the tea.

"Why thank you for your respect. When I was working I was always Mrs. Godwin. I just hate it when nobody calls you anything but your first name just like you was a child. I told my doctor he better get his nurse to call me Mrs. Godwin. That girl's got the manners of a pickaninny. I don't know where they get them from. When I was working we didn't hire that kind except to do the cleaning after hours."

"Where did you work?" Ran asked, hoping to shift the conversation back to higher ground.

"I worked for Arkansas Life. We had the best insurance office in the state when I was there. We had representatives who'd come to your house in the evenings. They dressed up in dark blue suits and shirts with *starch* in them so they wouldn't shrivel up in the summertime. And they were handsome! You just wouldn't believe how handsome an Arkansas Life salesman can be. Hair combed and parted neat and shaved so close and perfect. I wanted my boy Reece to be an Arkansas Life man, but he rejected it. Utterly rejected the whole idea. I will never understand it, not to my dying day."

Ran turned back to the canvas. "I need to keep working, Mrs. Godwin. Otherwise the paint will dry.

"And such a pretty, pretty picture too. Why I can see the cat there in the tree, and I can see the little birdie on the grass. Oh, he's going to be in trouble if he doesn't fly away before that cat decides to pounce."

Ran lowered her brush and looked carefully at what she'd been painting.

"You sure have some bright ideas, Miss Randa Robisson. Your mama and your daddy must be real proud of you." She stopped short, hand across her open mouth. "Oh, I misspoke. Your Daddy's gone. I was so sorry for your mama when he died. But look at you now. Painting like this, just like an artist."

Ran suppressed the impulse to blot out the corner Mrs. Godwin pointed to.

"Did you hear that?" Mrs. Godwin said. Ran heard the birdcalls and the distant sound of children playing. "I think I hear my telephone. Arkansas Life calls almost every day with some question about the office. 'Where did you leave the extra rolls of scotch tape?' one of them wanted to know. How am I supposed to know where they are now, after that colored girl they hired rearranged my desk?"

Ran watched her make her way down the drive and over the blacktop street towards the front door of her house. She turned to wave, turned back towards the door, then offside to it, back on course, offside. Dead on.

*

Ran spent the rest of the day and part of the next at her easel on the carport, stubbornly resisting her mother's reminder to call Brother Gulley. The painting wasn't going well. Between brush strokes she heard her noisy conscience nag at least as much as Faye. At last she laid aside her brush and dressed in what she thought of as job-hunting clothes. She parked along the courthouse square and made a quick circuit of the area on foot, trying to imagine herself employed in downtown El Dorado. The air conditioned lobbies of the local banks hummed with activity, but none of them had advertised in the help wanted section of the paper. She had no idea what she might do in a bank, but she noticed that a lot of women worked there. Women, she noticed, who weren't wearing handmade sandals; women with makeup and curled hair.

Across from the courthouse she spotted a bookstore. She hadn't thought of selling anything. But books? Better than selling shoes, she thought, and then she thought again. In the time she paced to the corner and back, planning her approach, no customers went in or out. A shoe store might more likely need another hand. But the only downtown shoe store she could find was closed and empty, one of half a dozen empty store fronts near the square. Strip mall development on North West Avenue, and Wal-Mart most of all, had evidently changed the commercial landscape of the town. She was looking in the wrong place for a job. Her spirits sagged as she reviewed her options: prepare to wear the blue Wal-Mart employee's vest or call Brother Gulley.

Her mother's little car was in the carport when she arrived and pulling out of the driveway was a larger one marked "El Dorado Police." Faye was waiting for her at the door. "The police just came to ask me about Mrs. Godwin. Someone found her early this morning, barefoot in her nightgown, walking down the center stripe on Main Street. She got halfway to downtown before they picked her up."

"Did her son know she was missing?"

"I don't see how he would." She pulled the metal lever on the ice cube tray indignantly. "He only goes there to do the yard work and take her to the grocery store. The police wanted to know whatever I could tell them, which was precious little. I haven't seen her for the last two months." She put the ice in two tall glasses and tipped the two liter 7 Up to fill them.

"When she was over here the other day, she didn't seem like someone who'd be wandering in the middle of the night."

"She's probably got Old Timer's." Faye had never mastered the right term, and Ran had given up correcting her. "They put her in the hospital overnight to see if they could tell what's going on."

*

After Faye left for school, Ran took her second cup of coffee to the carport, trying to prepare herself to make the call to Brother Gulley. Across the street a red pickup marked Godwin Portable Storage turned into the driveway. Inside the cab she could see Mrs. Godwin, for the moment at least returned to her own home. The driver, evidently her son, opened the tailgate of the truck and took out a red toolbox. Ran turned back to the carport and began to lay out all her paintings, the one she'd just finished, and, from the storage closet, wrapped in dusty sheets, several canvases from her MFA. After a few minutes, she heard the sounds of power tools, but from her vantage point all she could see was the open back of the truck. She returned to her paintings, determined to face the truth the canvases revealed, but whatever Reece had done at the back of the house he'd also started doing at the front door. Willing to be distracted, she dusted off her hands and walked down to the edge of Faye's driveway.

"I'm glad to see your mother's home," she called across the street when he had finished.

"What's that?" He hadn't seen her watching.

"I said I'm glad to see your mother's home." She wasn't sure how much to say.

"She's home all right. Now all I got to do is keep her there."

"I heard she got lost." She couldn't think of a gentler way to put it.

"She was walking in the traffic in her night gown in the dark. It's a lucky thing she didn't get herself run down and killed. Old woman's crazy as a bat." His job finished, he opened the red metal box and put the tools he'd used back into it.

"She didn't seem like that when she was here the other day."

"She covers up real good for people she don't know."

"Then maybe it isn't such a good idea to bring her home."

He finally looked in her direction. "You got an idea what to do? Maybe someplace cheap'll take her off my hands?"

The harshness of his question took her by surprise. "I know that nursing homes can be expensive."

"The ones in El Dorado cost a bundle. Anyway they don't have a bed for her right now. I'd have to take her up to Fordyce, and anyplace she goes, she can forget about Medicaid as long as she's got money in the bank." From the carport across the street Ran heard the sound of someone calling, drumming on the windows of the truck. "I better get her back into the house before she loses it." He stepped away from the entry, and Ran was able to see what he had done. A padlock on a strap secured the front door to the jamb.

"Wait," she called. "Is this safe?"

"It's safer than a lot of things."

"If there were a fire, how would she get out?"

"How would she get out now? She'd sleep right through a fire alarm. The Fire Department'd have to come and ax the door down with or without the padlock."

"But how can you be sure…"

"If I don't lock her up I can be sure she'll run off down the street the second my truck is gone." He turned abruptly and continued across the property towards the driveway and his truck.

She met her mother as she turned into the carport. "I can't believe he'd lock his mother in the house like that," Faye said.

"I think we ought to call the police. Surely it's against the law to lock up someone."

The thought of another visit from the police made Faye put her usual indignation aside. "I don't think we ought to interfere. I think he's probably trying to do the best he can under the circumstances."

"Couldn't he hire someone to stay with her while he's at work?"

"If he could pay for it he could. But she went walking in the night, so anyone he hired would have to be there around the clock. I doubt that he could pay what that would cost. Assuming he could even find someone reliable to begin with."

"Still..."

"Still it's his business, Randa. Not yours nor mine. We have our own lives to look out for. Speaking of which, have you called Brother Gulley?"

*

After her mother left for work, Ran poured a second cup of coffee and opened the phone book. The Savior's School was listed. She checked the clock and took another sip of coffee. In an hour she would call, she told herself. If she couldn't think of anything by then, she'd have to call.

The paintings she had taken out of the storage room still stood unwrapped beside the freezer. She ought to use the hour, perhaps her last, she thought, to see what she'd accomplished as an artist. As she had begun to do the day before, she lined up the canvases along the back wall of the carport. She could remember how she'd felt as she worked on the paintings for her MFA. Like Rothko working in a New York loft the size of a hangar, like Pollack throwing aside his brushes to pour the paint straight from the can. She'd had her heroes; working with her oils she had imagined she was one with them.

A sound distracted her, some kind of thumping on a hollow surface. She looked around but couldn't see a source. Her concentration broken, she started to go back into the house for coffee when the noise of breaking glass caught her attention.

"Miss Randa, Randa Robisson," an urgent voice called from across the street.

"Mrs. Godwin?" She hurried towards the neighbor woman's house, concerned about the broken glass.

"Now just see what I've done," Mrs. Godwin bent to speak to her through the broken pane. The screen still formed a barrier between them but Ran could see the woman reaching through the jagged opening as if to try to take her hand. A hammer lay beside her on the windowsill.

"Mrs. Godwin, there's sharp glass around you. Keep your hands inside so it doesn't cut you."

The woman, obedient, put her hands back at her side.

"Are you wearing your shoes?" Ran asked. "I don't want you walking barefoot on the broken glass."

"I have my shoes on." She seemed a hair less urgent now. "I meant to get you over here to talk to me. It was important, and I couldn't see another way."

"I'm here now, Mrs. Godwin." She hoped her tone of voice was soothing.

"Reece'll be angry when he sees the broken window. I'm not supposed to make him any trouble."

"I'm sure he'll understand it was an accident."

"It was *not* an accident! I had to tell you about your father."

Ran could see that she was becoming emotional again. "What did you want to tell me, Mrs. Godwin?"

"I saw it happen. I was looking out this window when they came. They carried him out, but he wasn't dead. Your daddy wasn't dead. It's a terrible thing to say, but I think you better ask your mother what they did with him. Maybe she knows or maybe she doesn't. Either way, it's up to you to find him."

"I know where he is, Mrs. Godwin." The narrow grave in New Hope Cemetery had barely been sufficient for his sturdy coffin. "You don't have to worry."

Reacting to her tone, Mrs. Godwin finally relaxed. "Well then, that's not a problem after all. Your mother, bless her heart, didn't tell me where he went, and I've been worried all for nothing." She smiled and drifted off into the house.

"Stay away from the broken glass," Ran called through the opening, but she couldn't tell whether her neighbor heard her.

Reece didn't come to fix the glass until that evening. Ran heard his truck drive up and watched until he'd finished.

"She was trying to get my attention to tell me something. If she'd been able to get out, she wouldn't have broken the window." A few steps back Faye watched, a witness to the scene. Reece, packing up his tools, didn't respond.

"I really think the padlock is a bad idea," Ran continued. "It's dangerous to leave her locked in. And because she can't get out, she broke the glass trying to get my attention. She could have cut herself. She could have bled to death." She paused and waited, but Reece didn't look up from his work.

"There must be some other way, don't you think?" She felt the argument had ended weakly. She looked towards her mother for some help, but Faye, uncharacteristically quiet, only watched.

Finally Reece looked up. "I got an extra key I'll give you since it worries you so much. But if you let her out, it's on your head to see to her. What comes of it is your responsibility, not mine. You keep her safe and get her home again."

Ran paused. "An extra key?"

"I'll get it for you." He took the toolbox, ready to be done.

Faye found her tongue at last. "That isn't reasonable. It's putting the burden on a neighbor when it's your own mother here, and you're the one who needs to be taking care of her."

"Your daughter," he nodded towards Ran but didn't look at her, "is the problem here. She's the one who's butting in on things is not her business. When you mix in other people's trouble, you got to be ready for the consequences."

*

When she went out to get the morning paper, she found the extra key in an envelope marked Godwin Portable Storage. "Should one of us go over to check on her?" she asked.

"I do *not* think so, Randa. That would be accepting a job that's rightfully his. If he doesn't want to look after his own mother, he has to hire someone to do it."

"What if he doesn't come back for a few days?"

"That's his choice. You only worried that she couldn't get out in an emergency. You didn't offer to be a home health worker. Leaving you the key doesn't make you her caregiver. You never should have got involved in the first place." She was ready to leave for work. "You have to use your time to benefit yourself. Right now you need to spend it looking for a way to earn a paycheck."

She watched her mother leave for school. The children on the playground a hundred yards away played noisily until their teachers called them in. The time to make the call to Brother Gulley was approaching. Until it came she might have taken out the paintings one more time and faced the terror of self-evaluation, but instead she listened for the sounds of breaking glass, for her neighbor calling, for the ringing of the phone that signaled Mrs. Godwin's call from Arkansas Life. All she heard, at last, was silence. She put the key that Reece had left her into her pocket. Drawing in a breath for courage, she crossed the street and knocked. "Mrs. Godwin? Are you OK?" She waited.

"Mrs. Godwin?" She tapped lightly on the kitchen window beside the door.

"Is that you Randa Robisson?"

A wave of relief swept over her at the sound of Mrs. Godwin's voice. "It is. I came to see if you're OK."

"Aren't you the sweetest thing to do that, Randa Robisson."

"Are you OK?"

"I am, but Reece says not to open up the door or window curtains. He says I have to stay away from glass because it breaks."

"He's right, Mrs. Godwin. You should do just what he says."

Speaking with her neighbor silenced a nagging voice inside. To take care of the rest, she put aside her painting for the morning, determined to face the call to Brother Gulley. To prime herself, to make the project real, she drove to central El Dorado and slowly cruised the neighborhood around the Savior's School. As she approached the building, she noticed the busy playground of a public school across the street, its graveled surface filled with the standard galvanized steel jungle gyms and swings. The playground at the Savior's School contained the same equipment but less of it, fenced inside a smaller yard. Unlike the children in the public school, the Savior's children dressed in uniforms—white shirts and dark blue trousers for the boys, white shirts and pleated navy jumpers for the girls. One other thing distinguished them. The children of the public school were black. The Savior's children were all white.

Her mother had told her that public school assignments in El Dorado—like those in Boulder and, for all she knew, the rest of America as well—were based on neighborhood. The schools were technically integrated by law, but the neighborhoods were not. That might explain the public school across the street—the neighborhood around the school seemed, as far as she had noticed, mostly black. But the children at a private school weren't necessarily from homes nearby. Presumably their parents, wherever they lived, enrolled them there without regard to neighborhood. Why hadn't any blacks done that? The school was church related, of course. When she'd attended Sunday service with her mother, the blacks she'd seen were congregated at the storefront church across the street. Did blacks attend her mother's church? A church was not a country club. The issue for membership, as far as she remembered, was religious conviction. What kind of greeting would a black family receive if they attended Sunday service at her mother's church? She couldn't guess. She hadn't really paid attention to its racial demographic. Perhaps black families *were* members there. Perhaps black children at the Savior's School escaped her notice when she glanced across the playground.

She put the car in gear and circled the block again, seeking any clue that would resolve her quandary. She knew enough to guess the reason why white families, north and south, chose private schools and paid, sometimes handsomely, for the privilege: many found desegregation threatening. She'd heard her mother say a hundred times that racial turnover destroys neighborhood schools. The Westside School where Faye taught was her evidence and proof. "The blacks in El Dorado can't begin to pay what houses cost around that school. And people living there don't sell, or they sell to someone they already know without advertising it. That keeps the school white so it hasn't gone downhill."

"But a change in racial make-up doesn't automatically undermine a school," Ran insisted doggedly. It was an argument they'd had for years.

"I've seen it with my own eyes," Faye answered every time. Her argument, based on her own experience and prejudice, never convinced Ran, but Faye's belief was strong enough to make debating futile.

Unable to resolve the matter, she idled at the curb, sorting her memories. In the 1950s, the governor of Arkansas closed the Little Rock schools to stave off integration. The Robissons, newly transferred to an Oklahoma City suburb, were safely distant from the conflict, but Faye's pastor brother, Truman Ellis, seized the opportunity and opened up a private school at his church. "It's a segregation academy," Ran's father grumbled angrily. "He's not trying to help out Little Rock families. He's helping whites. What would he say if a Negro family wanted to enroll?" Faye hadn't had an answer. Or hadn't dared to put one into words.

Another memory: her own experience in El Dorado schools. Halfway through her sophomore year, her father took another Wage & Hour Office transfer, this time from Oklahoma to south Arkansas. El Dorado High was newly integrated, but the students in her classes were all white. That none of the blacks had qualified for college prep had not struck her as strange. Plenty of white kids hadn't made it either. As a late arriver in the school, an outsider in a town where families had gone to school together for three generations, she'd worked at simply blending in. It was an option students from the closed black high school didn't have, but at the time their situation hadn't crossed her mind. Was the quality of the school diminished by their presence? She'd never given it a thought. Nevertheless, what she'd picked up about the growth of private schools in towns like El Dorado made her suspect that Faye was not alone in fearing the effects of integration.

But her own school in Boulder had been essentially all white, she thought, beginning to argue with herself. Avoiding integrated classes hadn't been the motive for the families that chose the Children's School. Minority children in the Boulder schools, public and private, came from the handful of black and Asian faculty or from international students in family housing. Her school had taken one or two and would have taken more if they'd applied. And as her partner, Josh, had always said, parents had the right to seek the best education for their children. That's why they'd started the Children's School in the first place. How different, really, were the motives of the parents sending children to the Savior's School? Race, she decided, was a problem that the South was working on. Schools, public or private, couldn't be expected to solve it single-handed overnight.

The rationalization nearly worked, but no matter what she told herself, she couldn't quash her doubts. Working at Brother Gulley's school would mean silencing her concern about the motives that had led to its existence. Until she knew more about the Savior's School, at least until she'd given it more thought, she'd wait to make her call. In the meantime, she could look for something else. She circled the block again. The children at both schools had left the playground. The afternoon of classes had begun, invisible to people passing in their cars.

*

An ambulance stood in front of Mrs. Godwin's house. Ran parked in time to see them load the body into the vehicle's rear doors. The EMTs had pulled the sheet over her face, but it was Mrs. Godwin, clear enough, Faye said. She was standing on the edge of the carport, watching. "I better go inside and make some food for him," she said, meaning Reece, whose truck stood in his mother's carport. Ran stood on the driveway for a moment, trying to decide what she ought to do. The EMTs closed up the back door of the ambulance and drove off slowly. There was no need to rush. The side door of the house opened again, and Ran saw Reece come out onto the covered carport where the ambulance had been. In Boulder she would have gone across the street to see what she might do for him, but she was still a stranger in the neighborhood. She went inside.

"I bet Reece hadn't visited her since he put the padlocks on the doors," Faye said. "You could see that she was stiff. She'd probably been lying there alone for days."

"I spoke to her through the side door the day he left us the key," Ran said, remembering.

"You didn't go inside?"

"No, but she heard me knocking, and she came to the door. She sounded OK." How would she have known? Ran asked herself. "She knew who I was."

She looked out the living room window. After the first anxious visit, she'd meant to check on her neighbor again, but, preoccupied by job search worries, she'd only looked and listened from her mother's carport. As Mrs. Godwin herself had said, *she* was the watcher for the neighborhood, not Ran. She hadn't seen Reece's truck, but she hadn't watched the driveway every minute. He might have come and gone without her noticing. She had no reason to think he would desert his mother. And as Faye said, Mrs. Godwin wasn't her responsibility. But still, the woman had died some days ago, alone.

"I think I was the last to speak to her," Ran said guiltily. "Perhaps I should have used the key to go inside and check."

"I think it's up to her son to look after her."

"Still..."

"Still you have your own business to take care of. And so do I." She put the casserole into the oven shelf and closed the metal door with a thunk.

As Ran got the morning paper from the driveway, she saw Reece at his mother's house, bringing out filled trash bags for the garbage pickup. When she went outside to take Faye's cans down to the curb, he called her from the bottom of his mother's yard. "I thought maybe Faye would want to take a look over here," he said. "Mama had two closets full of clothes she'd hardly worn." She noticed that he looked her over with an interest that she hadn't seen before.

"I'll ask her." Even at a distance, she could see that his tight red tee shirt with the drawing of a building failed to camouflage his belly. "I better give you back your key," she called. She opened the back door and got it from the counter. "I'm very sorry about your mother. When I last spoke to her she said she was OK."

"She prob'bly was. The doctor said this kind of thing comes on real quick. She had a stroke and died like that, the doctor said. Wasn't a thing anybody could'a done."

"Still, I was sorry that I didn't check on her again. Since there wasn't anyone else around."

He shrugged, missing the judgment that came with her apology. "You planning to stay on with your mother for a while?" he asked. She thought he still looked interested.

"I haven't decided. I'm looking for a job, but so far nothing much has turned up."

"What is it that you do?"

"I'm an artist," she said, trying to make the words sound natural.

"I never met an artist before."

"Well. Now you have." She tried to think of the next thing to say. He was waiting for it at the curb. "What do you do?"

"I sell these portables," he pointed to the drawing on his belly. "Like the one you see over there behind her place."

Ran looked across the street and saw a garden shed like the one in Faye's back yard where her father had kept his mower and his tools. "I guess they're pretty useful around here."

"They surely are. I got a model big enough for a tractor and another one just the right size for a lawn mower or two. I can put them up on your slab or I can pour you one." He stared at her expectantly as if awaiting her decision.

"I'll tell my mother about having a look at the clothes," she said, half turning back towards the carport. "She'll get back to you right away." She watched him wait another moment, still expectant. Finally he nodded as she turned away. A man with a good product isn't used to much rejection, she thought, and the idea made her laugh.

*

"I asked him was he planning to sell the house," Faye reported. She hadn't wanted any of Mrs. Godwin's clothes, but she'd used the opportunity to find out what she could. "Just like I thought, he's going to get a renter. I asked him was he going to rent it with the furniture. She had enough in there to fill two houses full. A renter who had anything at all would have to leave it on the carport. He said he'd rent it either way. If someone came with furniture, he'd put his mother's things into an extra portable. I don't know if he meant he'd use the one in back, or if he'd get another one or two and just fill up the rest of the yard."

"He's in a handy business," Ran said.

"Well, I guess we lose out either way. If somebody with some actual possessions of their own moves in, we get to see Reece put his tacky buildings across a perfectly good yard. And somebody without furniture won't be much of a contribution to the neighborhood. That's what I told him, and he didn't like to hear me say it either."

She watched Faye leave for work and then began her preparations. She lined up all her paintings along the back wall of the carport and studied them the way she'd seen her teachers do, hard-eyed, refusing to yield to the desire to love her work. In El Dorado, where landscapes of barns and flower gardens decorated every bank and public building, her paintings would jangle. But even in Boulder, where Rothko and Pollack were familiar names, even there her work would not escape the kind of judgment she'd been trained to make. After a long look, the verdict was too clear. Even her best work reflected only what her teachers had valued when she was in school. Whatever she'd been trying for, a vision of her own had not emerged. And she had nothing more to bring to a canvas, at least not now. She was unemployed and living in her mother's house in El Dorado, Arkansas. She needed a plan, and so far she had failed to make one.

As she locked the storage closet, she glanced towards the house across the street. There'd been no funeral for Mrs. Godwin. No one to come to it, Reece said. Ran had been ready to protest, but held her tongue. Clearly her objections carried little weight with him, and in fact, he might have been quite right. She had no idea how long ago his mother had retired from Arkansas Life or had a social life beyond condolence calls to Faye. Watching the neighborhood had been her life, Ran guessed, the fate of lonely women with no contacts in the outside world.

She'd just described herself. Since she'd moved to El Dorado, how often had she gone beyond her mother's carport? Her life was as blank as a fresh canvas, and if she had no artist's vision for a painting, she had almost as little for herself. And worse—while she'd been failing as an artist, a lonely neighbor woman died across the street from her, alone. In

Boulder she'd believed that teaching little children helped to build a better world, and she'd been willing to commit her life for that. What commitments had she made in El Dorado? In Arkansas the rules of ethics still applied. If she could make a contribution to the lives of others, she should make it. The time had come to make a choice about her future. She went into the house and made arrangements to discuss her prospects at the Savior's School.

*

Brother Gulley, sweat glistening on his rising forehead, met her at the entry to the school. Beside him, on a wrought iron bracket, hung a large old fashioned school bell with a heavy clapper. Without thinking, she reached out a hand to tap it. "I'll have to ask you not to do that," Brother Gulley said. "The principal's the only one can touch the bell."

Restraining laughter, Ran followed him inside. In honor of the heat Brother Gulley wore a short-sleeved shirt, slightly wrinkled on the back between the shoulder blades, and a skinny clip-on tie across his widening middle. Inside the entry way, he held his finger to his lips and seemed to rise on tiptoe as they passed the open doorways of the classrooms. Ran tried to look inside but their hurried passage gave her little opportunity.

In his office he gestured towards a chair and quickly took his place behind a dark Formica desk. A sign on top read "Principle."

"We had to start when the public schools opened," he began, his voice still somewhat hushed, "so we've been limping along without a music teacher."

Ran's heart sank. The time spent on her worried vacillation had been wasted. "I'm really not qualified for teaching music, Brother Gulley. At the school I started in Boulder, I taught art. That's where my background is."

"Now don't you worry," he said, smiling. "We won't expect too much at first. If you want to spend some time on art, that's fine with us. But we promise parents the children will get all the education that the public schools offer, so we have to give them music. Come to think of it, Mrs. Owens probably did some art, too. I know she put some student pictures out at Christmas and at Easter." He stopped, reflecting. "For Easter, one of the children drew a picture of Jesus on the cross that made you really stop and think about His suffering. As for the music," he continued more energetically, "I think she played a lot of records from the church collection. She let the students sing along, and at the end of the year when she had them sing for Sunday service, they knew those songs better than the choir. From what I heard, the parents were very impressed."

Finger to lips, he led her on a slower trip through the school hallway. Outside a classroom door they paused, and she could see the room arranged into conventional rows of student desks with the teacher's desk up front. Children in their seats bent to the task in front of them, silently writing. "It seems so quiet," Ran whispered.

"We put a high value on decorum," Brother Gulley said. "We like to see our students focused on their work."

"How many students do you have?"

"Ninety-seven as of this morning," he whispered. "We grow a little bit each month. The public schools have got some problems, as I'm sure your mother's told you. Their problems are our best referral system."

She saw an opportunity to ask if racial integration was one of them, but before she could begin, he raced ahead.

"We're set up to offer kindergarten through sixth grade, but right now we stop at third, and in fact that class is small enough it meets with the second grade teacher."

"So most of the students here are younger?"

"Yes, indeed. Our kindergarten is ready to pop with fifty students as of this morning. If you don't want to be our music teacher, we'd be glad to have you help out Mrs. Sweeter there." He led her to the stairway to the basement. "The music room's down here."

"What sort of art equipment do you have?" she asked, trying to turn the discussion towards her own domain.

"I guess we have the usual. I don't recall Mrs. Owens ever saying much about needing any special supplies."

At the bottom of the stairs he switched on the light that revealed a long, ugly room. In the dismal space a few oak desks suitable for high school students stood at random, waiting. An old upright piano filled one wall. A few religious pictures decorated the green walls, along with a poster of a Bible verse: "Suffer the little children to come unto me."

"We can try to round up a few more desks for you. Mrs. Owens just had the littler children sit on the floor."

Ran looked at the dirty dark shag carpet. "Where did the children do their art work?"

"Well, now, to tell the truth, I just don't know. I guess they must've done that on the floor, too. I don't remember much of what she did. It's possible she read them stories about art. Maybe she showed them pictures. A kind of art appreciation class would be just fine, you know. It gets a little noisy with too many children up and doing things. We take the rules about decorum pretty seriously. That's why we put the music classroom in the basement."

The dark space was becoming claustrophobic. "Could we go back upstairs?" Ran asked. "I'd like to get more of a feeling for the school as a whole."

He gave her a broad smile. "I'm glad to hear you ask about the school itself. This is the Lord's work that we're doing here. He's blessed us with these children. With His help we give them what the public schools have failed to give."

"And what is that?" she asked, prompting him, she hoped, towards the topic that had troubled her.

"Religious morals that the government has made the schools stop teaching." Brother Gulley stopped a few steps above her, turned and looked down as if speaking from the pulpit. "When you and I were in school we learned about morality along with Christmas and Easter. Now the public schools can't teach anything but Santa Claus and Easter Bunnies because the Godless courts are watching every move a teacher makes. And what is the result? The children are deprived of moral teaching. The public schools say they have their hands so full with discipline they can barely cover academics, but if their students were receiving a religious moral education along with the three Rs, the teachers wouldn't have to spend all their time on keeping order. Religious morals give the basis for decorum that lets the children to learn."

Unable to resist, she countered with her best example. "I'm sure my mother manages to teach her students what they need to know."

"I know she does. Your mother is a good God-fearing woman. But in the public schools her hands are tied. The minute she says right or wrong, somebody brings a lawyer down and takes the schools to court. And if she says a word about religion, Lord God help her!"

"I think she mostly works on reading and arithmetic, Brother Gulley."

He plunged through the opening she gave him as though to reach the end of the familiar presentation. "In our school, students learn to read and do arithmetic, but we also prepare them to live a Christian life." He said it emphatically, as if no further words were necessary.

Ran could see what she was up against. She used the pause to press a new concern. "Do you have a set curriculum for the art classes? And, of course," she finally remembered, "for music?"

"You can use whatever Mrs. Owens left by way of lesson plans. To tell the truth, that's one little problem here. We have a programmed curriculum for the regular classes that comes from Love of Jesus Publishing. The way it works is almost anyone can teach it. That's why we don't have to ask for teaching certificates. The children can go through their workbooks at their own rate, so some children could do a couple of years' work in a semester or two. The publishers say that the gifted students really advance fast. But the ones who aren't so gifted, they make good progress too, because they always know exactly what they need to do. The teacher just has to guide them through the workbooks. But there aren't any workbooks for the extras like music and art, so a lot is in the hands of the teacher. As a result, we have to be very careful about who we hire. I can assure you that I wouldn't even be talking to you if I didn't know your mother and your dear late father. The souls of little children are in the teachers' hands, Miss Robisson. That's a heavy responsibility. Are you ready for it?"

An electric bell buzzed loudly, startling them both. In the classrooms on both sides of the hall, teachers cried out, "Line up, form your rows" as the children popped up from their

145

desks and rushed towards the doors. Brother Gulley led her to the far end of the hall where she could see the columns of uniformed students walk quickly towards the doors to the playground. At the doors the columns broke as the children rushed towards the play equipment. Ran lost count of their numbers, but clearly the equipment was insufficient for so many. The bigger children pushed little ones away from swings. Some of the larger boys took control of the jungle gym. She saw one boy stamp on the fingers of a smaller one until the smaller child began to howl.

"We need a bit more supervision here," Brother Gulley said. "That's one of the things the music teacher always did, because she knew all of the students by name."

"The playground is a little small for so many kids. Why not stagger the recess periods?"

Brother Gulley beamed at her. "That is a first rate idea, Miss Robisson. I can see you'll make a real big contribution to our school."

She watched the playground for a moment, remembering the garden where the children at her school in Boulder played. By this time the frost would have taken all but the hardiest plants from the rows of vegetables, but the root crops would be still awaiting discovery. Between snowfalls she helped the children dig for carrots and parsnips and potatoes, and then they'd come inside to make a pot of soup. The children that she'd taught were better for her efforts. Would she feel that way about these children, too? She scanned the crowded playground where the scramble of uniforms suggested something almost military gone wrong.

"If you're willing," she said at last, "I can do my best with teaching music. But I'll need a separate room for art. I'll need equipment—paints, brushes, scissors, lots of paper. Shelves for storage and for books. I'd like to put corkboard on the walls so I can hang the students' work. And I'll need to have a room with lots of windows."

Ω

Broken. Everything.

by R. Daniel Lester

Mrs. Ashley wants her teeth back, reaches for them. In the large, wood-frame mirror on wheels beside her bed, Crill poses with the teeth in his mouth. Playing monster, only it's spit not blood dripping down his chin. It is something to do. He plays games in all their rooms. When he's done, Crill takes the teeth out of his mouth and places them in the palm of Mrs. Ashley's tiny, wrinkled hand. "Oh, you little rascal, Ethan," she whispers, smiling a gaping black hole at him.

Crill was there once when the real Ethan visited. Poking Mrs. Ashley with the end of her hairbrush to see if she was still alive—another game—when he heard footsteps and saw the door to her room being pushed open. Crill hid in the closet, peering out between the angled slats. A bald man entered and sat down on the edge of the bed, taking Mrs. Ashley's hand. Saying he shouldn't even be here, that it was dangerous because of the road bandits, the checkpoints. And that he had a way out and a place lined up for his family but he was sorry he couldn't take her with them. Mrs. Ashley slept through it all. When she finally woke up, as the bald man was leaving, she called her visitor "Thomas" even though he kept saying, "I'm Ethan, mother, remember? Your son." But Mrs. Ashley wasn't having any of that and called him Thomas and said he was a rotten son of a bitch for all the drinking and the whoring.

Ethan didn't stay for too long after that.

Crill doesn't have to hide anymore. No one visits these days, not since the sirens sounded again. Probably another evacuation. Maybe another civil war. Definitely an emergency. So no more footsteps in the hallway. Really no sounds other than his own. Other than the residents' slow shuffles, muffled moans, low whispers and wheelchair squeaks.

Mrs. Ashley puts her teeth in and sits up. Crill hands her the hairbrush, pulling the mirror to the bedside, angling it just so. Mrs. Ashley combs her long, white hair in the mirror, staring at her reflection. Singing quietly to herself.

Bored, he leaves Mrs. Ashley's room and wanders down the hall. He wants food, the emptiness in his gut a tiger clawing at his insides. But the kitchen cupboards have been empty for a long time now. And the van doesn't usually arrive until dark. Used to be three times daily. Then twice. Now, once, and they sometimes skip a day.

In the hallway, Mr. Tyler pushes himself along in his wheelchair, backwards, with his one good leg. When he sees Crill his eyes go wide and he pushes faster to get away but he isn't fast enough. Crill easily catches up, grabs the wheelchair by the handles and guides Mr. Tyler back into his room, stopping in front of the wooden trunk with the combination lock that sits at the foot of the bed.

Crill waits. Crill coughs. Crill pokes the old man in the back of the head.

Mr. Tyler only stares at the wall.

This is the game they play.

Crill walks around the wheelchair to face Mr. Tyler. The old man looks anywhere but at Crill. Crill slaps him across the cheek. The crack splits the silence. He slaps him again, harder. Still nothing. No response. Raising his hand a third time, Mr. Tyler finally lifts his eyes to meet Crill's and the ancient gaze is full of hate but the ancient body can do nothing about it.

Crill steps away from the trunk. Mr. Tyler leans forward and slowly spins the lock. Crill knows the secret combination but also knows that the real secret is getting Mr. Tyler to open the lock for him. He swings the lid up and removes one candy bar from the old man's stash. The trunk is full of them, stacked neatly. Hundreds left. He closes the lid and sits on the trunk, legs swinging back-and-forth as he eats the candy bar in front of Mr. Tyler. The chocolate tastes good, calms the tiger in his stomach. Later, he pushes Mr. Tyler into the lounge, places him next to Mrs. Hannah, who's sitting with Mrs. Brittney. Mrs. Hannah thinks she's still a teacher and introduces Mr. Tyler to the rest of the class. Twenty students, and she knows all their names. The names are different everyday. Today's lesson, the massive quake of 2024. But Mrs. Brittney can't hear anymore, so she cups her palm to her ear and says, "Speak up, dearie, I can't hear you" pretty much all day, over and over.

Crill leaves the lounge, walking back down the hallway. Past Mr. Tyler's room. Past Mrs. Ashley's room. Past Mrs. Hannah's room. And past the closed door to Mr. Jacob's room. He doesn't go in there anymore. A while ago, he had to stuff blankets under the door it smelled so bad.

He enters the nurses' office and spins on the office chair until he is dizzy. He stares at an outdated calendar on the wall. He toes the empty prescription bottles spilled on the floor.

The nurses are gone, too. They left shortly after Crill got there, along with the cleaning and cooking staff. Most of the adults ignored him—just another wild animal looking for food. Just another lost soul. All except for Nurse Elizabeth. Pretty Nurse Elizabeth with the cigarette dangling from her lip. She took one look at Crill, grabbed him by the hand, led him to the dining room and fed him a sandwich. Scattered at tables throughout the room, bent over sandwiches of their own, were a handful of old people wrapped in thin blankets and propped up in plastic chairs and wheelchairs.

"They're the ones left behind," she said. "The ones too sick to leave, too old to be packed up like luggage and stuffed into SUVs hell bent for the safe zones, wherever those are anymore. So, kiddo, what's your story? Parents?"

Crill shrugged. They were a concept. A certain smell, maybe, might remind him, but only then a small piece of memory he couldn't fit in the puzzle. What he remembered was being passed around, traded, people taking him in mostly for his pouty face and sticky fingers. One woman braided his hair. One woman burned him with matches. Seemed to Crill like the bad people far outweighed the good and it was the good ones that never stuck around. The last to take him in, a sweaty, pale-skinned man named Otter and his teenaged bride, Nancy, got shot to death robbing a pharmacy for antibiotics for Otter's infected, green-black leg. After that, Crill decided to fly solo, be his own man. He wandered. He stayed safe. He slept whenever, ate hardly ever.

Nurse Elizabeth considered the boy sitting in front of her, his wordy silence that said it all. She blew smoke and tapped the end of her cigarette onto the floor, stepping the ash into the carpet with her white nurse shoe. Then, she lit a new cigarette off the end of the one in her mouth, puffed both for a second, and ground the old one into the table until it was bent and dead.

"Yeah," she said, "it's all broken. Everything."

The words hung in the air, as poisonous as the cigarette smoke. Nurse Elizabeth's sobs were wet and loud, chest heaving with the effort. She let the sadness take her for a few more breaths then slapped herself on the face until the tears stopped.

Now, Crill wheels the chair out of the office and towards the front door. He puts his ear to the door. Listens. Hears nothing. He checks the padlock attached to the thick chain that is coiled around and through the handles of the door like a snake. The lock is sturdy, closed. He stops and listens again. Still nothing. It was Nurse Elizabeth that gave him the chain and the padlock, on the day she left. Said to secure the door behind her and never open it for anybody that didn't know the special knock, no matter what they said. After he agreed, she ruffled his hair. Then she tilted his chin up so their eyes met. "You be good, okay?"

He nodded.

"I'll come back. Some people I have to find first. My people. Till then, you stay here and look after these folks the best you can. You're all they've got."

He nodded.

"My my," she said. "Pitter patter goes my heart." Crill watched from the window as she vanished down the road, head down, walking quick little footprints into the dust.

Beside the front door is a window with the shade drawn. He lifts the shade, steps up on the rolling office chair and hoists himself up onto the sill. He peers out. The road is empty. The world is still. He pushes the sliding glass to the side and crawls out, letting himself drop, landing in the soft earth of the garden.

He collects the stones from under the tree and puts them in his pocket. He smoothes his hair back. He spits on his palms. He climbs the tree. Crill is good at climbing and quickly finds his favourite branch, which he straddles and inches out on, slowly, like the worms he sometimes plucks from the dirt and squishes between thumb and forefinger. He takes the rocks out of his pocket and lays them out on the branch, lining them up, at the ready, just in case. Then, he waits. He is good at this.

And Crill is good at watching too. Watching the road, the tank in the distance, rolling, patrolling, the three, no, four plumes of smoke spiraling into the blue, the caterpillar crawl across his hand, and, through the leaves, the clouds go past the sun.

And as quiet as his world outside is, Crill knows inside the home it is not quiet. There are shuffles and squeaks and groans and moans. He knows life is going on, and on, often longer than it should, and the experience is not pleasant. But he can't be there for the old people all the time. Watching is his work. Protecting. This is where he needs to be.

The one thing he really hates is the piss on the floor and the soiled diapers they fling in the corners. Later, after he cleans up the mess, for those that offended, one-by-one, he will pinch the thin, paper-like skin on the backs of their hands until tears form in the dry corners of their milky eyes.

Before dark, Crill shimmies down the tree and climbs back through the window. The smell always gets to him then. After hours of outside air, the inside air is thick and warm and sweetly sickening. Perfume sprayed on a steaming pile of dog poop. Next, he puts his back to the front door and waits.

When it's full dark, the van arrives. Crill hears the special knock against the door and then the sound of a cardboard box scraping against concrete. Then, the sound of the van driving away. Then, nothing.

Crill opens the padlock with the key hanging around his neck and bends down to drag the sandwiches inside. The sandwiches are wrapped in plastic and hastily put together. Usually the bread is mouldy, the meat grey, indistinct, and the lettuce limp and stringy. But food is food. Tigers must be fed.

"Hey, kid."

Startled, Crill looks up. His eyes make out the shape of a man standing in the shadows, leaning back against the tree. Like him, the man is good at waiting and watching too.

"I've been wondering who was feeding the old fogeys. Turns out to be the kid she talked about. The nurse, I mean."

The man comes forward out of the night and into a slice of moonlight. He looks fed but his eyes are still hungry. Crill wishes he had his rocks.

"She's gone now, though. Weeks back. Don't know if she's dead or alive."

Crill edges in front of the door, blocking the entrance.

"I could help you in with those sandwiches, if you want. Maybe take a tour of the establishment." He looks around Crill and inside. "Sittin' on a gold mine in there, I bet. TVs, jewelry, antiques, cash money. Sure, everything may have gone to shit, my young friend, but let me tell you this: commerce is alive and well."

Crill says nothing, does nothing. He is a wall.

The man grins. "Okay then, little man," he says. "As you were."

Crill watches the brake lights vanish into the night. When he's satisfied the van is truly gone, Crill drags the sandwiches inside and padlocks the door shut.

*

At night, he dreams of exploding bombs.
>Of fire and smoke.
>And panic.
>As a city burns.
>Riots and riot police.
>Being pulled through chanting, screaming crowds.
>Empty grocery store shelves.
>Wire fences, evacuations.
>Yellow school buses lined up on the street.
>A woman says, "Please help us."
>(This might be his mother.)
>A man says, "Hold on to me."
>(This might be his father.)
>TV news reports:
>Anti-tech terrorists seize downtown!
>Mayor kidnapped!
>Mayor beheaded on webcam!
>Tanks roll through the streets.
>Drones hover.
>That high-pitched squeal of incoming missiles.
>A city burns.

*

The next morning, Crill starts off with Mrs. Ashley. The sandwich he delivered the night before is on the bed beside her, still wrapped in plastic. He pokes her with the hairbrush, jamming the end deep into her side. She makes not a sound. And she doesn't stir.

Crill sits on the edge of her bed, considering this. He will need to play Mr. Jacob's golden horn later. Make the awkward sounds with the instrument and then close the door to her room forever. And put the blankets under the door, he won't forget to do that. The sandwich he takes, for the tiger. The teeth he will keep for himself, as a souvenir. Like Mr. Jacob's horn. And Mrs. Lauren's necklace. These things to present to Nurse Elizabeth when she returns, as a reward for the faith she put in him.

That day, he will wear a costume made of bed sheets and towels and chant the names of the dead. He will tell stories. He will put on a grand show in her honour.

So, he must practice. Because practice makes perfect.

Next to Mrs. Ashley's cold body, Crill stands in front of the mirror, baring his fangs. He is a monster. And he is patient.

Ω

Cigarettes and Birdhouses

by Jenna Loceff

He said he was going out for a pack of smokes; it wasn't for over an hour that it occurred to me he didn't smoke. He called six years later, I was married and had two kids by then, and he asked if he could come by and pick up his things. I was nineteen when he disappeared and I guess the heart heals quicker in the young, though I would argue that the wounds go a bit deeper than in the old.

When he called I told him that when Warren moved in, we sold all of his things at a garage sale, but if he wanted $87.25, which was how much we got, I would gladly write him a check. At the time, I realized that what with inflation and all it was probably worth maybe $112 or so, but I kept it to myself, seeing as money is money, and I didn't have a lot of it.

At the time of the phone call I was 25 and Betsey was four and Caleb was two and I worked in a grocery store. It was a good job with benefits which we needed because Warren sat on the couch all day drinking Hamm's beer and making bird-houses which he stacked against the wall in the bedroom. He would draw up a detailed plan for each one and was working toward the perfect model so he could make a bunch and sell them and we could finally buy a house. This was his retirement plan. By the time of the phone call, Warren had 273 birdhouses all stacked against that wall. I guess it is a good thing we didn't live in California anymore, because if there had been an earthquake, well let's just say we would have had a lot of splinters at best.

The first fifty birdhouses had a pinkish color because they were made with used Popsicle sticks. Warren would go down to the ballpark and dig through the garbage after the little league games and bring home sacks filled with them. I made him clean them in the back yard because with Betsy around and Caleb on the way, I didn't want all kinds of strangers' germs and spit all over the house.

When I got sick of that I went to the drugstore and got tongue depressors and he started using them to make the birdhouses, which I guess was good because they were bigger anyway and he could make the unusable birdhouses faster. He could also order the depressors by the boxful and stop rooting through the trash like a regular hobo, which made me happy but I think he kind of missed.

At any rate, there I was on the phone and when he heard that I had sold all of his things and that I would write him a check for $87.25, he asked when he could come over. I told him it didn't matter and that next Sunday was fine and if he came in the morning he could meet the kids and have waffles which were the Sunday morning specialty.

When next Sunday rolled around I had forgotten I had forgotten he was coming, what with the kids and work and Warren and his beer and his birdhouses, so when the doorbell rang, and I pulled apart the curtains to see who it was, I almost had a heart attack to see him in a light blue leisure suit with a handful of limp daisies and broken toothed smile.

I stepped out on the porch and he kissed my hand like a regular gentleman and handed me the flowers and said how he missed me but couldn't call on account of his being in jail the whole time for holding up the liquor store where he went to get the cigarettes he didn't even want, and how he was sorry for leaving like that and did I think it was funny that he started smoking in prison where he was for stealing cigarettes that, like he already said, he never really wanted.

Well the whole thing seemed crazy to me and I didn't believe a word of it. For one, I thought that if he had been to jail I would have heard about it, and for another thing he didn't smell at all like cigarettes which, as I had noticed my whole life, anyone who smokes is sure to do.

But I let him tell me about jail and like a regular war hero he described fights, and a whole lot of other stuff that I didn't really listen to, and when he was done with all that, I asked him if he wanted to have that check and come in for some waffles, but he said no, He really had just wanted to see me, and would I like to go for a ride in his shiny new car.

After thinking about that for about 42 seconds, I told him that against my better judgment I would because I had been driving around in an old truck for the past five years as that was what Warren had when we married. So I went inside and got my coat and purse and one of the birdhouses and stuck my head in the kitchen where Warren was making waffles and said "Warren, I am going to go out, I need a pack of cigarettes."

Ω

Crazy Talk

by Louise Marburg

Once a month, Jenna saw her psychopharmacologist, Doctor Pryzansky. For fifteen minutes, she told him how she felt and what she'd been doing, and then he wrote out her prescriptions and presented them to her in a neat little fan. Though she had been seeing him for a year, she still thought of him as "new," and suspected he felt the same way because he sometimes forgot who she was. Once he asked her how her children were, and she had to remind him she didn't have any, and another time he asked if she enjoyed her vacation when she hadn't been anywhere. *It was lovely,* she told him to spare them both the awkwardness. *So, relaxing, I didn't want to come back.* Then just for the hell of it, she went on to describe a vacation in Bermuda a customer once described to her. She wondered if the patient Pryzansky was thinking of had gone on a different kind of trip, had taken a cruise to Alaska, or bicycled through the south of France, but he listened impassively to her description of pink beaches and turquoise water until their time ran out. For a moment she thought of telling him the truth: *I'm just shitting you, Pryzansky, I've never been to*

Bermuda. But that would make her seem crazy, manic, and who knew how he would react. The last thing she needed was for him to take an interest and start screwing around with her meds. The doctor she saw before Pryzansky had died of a stroke, and through some arrangement she never fully understood, Pryzansky inherited his patients.

Lying about the vacation had been more entertaining than talking about herself, so the next time Pryzansky mistook her for another patient and asked if she'd gotten that promotion, she told him with feigned pride that she was a vice president now, and making double her former salary. The look on his face made her think he'd realized his mistake, but it turned out he was only surprised that she had gotten such a big raise. He had a point; people were losing their jobs every day. She decided to say that she worked for a chain of funeral homes.

"People pass away regardless of the economy. Of course, their loved ones aren't springing for the top-of-the line caskets anymore, but fortunately that's not my division. I'm in Remains, Vice President of Cremation. It's a tough job, long hours, but, as you are no doubt aware, the perpetual abundance of human remains is an undeniable reality." She leaned forward as if to confide a secret. "Death is recession-proof, Doctor."

"I guess so," Pryzansky said, and took out his prescription pad.

*

In her real life, Jenna was a waitress at an expensive restaurant that specialized in childhood foods. Five nights a week, she served nostalgic adults grilled cheese sandwiches and chocolate pudding. At one time she had been an actor who supported herself by waiting tables, but after years of rarely getting any acting jobs and waiting on ever more tables, she now thought of herself as a waitress who used to be an actor. She hadn't been much of an actor, but she was an efficient and popular waitress; she made enough money in tips to live alone in a small one-bedroom apartment. She didn't care what she did for a living, as long as it paid the bills, because she felt lucky to be alive. Six years before, she almost succeeded in killing herself by putting a plastic bag over her head and cutting her wrists with an X-acto blade. "You were serious," the doctor in the psych ward had said, almost in admiration. Waking up alive had been an astonishing relief at first. She could not fathom what made her do it. Then the suffocating gray veil that obscured the future wrapped itself around her once more, and she felt the old craving to destroy herself. "Why?" her mother asked repeatedly. She could not put it into words. The only thing she knew was that she desperately needed to die. "No, you don't," the doctor told her, as if she'd said she needed an elephant. She was given a spectrum of pills that made her feel nauseated and dizzy, then a new combination that didn't, and was released from the hospital thirty days later into an entirely different world than the one she had attempted to leave.

*

She told the guy she was dating about lying to Pryzansky because she thought it would make him laugh. He did laugh, they both did, but then he said, "You should really find a better shrink, Jenna. This joker sounds like an idiot."

"I don't pay him to think, I pay him to write my prescriptions."

"Well, now he thinks you work for a funeral home."

"A *chain* of funeral homes," she corrected, and they laughed about it again.

The guy, Brad, was a successful actor. He was Ken-doll handsome and did a lot of commercials, which made it possible for him to take on theatrical roles. On her nights off from the restaurant, Jenna would go to whatever play he was in and admire him from the mezzanine. "Isn't he a wonderful actor?" she would say to the person sitting next to her. "Don't you think he's handsome?" It thrilled her to hear strangers agree. Brad knew that Jenna had been an actor once, and thought she should try it again.

"You're beautiful," he said, twirling her long red hair around his index finger. "You gave up on yourself too soon."

"You don't know what giving up on yourself is," she said. She had an irrational fear that if she went back to acting she would want to kill herself again, as if the one thing had led to the other, both entwined in the veil of gray. She knew this wasn't true. She told Brad she was a mediocre actor. "It's exhausting trying to be better than you are, trying to believe in this person who really isn't you at all."

"But that's acting," Brad said. "Pretending you're someone else."

"I said believe in, not pretend." But she could see he didn't understand. She marveled at his simplicity. He was solid, indestructible; he had been the King of his senior prom. He would give her indestructible babies who would be exactly like him. She had been told by her doctor before Pryzansky that having her own children would be unwise. She would have to cycle off her medications to avoid damaging the fetus, and there was a genetic possibility that the child would share her illness. But she could not imagine her defective genes prevailing over Brad's solid and healthy ones, and she had found out from the Internet that only two of her medications were strictly contraindicated during pregnancy. Two out of four. She could deal with that. Nine months wasn't such a long time.

*

"I'm in love," she told Pryzansky. He asked her with whom.

"Whom?" she said. Whom? What a priggish word. She changed her mind. Her love for Brad was none of his business.

"Yes," Pryzansky said, a little impatiently. "With whom are you in love?"

"I am in love with a female impersonator," she said. "Oh, I know what you're thinking, and no, he's not gay. Everybody assumes that. He's quite virile, actually. I mean in bed. Let's just say he's ample." She paused to see Pryzansky's reaction. He reached up and lightly touched his comb-over, which was greasy and complex, the hair piled up from both one side and the back. She wondered if he believed this hairdo disguised the fact that he was bald, and if he cared so much, why didn't he get plugs or a weave. "Lon—that's his name, Lon—does all sorts of impersonations, but his specialty is Cher. He wears this long black wig and sings, *'Babe, I got you, babe.'*" She stood up and swung her long hair in imitation of Cher while holding an invisible microphone to her mouth. He also does Madonna. *'Like a Vir-gin,'*" she sang, jutting her hips. *'Touched for the ve-ry first time.'* Early Madonna, of course. Late Madonna is a bore." She sat down again and crossed her thin legs, hooking one around the other. "Anyway, I went to his show with a mutual friend and we were invited backstage." She rolled her eyes and giggled. "It was love at first sight. I mean, even though he still had his wig and makeup on, I was irresistibly attracted to him. It was weird, though, to hear this deep voice come out of him when he said hello. He sounds like James Earl Jones. Then the three of us went out for a drink, and after that, since he and I both live downtown, we shared a cab and made out the whole ride. Then he came back to my place and we humped like monkeys."

"Well," Pryzansky said. He picked up his pad and wrote out her prescriptions. "Here you go. See you next time."

*

She told Brad about it and they laughed until they cried. "It was the first thing I thought of, isn't that weird? I made up a whole story."

"And you say you're a bad actor," he said.

"It was fun. I don't know if he believed me or not. I doubt he was paying attention, to tell you the truth."

"Then he missed a good show," Brad said.

She began to think about going back to acting. She took a class where she did basic exercises such as imagining she was a tree, then another where she sat at a table with other actors and read dramatically from famous plays. A friend of Brad's produced a showcase in which she played a drunken prostitute, her hair piled messily on top of her head and a cigarette dangling from her lip. The cigarette had been her idea. Emboldened, she auditioned for a stage play, and won the part of the waitress.

"Of course I got the part, I *am* a waitress," she said when Brad insisted on celebrating. It was a tiny production in a makeshift theater on the Lower East Side; the only people who came to see it were the families and friends of the actors. She knew it was the best she could expect. At thirty-three, her looks were on the wane. Her once brilliant blue eyes looked sleepy and faded, and there was a geyser of creases above the bridge of her nose. If she had any ambition, these signs of aging would have bothered her, but she still associated acting with sadness, and the bleak little Lower East Side production had made her feel sorry for everyone involved.

Brad was playing Macbeth on Broadway. He was breath-taking, Jenna thought. Then suddenly he was cast as a New York detective in a weekly television drama.

"I want to have your baby," she told him. Getting their girlfriends pregnant was a fad among celebrity men. "Baby bumps" and "Baby Daddies" were a sensation in the enter-tainment news. She imagined herself elegantly gowned and round-bellied at a red carpet event with Brad. "Think of what beautiful children we'll have." He was making a ridiculous amount of money.

She stopped taking the medications that were contraindi-cated in pregnancy and waited to feel the difference. A month passed and she felt fine. In fact, she felt better than ever. The future welled in her throat and sparkled in her mind.

*

"I'm so happy!" she told Pryzansky. She couldn't help it. She was pregnant. She pressed her lips together and hugged her-self, as if physically holding in the news.

"Tell me," he said with unusual interest.

She grabbed for anything. "I just graduated from Clown College!"

"Clown College. I didn't know such an institution exist-ed."

She stifled a laugh. "Oooh, yes. Clowns don't just appear out of thin air! They have to be educated! I got a job as an ap-prentice clown. Luckily! Because it's not as if there are a ton of clown jobs out there. I'm a female clown, of course. I wear a blue gingham dress with ruffled knickers, and a floppy hat with a big pink flower on top." She stroked her hair. "And long red braids. Because my hair is red already, I don't have to wear a wig, which is great because wigs are so uncomfortable." She looked at Pryzansky's comb-over. "I'm sure you can imagine. I'm one of those clowns that pop out of a tiny car with a bunch of other clowns. A clown car, you know? We come scurrying out of the car and spread through the audience being silly and blowing horns, the usual clown behavior. We aren't really all stuffed in the car. We come up through a trapdoor in the floor and then out of the car. Did you know that? You probably did." She sighed and sat back. Her lower abdomen felt heavy and she was suddenly tired. She wasn't sure she had the energy to think up much more. "I don't know how you feel about clowns, but there are people who don't like them. There's a certain prejudice against circus and carnival professionals in general: your clowns, your jugglers, your knife throwers; fat ladies, midgets, carnies—carnies especially. Everybody dumps on carnies, even the midgets. If clowns are royalty, carnies are peasants. Actually, the circus hierarchy goes like this: acrobats, lion tamers, *then* the clowns. The other day during a performance I was—"

"This is preposterous," Pryzansky cut in.

"Well, I'm sorry you feel that way," Jenna said. "If you can't tell your psychopharmacologist you're a clown, who can you tell?"

"You are not a clown," Pryzansky said. He looked at the clock on his desk. Their time was almost up. "I don't know what moves you to tell these lies. Psychoanalysis is not my specialty. Here is the name of a doctor I want to refer you to. I'm afraid I can't treat you anymore."

"You're firing me? Who will prescribe my medications?"

"It appears that your medications need some adjustment. But unless you are honest with me, I can't help you, and I don't think, in any case, that medication is the only therapy you need. Doctor Radley is an excellent psychiatrist." He tore the page off his memo pad and handed it to her. "He will prescribe your medications from now on. I beg you to call him immediately."

"But I've never felt better in my life!" Jenna said.

"That's what worries me," Pryzansky said.

*

She sat on the couch and stroked her stomach, where sturdy little Brad Junior lived like a troll. Pryzansky had to have known she was kidding around. Anyone else would have laughed. And yet a finger of chagrin tap-tapped at her mind like a woodpecker at a tree. Clown College? She had no idea where that came from. She didn't mean him to actually believe her. Obviously! Or she did mean him to, and then she didn't. She couldn't remember what she meant, but she knew for certain that she'd been misunderstood, and felt injured, irate: people were so goddamn stupid. She heard her voice like an echo—*Clowns don't just appear out of thin air!* —and understood it had been too loud. "Use your indoor voice," her mother used to admonish. Pryzansky's office was the size of a closet: a whisper came out like a shout.

"Good day," she said as a test, addressing a crack in the wall. "My name is Jenna. I am seven weeks pregnant." Her voice was modulated and she spoke the truth. "Myron Pryzansky is a prig."

She got up and went to the bathroom and kneeled in front of the toilet. A tide of vomit roared out of her mouth until she was gagging up strings of bile. Her OB/GYN had told her that feeling sick meant the baby was healthy. She thought about phoning Pryzansky. She would tell him she was pregnant and didn't need him: he was contraindicated. She went into the kitchen and ate a bagel and washed it down with a Coke, then went back to the bathroom and vomited again for the pleasure of knowing Brad Junior was growing.

"I *love* being pregnant!" she told her mother on the phone. "Didn't you just love it?" She heard her mother sniff at the other end of the line. She was the kind of woman who kept tissues tucked in her sleeve. Jenna heard a long, honking blow. *Come on*, she thought impatiently. Everyone was so slow! That morning, she had to tell the kid who bagged her groceries to get the lead out and make it snappy.

"Well, not really, darling. I felt awfully sick in the beginning, and then later I—"

"I *love* feeling sick!" Jenna said. "It's this constant, amazing reminder that there is life inside me!"

"That it is," her mother said dryly.

"I can't wait to get really huge." She would be one of those women who let their big bellies show beneath tight T-shirts and slinky dresses. She would be sexy as hell. "There is nothing sexier than a pregnant woman."

Her mother laughed.

"I'm serious! Why is it that when I am being serious, people think I'm funny, but when I'm being funny, people think I'm serious? It's fucking annoying."

"Jenna! Is something the matter?"

"Yes. People are fucking idiotic is what the matter is."

"I wish you wouldn't use that word."

"What, idiotic?" There was a silence on the line. "Nobody gets a joke anymore."

"You're in a bad humor," her mother said.

"I am in an excellent humor, Mother." She rarely called her mother Mother. She called her Mom, like most people. What would Brad Junior call her? Mommy, Mom, Mother, Mummy?

"You might have a girl," her mother said.

"What are you talking about?"

169

"You just called the baby 'Brad Junior.' You were saying you wondered what he would call you."

"I was not," Jenna said. "I was thinking about it. I didn't *say* anything."

"You certainly did, Jenna. I'm not a mind reader."

"Remember how you used to tell me you had eyes in the back of your head?" She laughed and squeezed her aching breasts. She loved the idea of having eyes in the back of her head. Or just one eye, like Cyclops. She walked into the small room that was to be Brad Junior's nursery. Shimmering light streamed between the slats in the blinds, spangled with motes, striping the floor and wall. It was so beautiful she wanted to photograph it. Aiming her phone, she took pictures from several angles while her mother's voice bleated, "Hello? Hello?"

*

Brad was cast in a movie in which he played a man who was charged with a brutal murder that was actually perpetrated by his late brother's spirit. "Sins Of My Brother," it was called. It was a silly idea for a movie, Jenna thought. They moved to Los Angeles, and he worked night and day. When he came home, he was so beat he could hardly pay attention to her. But she liked the house they rented in the hills above Silver Lake. The lake itself was a disappointing reservoir surrounded by chain-link fences, but she could see the snow-capped San Gabriel mountains through the back windows of the house, and the downtown skyline from the front porch. She had stopped being sick and was showing now, but there was nobody to see her belly unless she got into the car and drove through the traffic to the mall, or visited Brad at work.

"Can't you find something to do?" he asked. "Why don't you take a class again? Audition for something."

"I don't want to audition. I'm pregnant."

"You have four months to go. You can't come to the set every day."

What she wanted to do was to sit in a fat, flowered chair all day long and gaze at the snow-capped mountains. Eventually she succumbed to the urge. It was winter, bright and chilly. The sky above the mountains was an empty wall immune to passing clouds; the valley below was a flat gray grid that stretched for hours and hours. One morning she woke up and the mountains were brown. The snow on the peaks was gone.

"The snow disappeared!" she told Brad when he finally came home. "Yesterday it was there and today it's gone." Did she mean yesterday? Yes, she did, because today was the first day the snow hadn't been there. Or maybe today was the day after the first day. Between Brad's erratic schedule and her habit of dozing off in her chair, it was hard to cut the days apart. She imagined each day as a slice of bread falling away from a loaf.

"What snow?' Brad said.

"On the mountains."

"I don't know what you're talking about."

"Yes, yes, you do! The snow on the mountains out back!"

"Listen. I've been working for eighteen hours. I need some sleep." His hair was sticky with gel, and there was a trace of tan makeup along his jaw. The wrinkles at the corners of his eyes looked like claws, she thought. He was getting old, and so was she, closer to death every day.

"I love you," she said. "God, I love you so much."

"You too, babe." He flopped onto their bed and was immediately asleep.

She went out to the front porch and looked at the skyline. The eucalyptus trees rattled in the breeze. The owner of the house had planted poinsettias by the front steps, but instead of

171

the thick red domes she thought of as Christmas, these were tall and thin and nearly leafless, struggling transplants from holiday pots. By Christmas, Brad Junior would be six months old and she wouldn't be pregnant anymore. She wished there was a way to keep him in her womb forever. That he might be a girl was an unwelcome idea that passed through her mind too often.

"Don't tell me the sex," she had said to the ultrasound technician, turning her face away from the monitor in case she could see it herself.

"Relax," the technician said. "I'm not allowed to tell you anyway, that's the doctor's job."

"Don't let her tell me!" Jenna said in alarm. What if the doctor blurted it out? You couldn't un-hear something once it was spoken.

"I won't," the technician said. "But it's not the worst thing in the world to know the sex of your baby."

"It *is* the worst thing! Don't force me to hear something I don't want to know."

The technician wiped the lubricant off her belly and turned off the monitor. Jenna got off the table to get dressed. "What a nut," she heard from inside her blouse as the technician left the room.

Remembering this, she asked, "Do you think I'm a nut?" when Brad woke up from his nap.

He frowned at her. "Of course not. Is there anything to eat around here?"

She made him a peanut butter sandwich and a bowl of chicken noodle soup, a combination she had served at the restaurant hundreds of times. She wished she were there now, joking with customers, balancing her tray on her shoulder. She was the best waitress who ever worked there. It had been a perfect life.

"Remember?" she said to Brad. "Remember how it used to be?"

She sat down at the table and began to cry. Brad had come to ignore her when she was like this, because she could never say what was wrong.

He stopped eating and looked at her for a moment. "Hey, babe, stupid question. Are you taking your medications?"

Jenna laughed at him, incredulous. "Of course I'm not! I'm pregnant! That would be crazy."

"What?" His eyes widened. His face went slack and pale.

"Oh, Brad," she said sadly. "You're melting."

*

It was like being in the hospital, except her mother was the nurse, and she slept in her childhood room instead of a ward. A village of pill bottles sat on her night table, each printed with instructions: once a day in the morning, twice a day with meals, two at night before bed, three a day as needed. Her mother dispensed them. Brad was still in Los Angeles playing the murderous spirit's brother.

She lay in the narrow bed and watched her belly grow so large it seemed the baby would weigh a hundred pounds. The view from her window was of rooftops, cylindrical water towers wearing conical hats, and a taller building farther away whose glass facade was gilded at precisely 3:12 every day. On fine days her face was turned to the window, and time passed according to the movement of the sunlight and the shadows. On overcast days her face was turned to the door where her mother checked on her every hour or so. She got up on the days she saw Dr. Radley.

"How is your mood?" was always the first thing he said. Unlike Pryzansky, he had all his hair, and paid close attention to what she said. She had to be careful not to concern him, or her mother, or Brad daily on the phone. They were waiting for her to retrieve herself. She wasn't allowed to be alone.

"Have you been taking pleasure in any activities?"

"I did the crossword puzzle yesterday. I played with my mother's dog."

But he was sharp, nobody's fool. "Your mother doesn't have a dog."

"No."

"Jenna. Why won't you be honest with me?"

He didn't plead, as her mother did. He didn't feel sorry for her. He sat straight in his chair and wore a suit and tie. She was an exasperating patient, she knew. "You have a disease," he had explained the first time she saw him. "Think of yourself as diabetic. Would you neglect to take your insulin?" What could she say to that? She wasn't diabetic; she had no idea what she would do.

"I don't want this baby," she said. "I don't want him in me." As she said it, she felt an elbow, a foot, maybe a head, knock briefly against her bladder.

"What do you mean when you say you don't want your baby, Jenna? Are you trying to shock me the way you tried to shock Doctor Pryzansky?"

"No, I'm not. Pryzansky is a fool. I wasn't trying to shock him. I assumed he wasn't listening."

"Why is that? Do you feel unheard? Do you think I'm listening to you now?"

"I don't care if you're listening or not."

"That's because you're depressed, Jenna. I am listening. You'll realize that when the medications do their job."

"When will that be again?"

"Four to six weeks. You should be feeling better very soon.

"That will make everyone happy."

"Most importantly, you."

"Yes."

"Isn't that what you want? To feel better?"

"I want to kill myself, I told you that."

Radley sighed. "That's your illness talking. You know that, don't you, Jenna."

Jenna nodded. She did know it, and there was some relief in that. Brad Junior flipped and rolled like an eel inside her, insistently alive.

Ω

The Amazing Adventures of
Hannah O'Hare

by Karen McIntyre

All morning long, on that day I stopped being a regular ten-year old and discovered my superpowers, the wind was trying to tell me something. It blew in fitful gusts, like a baby crying, and shook the back door hard and urgent while I crunched through my bowl of Froot Loops. When I stepped outside, it yanked the screen door from my hand and slammed it hard against the doorframe, as if to shove me out there with the balding grass and someone's old newspaper blowing across the yard.

If my friend Maribeth were there, we'd have run around with our model horses, playing out complex scenarios involving lost foals or the desperate need for a watering hole. But she was sick that day, and she was the only friend I'd made since we moved to the new town. So I did the other kind of playing you can do with toy horses, the kind that's more like being a museum curator where you poke twigs in the ground and set them up in realistic tableaus. It wasn't fun, exactly. But it absorbed me so fully I didn't see the little boy until he was looming over me in his Sears Toughskins jeans and dirty wind-breaker. It was Davey, the boy who lived on the other side of our duplex, a boy my mother had warned me about.

"What's this?" He plucked Midnight, my big black stallion, from the herd. I grabbed but Davey spun away. A slow, mean smile spread over his face.

"Hey, ever seen a horse fly?" He threw Midnight over his head. We both watched with our heads tipped back as Midnight went up, up toward the cloudy gray sky, then fell past my reaching fingers to the ground, where his leg snapped off.

I knelt on the cold grass and looked at the little leg with its shard of plastic on one end and the tiny, perfectly detailed hoof on the other.

"It was a *acc*ident," Davey said.

And somehow that was the last straw: that terrible blank "A" bumping against the other "A" and he couldn't hear it, and probably never would, because that was how people talked in Syracuse. And there, right in front of me, was Davey's white ankle glaring out between his high-water jeans and the lumpy sag of his tube sock. My hand leaped out and closed around his ankle and jerked it toward me and Davey fell to the ground with a *whump*. How quickly I moved, springing onto him so my butt was solid on the scrawny bird bones of his pelvis, my left hand pressing firmly to pin his shoulder to the ground. It was as if my body had always known how to jump on a boy and hit him. I remember seeing his mouth open and his tongue tinted Popsicle blue. Then my fist came down. Shockwaves of pain went up my arm but it felt good, like something I was meant to be doing, while my real part stayed enclosed and safe like a nut in a shell, watching calmly from behind my eyes as my knuckles connected with his blond eyebrow and the wobbling soft eyeball underneath.

A sob. His face turned sideways. As if someone had blown a whistle I got up, and he got up and wiped a streak of dirt across his teary cheek. I stood there with my knuckles smarting in the wind and watched him run into his side of the duplex. The aluminum door bounced on its latch and hung open, flashing in the weak sunlight.

Inside, the air was warm and smelled like Windex. From the living room I heard my mom singing over the vacuum cleaner, "Bad girls, talkin' 'bout the sad girls..." then the *ther-thunk* of the vacuum sucking up a Barbie shoe. I went into the bathroom to see what had happened to me.

My hair was bunched up in a frizzy shrub. In my new school, all the girls had hair that bounced when they walked. I reached for the faucet. A spark zinged off my finger and cracked against the metal.

"Zap," I said, and met my own eyes in the mirror. I took off my pilly sweater and pulled it back over my head, on and off until my hair stood up in waving filaments. Well. This was not a girl you would bump in the cafeteria line, then give a sneaky laughing look to your friends because you knew she would just take it in and skulk away. Not a girl who would walk blindly up the bus aisle with her head full of happiness because her class was going to the art museum, only to have some boy stick his foot in the aisle to trip her.

Those kids.

They better watch their step.

*

Monday morning I sparkled down the school corridors, my superpowers zinging around me like those little circles they draw around pictures of atoms to show the hidden force fields. All around me rose the babble of kids and the occasional squeak of a sneaker. A locker slammed and the smaller boys jumped and pushed out a rough, showy laugh and of course it was him, Peter Giannetti, the boy from the bus who thought he was a big shot because his father was a fireman and let him wear suspenders to school. I watched him come strutting down the hall chest first, pulling the other boys behind him like the brown birds who flapped their wings a thousand miles north just to end up sitting on a power line waiting for the seasons to change.

I no longer felt my feet step automatically aside to let the boys pass. When Peter bumped my side, I bumped right back.

"What are you looking at, Ugly Face?" he asked.

"Nothing," I said. "Really. Nothing."

"What's that?" He put his hand to his ear as if trying to figure out where a noise was coming from. "Hey, I've seen a face like yours before. On a stopped clock."

"Shows how smart you are," I said. "You're supposed to say, a face that could STOP a clock. Not the clock itself."

A hard, high titter. Then a hush from the other boys.

"You're lucky I don't fight with girls," he said, and belched in my face.

And then time did stop, or at least, broke into pieces so I could examine them later: the heat of his insides wafting onto my face. A camera zoom into his open mouth to show the peanut butter packed around his molars with the gray fillings on top. Then the vomity smell of his burp, and time gurgled back into normal speed and I saw the circle of faces around us rocking with laughter, their eyes narrowed into shiny slits. Peter turned his head to bask in the glow and I punched his nose hard from the side, so fast his friends were still laughing when I got my second shot in, an uppercut straight to his Adam's apple. He bent forward choking and then the second bell was grating the air and kids were scattering, and I was gone, striding into art class to fasten my smock.

Afterwards, when I walked down the hall, kids stepped aside to avoid me. "It's *her*," they said. "She hit a *boy*, and it was *Peter Giannetti*."

*

Back then there were no good superhero female role models. Fake as Batman's fighting was, Cat Woman's stylized high kicks wouldn't hurt anyone but a choreographer. Wonder Woman was even worse. The brazen way she stood with her thighs apart, hands on her hips, both breasts pertly defined—she *embarrassed* me. There never was a Superwoman, though that blond cheerleader they called Supergirl came and went over the years. The closest they ever came to a Superwoman was in the old DC comics when some evil sorcerer put a spell on Lois Lane so she ran around town making a fool of herself—trying to stop trains with her index finger or leaping off skyscrapers to rescue a sputtering propeller plane in her dainty little high-heeled shoes. She didn't save anybody. All she did was make double work for Superman, who had to interrupt his own busy schedule to rescue her using Super Speed so she wouldn't get huffy and notice. It made me mad because they wrote it so Lois was doubly duped, feeling all proud with her newspaper lady nipped-waist suit and roller-set hairdo, until the spell was broken and of course she snapped out of it in Superman's arms, gazing up at him adoringly as he flew through the air with his cape streaming behind him, making some flirty remark about sweeping her off her feet.

It was clear I would have to teach myself.

I started by making friends with pain. I lay in bed at night rapping my knuckles against various parts of myself, mentally cataloging the various astonishments: That flash of cosmic light from my eyeballs. The twanging sinus twinge that spread up from the bridge of my nose when struck with my palm, versus the stabbing ice pick when my nose was hit straight on. I no longer feared pain. Even if I flinched I knew it was just a thing to be endured on my way to getting what I wanted: to win. Punches still hurt, but it was just that, just pain. Part of me thinking, *this is the worst you can do?* Practicing with my brother Patrick, I let him twist my arm back until a white-hot spear pierced my shoulder. But I wouldn't say "uncle." I knew if I waited long enough he would just stop.

"What's the matter with you?" He let go and I dropped to the floor. I stared up at his face with its erupting red acne crusted by Clearasil.

"I'm telling Mom," he said, backing away.

"Why? Cause you hurt me and I didn't cry?"

And all he could do was give me the finger and slam his door with the grinning Farrah Fawcett poster hanging crookedly from two pieces of tape. Because while both of us knew I had done something against the rules, neither one of us had a name for it.

In our old house, we shared the same room, and Patrick's friends were the brothers of my friends. It wasn't me tagging along, it was all of us together, running barefoot across the summer lawns. But in our new town, he was suddenly visibly older, chunking a basketball down the street with his lank-haired junior high school friends. I barely saw him except at dinner, when Dad was just waking up for work, and Mom was rushing around still in her uniform, slamming the oven door and throwing a block of frozen spinach into a pot. My brother and I knew not to fight with each other at the table the way we used to; the tired face of my mother chewing, my dad sipping coffee and staring into space, took the bickering right out of us. But when we lost that friction, we didn't seem to have any other way to connect.

Sometimes I would slip into Patrick's room before he got home from school, and hide under his bed so I could watch him throw his knapsack down and play the same dim, home-made cassette of Led Zeppelin over and over while he stalked back and forth, jackknifing his skinny body over an imaginary guitar, trying to throw his hair around. I'd lie there dozing until my mom came home from work and yelled at Patrick to move his damn sneakers from where she'd just tripped on them, when I could run back to my desk to scribble out my homework, blood still beading from my knuckles.

*

Like all superheroes, I managed to keep my flimsy disguise in place. Come *on*, a person might reasonably say, can *no one* recognize Superman's square jaw and steely gaze behind Clark Kent's glasses? You'd think my parents would notice the band-aid slapped across my knuckles, or the wincing way I reached to place a fork and paper towel beside each plate. When Dad lumbered to the table with pillow marks still creasing his face, you'd think he'd see the flash of fear in my eyes as he clamped my head in a Papa Bear squeeze and asked how my big brain did at school that day. You'd think he'd notice how fast I ducked away, before his fingers could graze the scabs on my scalp where my head had banged against the pavement. But I soon realized if I put my schoolwork in the middle of the kitchen counter, the circled "98" on my math test would color their judgment about all that came after, the way Clark Kent's timid suit masked the muscles bulging underneath.

If I was going to be a superhero, I needed someone to save. Ravi Shoopur was a likely candidate. The school's lone Indian boy, he spoke in a lilting accent and wore slab-like lenses that flashed in the frames of his wire-rimmed glasses. But for some reason Ravi was now afraid of me. When I shadowed him down the hall, he darted into the boy's lav and stayed there until the next bell rang. I set my sights on Ilene Fleisher, a Jewish girl with hair worse than mine. She wore political buttons to school that read, "Don't blame me, I voted for McGovern" and staged a one-girl protest in the lunchroom because they didn't offer vegetarian entrees. I walked beside her down the hallways with a heavy, protective tread, my head swiveling for any sign of bullying. But she must've been too weird for Peter Giannetti and his friends to bother with, because even when she tried to hand them flyers for her mother's anti-Reagan rally, they just curled their lips and walked away.

I stood showily in places I didn't belong. In the middle of the hallway so boys had to make an effort not to bump into me, or near the basketball hoop, where if I taunted long enough they'd let me play and then inevitably hurl a ball at my head. The smack and pounce of pain, the cold schoolyard air rushing to the hot, hurting place and my feet running to Billy Rodgers to throw my whole weight behind the first punch—it didn't matter that he pushed me down and tore my tights on the asphalt, or hit me so hard in the ribs I couldn't take an all-the-way breath for the rest of the day. It was enough to just bloody my knuckles against his teeth and punch my blunt-toed ugly shoe into his abdomen while that high pure singing feeling tore out of me.

At the first punch a skittering excitement would blow across the recess yard. Girls let the Chinese jump rope fall from their legs and ran full tilt to form a circle around me and the boy as we rolled over and over, grappling and slapping and grunting. I would glimpse them over the boy's reddened, glowing ear, pumping their fists and shouting *Han-nah! Han-nah!* I understood these girls weren't really my friends. But they knew me now. They knew me as more than the bookish girl with immovable hair, even if they couldn't possibly know the Hannah O'Hare I really was, the one who still existed for me back in our old town, in the yellow house with the normal, single front door and the lilac bush on the side.

Sometimes, turning from the pencil sharpener or carrying my homework to the teacher's desk, I'd see the girls' eyes give a little flare of fear, with the white part showing all the way around the colored part. It gave me the courage to be nice, the way Clark Kent could put up with Perry White yelling at him for bumbling a scoop, when Clark would just give his mild smile and turn back to his typewriter.

With every smile and step to the side at the water fountain, I was pardoning them.

I also knew my parents hadn't moved to Syracuse to ruin my life, though that was my story and I was sticking to it. "You think Daddy likes working all night while we're here asleep?" my mother would ask, taking the clean socks from my hand and shoving them into my brother's dresser. "You think I wanted to leave Athenia for a place that uses the same cooking oil all week?" And it was true, in our old town she wasn't a mom who had to work as a waitress. She was a niece helping out her Uncle Tony at the renowned Athenia Diner, where they took pride in their fried chicken and I got to have my ninth birthday with all my friends and every dessert from the revolving glass case lined up in front of us. But Syracuse was where my father's new job was—in *management,* as he liked to say, with the same audible italics reserved for *college education,* something my parents would now be able to save money toward, with the understanding that my brother might not get in.

The year we moved, the Syracuse town fathers launched a new civic booster campaign. *There's Snow Place Like Syracuse!* a red banner proclaimed to the dying downtown with its shuttered department stores and sidewalks gritty with rock salt. Around it, pennants of primary-colored triangles whipped in the gray, diagonal sleet. Feet plunged into icy puddles. Shovels dented against frozen curbs. Yet our neighbors bragged in their flat accents that this was *nothing*—last year they'd gotten three feet by Halloween! "The most snowfall of any U.S. city," my dad said with quiet pride, hoisting another hundred-pound bag of sand into the trunk of our Plymouth.

To wake up morning after morning in the dark, blowing cold, to discover that even when I finally broke down and wore my bulbously wrong rubber boots over my shoes, my feet would still freeze into numb pads before I got to school—the whole town seemed to be conspiring to beat me down and make me give up. The way the shopping cart at Price Chopper slid sideways through the slushy parking lot. The stale blast of the car heater and my dad's thumb split by cold so you could see the meaty red inside, turning and turning the ignition key—it was all I could do to keep the memory of my old life alive inside me.

Sometimes as a treat, Mom would let me take the bus to her new job so I could do my homework at the counter while she finished her shift. She'd bring me a heavy, seamed parfait glass filled with cold rice pudding and pull the wad of singles and fives from her apron to count. She seemed so commanding, kicking through the kitchen door in her sturdy nurse's shoes, bearing down on a table with plates of burgers piled up her arms. But after a while it made me mad the way the men would hold up their coffee cups for a refill, not even bothering to use words to ask her, as if not willing to stop their chewing for even the moment it would take to say something nice. At home, I watched her pull off her shoes and rub the ball of her foot through her thick, putty-colored pantyhose, saying, *oh, it feels good just to sit* and I wanted to fly down to the diner and punch the men off their counter stools one by one, for the way they sat with their big butts overflowing the red vinyl, doing that stupid scribbling motion to make my mom come running.

*

In our old town, snow before Thanksgiving was magical and extraordinary. In Syracuse, the snowbanks were already splashed with dirt and squiggled with bright yellow dog pee. Maribeth and I were walking home on the stretch of Salt Springs Road near the snowed-over soccer field where no one ever shoveled the sidewalk. There was only a thin path meandering along the edge of the field, made by other people's feet packing down the snow. Maribeth was hopping from one footprint to the other, chattering about last night's episode of *The Waltons*. I was carrying my painting of a Horn of Plenty that Mrs. Wilner had compared favorably to Cezanne, for the way I'd worked squarish yellow smudges onto the red apples until the brush tore through the cheap paper. I was holding it carefully to keep from creasing it, when I saw Peter standing in the path up ahead. He had one arm raised like the Statue of Liberty, only instead of a torch he let his middle finger be the beacon for the world.

"Come on." Maribeth tugged my parka. "Let's cross." She already had one foot up on the snowbank. Cars hissed by, splashing slush. But I could no more avoid Peter Giannetti than Superman could avoid Lex Luthor tempting him toward the den of hidden Kryptonite. I knew fighting would be different out here beside the big empty field with no bells to ring or teachers to suddenly step into view. But if I crossed the street now I would be walking back to being a scared little nobody. The path of footprints stretched between us, marching me to my destiny.

Ten feet away. Peter shrugged off his backpack and set his Starsky and Hutch lunchbox on the snow. A thrill of fear spiraled up from my belly at the sight of his cheeks, which had an adult swarthiness in the afternoon light. It was rumored that he shaved.

Five feet. Peter ducked his chin and glared at me like the bad-guy boxer in Rocky III, the effect only slightly mitigated by his red plaid hunter's cap with the sporty earflaps turned up.

Maribeth's voice took on a maternal scolding quality. "Hannah! Right now! Come on!" Her stomping foot crunched the snow. I tried to hand her my cornucopia painting but she wouldn't take it, so I opened my hand and let the wind have it instead. For a long, silent moment the three of us watched my overworked apples and perfunctory grapes skid away across the sculpted top of the snow.

"Get out of my way," I said to Peter, my eyes at a level with his chest.

"Why don't you make me?" he asked.

We both stood there. Later, in high school, I would recognize this odd unmoving dance as the helium moment before a first kiss, when you're both trying to figure out how to start, and wondering where your noses will go. I stared up into his brown eyes. "Go ahead, Pube Head," he told me. I put both hands on his chest and shoved.

His hands came up and I fell backwards, ingloriously, like a tree.

I learned two things that day. First, how awful a boy was when he was on top of you, how much his knee hurt and humiliated as it dug into your belly. Second, superpowers are a relative thing. You can feel them surging and singing inside you but still be unable to unpin your limbs from the boy's massive bulk while snow seeps down your neck and up your sleeves.

"Ho hum," he kept saying, pretending to tamp down a yawn with his hand.

I found myself jerking in moth-like, fluttering movements until the unthinkable happened. I began to cry.

"Oh shit," he said. "Cut that out."

"No, YOU cut it out!" Maribeth took this opportunity to say.

His knee left my belly. Cold air trickled in through my hot, congested nostrils. "Come on. Stand up. You're not hurt bad."

Maribeth's mittened hand came down. I pulled myself to my feet.

"I'm going," Peter said. He inspected my face with a worried frown. "Don't you tell on me."

I punched him. It was a nice shot, clean from the shoulder, surging on a wave of pure despair.

He punched me back.

Fireworks of pain flowered down from my nose and fell in bright red drops on the snow. And then he was gone, running down the foot-beaten path, yelling "I told ya, stupid girl!"

*

In the comics, when a woman screams, Superman turns in mid-air, red cape roiling around him, and flies like a bullet toward her, one fist punched into the air ahead to make him fly faster. In our house, the last "ah" of my mother's scream hung in the air for eons while I kept my face stiffly upright on the Strawberry Shortcake pillowcase she still thought I liked, trying not to smear the SunGlo Beige makeup I'd snuck from her makeup bag to cover the giant purpling bruise on my face. Footsteps pounded down the hall. My brother gawked in at me, hanging in from the doorframe with his plaid shirt riding up his bony wrists. My dad shoved past, took one look and seized Patrick by the shoulders. "WHAT THE HELL HAPPENED TO HER?!"

"How should I know?" Patrick said.

"Who did this to you?" my father asked.

I wanted to crawl onto my mom's lap and bury my face in her polyester grease-smelling uniform while my father patted my back and made tuneless soothing sounds. But I was too far away from them now, too deep inside myself with all my secrets. Watching my father pace in his pajamas and my mother slump on the edge of my bed with her hands on her hairnet, I felt as Superman must feel when he pauses weightless in space, surrounded by blackness, gazing down at the blue little earth.

"I don't know who it was," I told them. "Just a … boy."

"But why you?" my mother asked. "Why would anyone want to hurt YOU?"

"He wanted my cornucopia painting," I said.

Then my parents started arguing about how they'd get me home safely from then on, with two jobs and only one car between them. It was one of those endless, ragged debates fueled by exhaustion where usually my brother and I would slip away but here we were, watching my father clench and unclench his fists and my mother slowly pull off her nurse's shoes, trying to decide if he could drop her at work in the morning so he could wake up early and pick me up in the afternoon, when it would only mean losing a few hours of sleep.

And then Patrick spoke up in his fluty-creaking changing voice. "I'll get her," he said. My parents stared at him, as if the lamp had spoken.

He leaned in close enough for me to smell the Juicy Fruit gum on his breath and the cigarette smoke underneath. "Wait for me inside the doors," he said. "I'll come get you." And then he snapped his head back, so the tight curls in front shivered.

"Well … good," my father said. "Thank you, son."

My mother sighed, patting her pocket with the wad of bills inside. "It's meatloaf tonight," she said apologetically to us all.

*

Winter went on. I never told on Peter, and he never bothered me again, though sometimes when we passed each other in the hall I saw his eyes slide sideways like he might be about to say something. Years later, I found out he'd become a firefighter like his father, and a few years after that my mom sent a clipping of Peter carrying a little girl down a ladder, saving her from the State Street fire.

Every day for the rest of the winter, Patrick came to get me. We didn't talk. We didn't even walk next to each other. I'd wait inside the big double doors until I saw him stop near the steps in his flapping Army jacket and busted-out jeans. I'd come out and he would just turn around and start walking and I'd follow. Only once did he even acknowledge my existence. It was a blizzard, one of the rare times they closed the Syracuse schools early.

Snow boiled down from a colorless sky. My scarf froze. My nostrils burned. Yet still my brother kept up his odd, lunging pace, plunging his sneakered feet into the snow and forging on five steps ahead. But when we got to the wide sweep of the

190

soccer field he slowed until he was just in front of me, sheltering me from the pushing wind. And on we walked past the field with its grass frozen under the snow, the two-wheel-drive cars going slowly past with chains on their tires and their wipers on, while in our house my father slept and downtown my mother raced between tables and the blizzard raged and the bright red and yellow pennants flapped hard in the wind blowing in from the lake, all of us just trying to make it to spring.

$$\Omega$$

Gathering Moss

by Jason Pollard

Eagle has it good. At least, he has it better than me. It must be nice to wake up in the morning on Mount Olympus, sun beaming onto his feathers, followed by a quick flight down to a guaranteed fresh liver from some fire-bringing sap. That's his life every day, man. He has a defined beginning and end, with things to look forward to. Not to mention he gets to tear into a dude every day. Talk about a sweet gig.

So let me ask you: if Eagle can get such a nice, cushy punishment job, why am I stuck rolling up and down this hill while getting manhandled by this Sisyphus jackass? Don't get me wrong, I'm not against the idea of rolling up and down a hill. I realize that I'm a gigantic piece of rock and rolling is what we're wont to do, but I feel like some variety isn't absolutely uncalled for, especially for a rock of my caliber. Eagle is the master of his own destiny. Yeah, at the end of the day he has to eat Prometheus's liver, but the point-A to point-B can be whatever he wants. Monday, he could just tear into the side. Tuesday, he could force feed him his own liver and then eat it out of the stomach. Wednesday, rectum day. The possibilities are as endless as the liver supply.

And what job do I get the great honor of having? Getting rolled up to the top of this hill, only to roll back down to the bottom. If you ask me, someone who kidnapped Hades himself should get a bigger punishment than rolling my ass around. But I'm obviously not the one making these decisions. I'm actually not quite sure who the one making these decisions is, but I'd like to lobby for his job because he seems to be slacking as of late. When you have such a good track record of punishments (liver-eating eagles, turning your victim so it may be torn apart by dogs, or changing it into a spider) it's pretty disappointing when the latest, greatest one is "roll this rock forever."

At this point, you're probably thinking, "But Boulder, you're not supposed to be able to talk! Why does your side of the story matter?" If your complaint is that a talking rock is too fantastical to be believable, I'd suggest you direct your complaints towards the three-headed dog guarding the gates over there. The gates past the river of fire and the *throne of the godsdamn underworld*. A talking boulder should be making you roll your eyes and yawn from boredom.

"I'm Sisyphus, by the way," he said. "You can hear me, can't you? I heard you sigh. At least I think that was you." This was probably a few thousand years from when we started. A little early to start talking to rocks, in my opinion. "I've gotta say, if I could go do it all again, I'd probably—" His sentence was cut short by a strained grunt as he heaved me over a chunk of brimstone the size of Priapus's dick. "—avoid the shit that got me here in the first place."

His hands now were a lot more raw than they had been at the start. Callused, more dirt than flesh. Those fingernails not chipped or broken off by my surface had grown long enough to curve in on themselves. It grossed me out every time they scraped along my side. At least the gods had been kind enough to disable his bodily functions (those probably took away from valuable me-rolling time). Only the normal smells of the underworld surrounded us: rotting meat and fire.

"We're nearing the top. See you at the bottom," he said. He rolled me up to the peak, and I came to a stop. In about five seconds, I'd start rolling back down. This was probably the most exciting part, even though it lasted all of a minute. I let out a heavy sigh before remembering that I'm a rock and should probably refrain from doing that. But I was already starting my descent, so it was not like he could have—

"I heard that," he said.

"Shit."

"That, too."

"So are you like a demigod of geology?"

"Nope. Just a rock, man. Keep pushing." This was my fault. I have a lot of trouble keeping my "mouth" shut, and now I was paying the price.

"So you're like my spirit guide, then? A messenger from Zeus or Hades to monitor my progress?" He had this annoying habit where every time he asked a question, he would stop pushing me up the hill. This was pretty counterproductive to literally his only task for the rest of eternity.

"No, dude. I'm just the boulder assigned to you for pushing. Two tons of rock you're destined to grope forever. Two tons of rock that, for some reason, is holding completely still at the moment. Think you might be able to do something to fix that, Sis?"

"Yeah," he said. "Yeah, of course. I'm sorry." The last few thousand years seemed to do his personality the favors that his body didn't get. He was starved for interaction and willing to do anything to please. Definitely not the hubristic murderer that had started rolling me a few centuries ago. "Two tons has to be a hyperbole, though. You don't feel any more than half that." Flattering.

"You could be right. Rolling around might have chipped a considerable amount off." Why was I encouraging him? I didn't have hands to be callused or fingernails to chip and curl. I'm better than this. Keep your head down and your mouth shut, Boulder, that's the best way to get through these things. Because when you encourage the people getting punished, they get attached, and when they get attached—

"I'm really seeing the error of my ways, you know? This has really showed me how selfish I was being." Fuck. Here it goes. "It's really great knowing you're sentient. I have someone to confide in."

"Listen, Sis, if you think I'm some kind of earpiece for the Gods, you're wrong. I'm not here to judge your character. I'm not here to be some symbol for your self-actualization. I'm here to get rolled up the hill and to fall down the hill, over and over."

"An earpiece? Gods no!" He paused and licked his lips before continuing, the dry smack reminding me that he hadn't had a drink of water in thousands of years. "I just thought, maybe, if you noticed that I wasn't the same guy I used to be, you could relay the message to Zeus, and we could negotiate some kind of release."

"You just described an earpiece scenario."

"Well, even so, couldn't you?"

"That's not what this is."

*

195

A couple dozen centuries went by without another word. It was nice. I started playing a game where for every full rotation I made, I'd think of a different way I'd kill Sisyphus with the first thing I saw. About sixty years into the game, I was imagining pinning him under the waters of the river Styx when he broke the silence.

"Eternity seems like overkill," Sisyphus said. I almost laughed right in his face. All this time to think of something to say, and it's that? Homer, he was not.

"Profound."

"I just think once a lesson has been learned, I should be able to get a second chance or something."

"As much as I feel a guy who enslaved the god of death for fun is deserving of a second chance," I said, "maybe you should take it easy on revising Zeus's punishment techniques. Thinking you're better than him is kind of what got you in this mess in the first place." That sat for a decade or so, the only sounds being me grinding on the surface of the hill and that screaming guy who had been getting stabbed with hot pokers across the river for the last fifty years. Those hot pokers had it good.

"True," Sis said after letting our friend across the river serenade us a little longer. "Just still having trouble accepting it, I guess." The guy had a point, really, though I hated to admit it.

"I went through that when I got the assignment to get rolled, no joke. It's tough accepting you're going to be doing something forever. Even if it was something you liked, it'd be pretty shitty without other things to compare it to." This was definitely against the rules to be talking to him like this.

"Exactly! I wish I—"

"Keep rolling."

"Right, sorry. I wish I didn't know it was an eternity thing. I'd feel like thinking there'd be an end would make me work harder. With no end in sight, why even bother?"

"Would going back to thinking I was an earpiece help your motivation problem?" I teased. "Because this is all stuff I bet Zeus would love to hear." Sisyphus started laughing, a hoarse kind of laugh. Exactly how you'd expect a man to sound when he laughed for the first time in over four thousand years: sick.

"I'll cut you a deal. I'll push you around that patch of thorns from now on if you go back to 'being an earpiece.'"

"You knew that thorn patch was there? You asshole."

"Do we have a deal?"

"As long as you know that that isn't what this is."

"I know."

"Alright, fine. But Zeus will be hearing about intentionally rolling me through the thorns."

"Excellent!" We both laughed, and he sounded less sick now. I couldn't tell if it was the addition of hope or just the fact that he had gotten a practice laugh in a few seconds ago.

"Keep rolling," I said.

*

Sis wasn't such a bad guy. It was kind of nice to have someone to talk to and pass the time. After a few centuries, it felt a lot less like a job and more like hanging out.

"So what would you be doing if you didn't have to shove me around?" Our conversations often contained hypotheticals because what else was there to talk about?

"I'm not so sure. If you had asked me that when I first started, I would have known the answer immediately. I'd go back to ruling Ephyra. Go back to killing and lying. But now? I'm not sure how life goes on up there. I'm so used to thinking

I was above something, too good to bother with it. If I didn't have complete control over something, the next step was always to gain that complete control over it, by any means necessary. I killed merchants who didn't want to pay taxes. I seduced a man's daughter only to get close enough to kill him. I enslaved Hades himself! All because of the notion that I was too good, too clever to be brought down." He hadn't given me a push in a while, but I let him lean against me, his head resting next to bits of finger skin that had begun to peel off and wedge themselves into my cracks.

"King Sisyphus was a master of all," he continued. "But I'm not quite sure what Boulder Sisyphus is." The fact that he used my name before his like a kind of marital hyphenate filled me with a mixture of pride and pity. We both sat there for a couple of months, the crackle of the fire river underscoring the screaming man. "What about you? What would you be doing?"

"I'm a rock."

"Right."

"What's the difference between you and those pokers, then?" Sisyphus asked me.

"What do you mean?" He was sitting next to me, tracing into the dirt with his finger while looking across at the guy getting stabbed. He hadn't given me a push in years.

"You said you got assigned to being rolled. Why'd that happen instead of some other kind of punishment? You seem to have gotten a bum deal." Where'd he get off asking me something like that? I do him a solid and let him take a break, and he asks me why my job is shitty?

"Luck of the draw. Get up. You need to start rolling." He rotated and faced me, staring straight through to my core. A futile gesture, since I lack facial features, but powerful none-theless, I suppose.

"You don't sound like you're convinced that it was luck." He stood up and dusted his ass off before gripping my side. "You sound bitter."

"Start pushing." He did. "I have nothing to be bitter about. It's my job to punish you for your hubris, so here I am, and here you are. Watch the thorns." He rolled me around the patch, per our agreement, and settled me near the top so I could begin my descent.

"Here you are, yes." He circled my perimeter and patted my side with a hard tap, pushing me over the lip of the peak, slowly tumbling down towards the foot of the hill.

While spinning, I'd catch brief glimpses of Sisyphus walking down the hill after me, arms stretched to the sky, popping his shoulders and elbows and wrists and knuckles. I'd see across the river to the hot pokers gouging into the screaming man's sides. If I drowned out everything else, I could almost hear the call of Zeus's eagle flying down to meet Prometheus. I could do that, easy. I could stab a guy with a beak or poker or with a fucking tree branch if I had to. The notion that I couldn't was insane, and the fact that they had put me here to get chauffeured up and down, back and forth was not only an insult to my integrity as a punisher but—

Oh.

Zeus was slick; I'll give him that. You have a mortal king who's full of himself and a punishment rock who's full of himself, and what do you do? Kill two birds with one boulder, and make them figure out their shit together! It all made sense now, that ambrosia drinking bastard. I couldn't wait to have a laugh about this at the assignment offices; Eagle and I could swap stories while watching the pokers do their thing. Just needed to get to the foot of the hill to get this sorted out.

I slammed into the weeping willow that had served as my brakes since we started and waited for Sis to catch up.

"You fucking earpiece you!" I yelled as he walked up and rolled me back from the tree.

"What?"

"That little speech you gave up there—you knew this whole time that this was punishment for me, just the same as you! But I got it now! It's all figured out, so you can call up Zeus and tell him that Boulder recognizes his hubris and politely apologizes for it." Sis spent a while just staring at me, eyebrow cocked. Behind him, I saw the pokers go in between the screaming man's ribs on his left side and exit his right, dripping cooked viscera onto the bank of the river. If I looked closely, I could have sworn I saw Eagle flying off with a piece of liver in his mouth. Business as usual. Jobs performed, punishments carried out. Sis shook his head.

"That's not what this is."

Ω

"Gathering Moss" first appeared in the *North Texas Review*.

Noblesse Oblige

by Karen Recht

The Cessna circles over a long line of elephants small as cockroaches. It tips its wings and swoops low. Jake, who is sitting up front in the co-pilot seat, has just spotted a bloated hippo in the shallow water, all four legs sticking straight up. The pilot wants to give us a better view. He thinks he is doing us a kindness.

Twisting to smile back at me, Jake, who I first spied in an antiseptic lobby in Silicon Valley, and whose name I wheedled out of the receptionist, and who I brazenly tracked to a bar—who I thought I was stalking, if I'm being honest—now, six months later, shouts into the microphone below his chin, "Good lord! No less than nine crocs are tearing at that thing!"

"I am Africa," he said to me in that bar that first night, his smile baring his teeth, all of them perfect except for the front right, which I later learned he'd chipped biting into something he shouldn't.

"I'm California," I laughed back. My face flushing hot, and not just my face, all of me burning, I didn't stop to ask myself why this man was so easy to follow. Only later would it occur to me that he knew I would come, that his sun-streaked brown hair, his worn suede chukkas, and the exotic sound of a nearly British accent were as breadcrumbs to a computer nerd like me. Breadcrumbs he'd laid like bait.

Now, four days married, or "mated," as Jake likes to put it; mated, sated and hopped up on anti-malarials, I'm staring down at what the pilot calls waterdogs. I'm the same woman I was yesterday in Customs and Immigrations. I'm not even twenty-four hours from rubbing shoulders with Jake, being flirty about handing over my crisp, new passport with my new, married name on it. Nothing has changed, only now I'm staring at a pool of red weeping from a gash in a hippo's skin unable to look away from the way its blood is clouding the murky water, thinking Jake may have overstated it when he'd said that Zimbabwe was like California, only less so. Less electricity, less clean water, less medical care, but familiar. There is nothing familiar about it.

Just yesterday, I thought that when I joked that the president of Jake's country, Comrade Robert Mugabe, looked like a frog, Jake would tip his head back and laugh as he would have done in California. In Palo Alto, he thought I was funny but in the airport, at the gateway to Zimbabwe, he elbowed me hard in the ribs and whispered fiercely not to mock old Bob.

"Mate with me," he'd said that first night when the dizzying tang was still upon me. I kept my eyes wide open. He tipped his head back and roared. It couldn't have been more primal, I remember thinking, if he'd ripped my clothes off with his teeth. I had no way of knowing that primal is a hippo whose skin is split like a sausage on a grill. Primal is the way crocodiles travel in packs, when I'd thought of them slithering through the water as loners, like snakes. Primal is a human who lifts his binocs to get a better view of an unholy cycle of life. There was nothing primal about coupling before a gas fireplace our body fluids divided neatly between condoms and sponges, in his and hers packages. I was wrong about that. Palo Alto wasn't primal; it was just loud.

And now, in Zimbabwe, I'm silently queasy in the second row of a little six-seater with an instrument panel held together with duct tape. I'm digging my nails into the armrest, peering through the grubby window while we do touch and goes, buzzing the hard-packed dirt airstrip to clear it of a family of wart hogs.

I hold my breath as the plane swoops over them yet again. This time they scatter, their tails straight in the air. We bank sharply, and the pilot puts it down onto the dirt runway, no second thoughts, no retreat.

Unsnagging my Raybans from my hair, I watch swirls of rust red dust shooting past my window thinking I should make a moment out of this, my first view of Jake's beloved Bush. I should snap a mental photograph. I should remember this exact minute the rest of my life. I tell myself that I should never forget the sight of the algae green safari vehicle chasing after our plane, but mostly, what sinks in as we rattle to a stop at the far end of the pitted runway is the sound of the pilot yelling from his microphone to my ears, "Remember: No running in Africa!"

I'm troubled that I don't know if the old guy is joking. I watch him smashing his felt safari hat onto his head, and pushing open the door even before he has shut down the engines, and I think maybe he's not. Maybe he is not joking at all.

A welcome wave of fresh air washes over us. Jake waves at the guys in the safari vehicle now parked in the shade of the wing, right outside my window, just short of the propellers.

"Got everything?" he mouths at me. "Camera? Laptop? All your bits and pieces, Syd? Got em all, do you? There's no going back for them."

The pilot and the guys from the camp, all of them dressed in dull, olive green, empty the plane of our small bags and several limp cardboard boxes holding fresh vegetables, beer, wine, and bottles of orange squash they tell me are destined for our lodge at the mouth of the Ume River, our driver introduces himself as Matuse. Jake and he perform a complicated handshake while our spotter, whose name I never do catch, stows our soft-sided bags in the farthest back seat of the safari vehicle.

As I remind myself to ask Jake if that thumb dance he and Matuse just performed was an official Zimbabwean handshake, or it was just hip in some African way, Jake comes to stand behind me.

Dropping his arms over my shoulders, he presses the length of his body tight against mine. "Your first elephant, Syddo."

Only three days out of California—and the first two of those days spent in the blur of transit—I am so sure the elephants we saw are miles away that I don't turn my head until Jake's long arm reaches over my shoulder and points past the red dirt of the airstrip, past the pilot who is now ducking beneath the plane's wings, kicking tires and checking fuel lines in preparation for his next leg.

"See?" Jake's long finger moves a little to the right, indicating a different thorny tree from the one I thought he meant, this one boasting bird nests dangling from it like Christmas ornaments.

"Do you see?" His deep voice is a near whisper, but I can tell he is excited. "Behind those Acacias? You can just make out the shape of his shoulder? Just have a look at all those broken branches. Destructive beasts, aren't they? They break off entire limbs just to eat the tender bark. The rest, like the mound of leaves over there, they leave lying on the ground."

I shade my eyes and squint along the line of his finger and see few tufts of grass in the endless dirt. I see loads of flowerless bushes well on their way to becoming tumbleweeds. I also see yellow flowers on pale green trees but I don't see anything of special interest besides a scar on the side of his finger I'd not previously noticed.

"Breathe in, Syddo," he says into my hair. "Eles are close enough to smell."

I lean back, enjoying the feel of his chin on my head. At 5'10, I never thought I'd find a man tall enough to form his body into a comma around mine, but that doesn't mean I breathe in just because he says I should. Of course I don't. But I do notice, now that Jake is talking about smells, that the breeze does seem to carry the warm summer smell of hay. I think I detect a bit of wet dog as well.

"See that?" He points again as the pilot climbs back into his sun-scorched seat, swaps his hat for his earphones and starts to taxi, one tan arm holding his still open door. This time Jake's finger directs my eyes to a gigantic pile of dung. Full of bits of grass, it is crawling with bugs and looks so damp that in colder weather it would have been steaming.

"See how it's too big to have come from cattle? That mess came from an elephant. And recently too. It would be a darker brown had it been left last night."

I watch the pilot pull the door closed at the last possible minute. I see him locking himself into the plane's stale heat. And I wonder, as Jake points again at the tree, if he will ever

come back. Surely a man wearing a uniform belt will be reliable. Surely he will return for us. *Oh lord,* I think. *Please.*

Covering my ears against the roar of the taxiing Cessna, I
look harder—partly because I'm interested, but mostly because Jake will never stop pointing if I don't. At first glance,
the tree appears to be a clump of wispy bushes, more air than
leaves. Though I don't see how anything can be hidden behind
it, much less an animal the size of a small house, I think I notice a shadow sweeping along the ground.

I relax into the curve of Jake's taut body telling myself I've
been seeing things. But then, while the duct-taped Cessna begins its gallop along the dirt runway, out from behind the
branches of Jake's chosen tree rises the massive grey head of
one of those elephants you see on the Animal Channel. This is
not the cute, tail-holding little baby everyone wants to adopt
and name Ellie. This is a mighty great bull that looks like he
rose out of the earth carved out of granite, his gigantic curved
tusks fully grown, and his flabby looking knees his only bad
feature. Before you think to laugh at his legs, don't: they carry
four huge round feet, each of which able to stomp me flat
without breaking stride. I saw that on the Animal Channel
too.

With anemic green leaves dangling from his triangle-
shaped mouth, the creature Jake was so excited about stares
straight at me, like, *girl, you are in the way.*

"Oh no!" I twist in Jake's arms to stare after my means of
escape, but it has already reached the end of the pitted runway,
and hopped itself airborne. As I watch it disappearing into the
blinding African sun, too late, it occurs to me that our cowboy
pilot wasn't joking: There is no running in Africa. And that's
because there is nowhere to run. Jake's favorite place is in the
middle of *actual* nowhere. But when I turn to bug my eyes at

Jake, the man my mother begged me not to marry—my husband of four days—allows himself an amused grin, just a quick one. Then, his arms tighten around me.

"Don't move!" he says, his breath lifting my hair. "Magnificent Beast, isn't he? Just watch: we're between him and the lake. He'll be crossing in front of us soon. He's heading for water."

Heat shimmers off Jake, cooking the small of my back while he looks back and forth between the massive monster and me asking if I see the ele's whiskers.

And yes, I do see whiskers. I see long, long eyelashes and dirt dry skin too. But what I hear is the sound of two elephant ears smacking the side of one elephant head. As I listen, wishing I could ask the bull if the sound of carpets being beaten is loud for him too, or if the noise is just there, no different to him than the pounding of his heart, my first elephant stares back at me with the saddest, most world-weary eyes I've ever seen.

Do I see the wet tracks near his eyes? Jake says into the palm of my hand. Not tears, he insists, but a gland that releases moisture when the beasts are stressed, as elephants would be this time of year, when food is scarce. Life in the bush is brutally unkind, but magnificent. Do I see what he meant all this time? Do I?

"Maybe my mother was right to give me med-evac insurance as a wedding gift," is all I can think to say back to him. This is not because Matuse is standing next to his oversized jeep, gesturing that we should climb on in. It is not because there is an elephant that thinks I'm so interesting he stopped chewing. It is because when Jake asked me to transplant myself in his Zimbabwean home he promised me candle-lit dinners by the pool. He promised parties with friends he'd known all his life. He said nothing of bench seats, each higher than the other. He never mentioned that stadium seating comes with roll bars but no roof—not even a roof made from canvas—and this becomes an important omission now that I'm close enough to see puffs of dust rising with every thwack of my first elephant's ears.

"Your mother was rude," says the man I waited just six months to marry, and even that seemed too long. He holds out his hand, palm up, waiting for me to twine my fingers through his. He is confident that I will and I do and the Jake fizz lights me right up. I stay lit until he ruins the buzz by saying that he feels like he should carry me over this threshold. By which he means the threshold of the truck, the only witnesses to our joy being two men roasting in uniforms too heavy for this heat and a thirsty elephant.

My mouth suddenly dry, I yank my hand away from Jake's, breaking the circuit, feeling the sharp opposite of a frisson, the emptiness, as the electricity stops flowing. What threshold? The truck doesn't even have door handles.

"All in?" Matuse says pointedly.

"Sorry mate," Jake says, laughing at the look on my face. He puts a foot on the rear tire and uses it to launch himself in over the low door. I follow after him. The spotter takes his place in a seat welded to the front of the vehicle, opposite to the side Matuse sits on. Now dangling in front of us like he's an appetizer, the spotter's only protection is a long stick that Jake tells me is to protect his eyes from any bushes we might drive through. This, he says even though he heard the spotter as clearly as I did. And what the spotter said is that the stick is to catch any snakes that are about to be flung into the vehicle. *Flung.*

My mother was rude, Jake's right about that. "Why is he trolling for a wife in America anyway? What's wrong with Palo Alto and a Green Card?" she said before she ever thought of the possibility of snakes dropping out of the sky onto my feet, or thorns mauling my pale skin, or elephants staring back at us like it is we who don't belong, not them.

The offer of a garden wedding never came. My mother refused to be my witness when Jake and I married at City Hall. But the odd thing is, I think she might like the road I'm on now. I'm the one elbowing Jake, asking how the guide can possibly know where he's going.

Jake hears me, but pivoting his head from one side to the other, says, "See those bushes? Its leaves curl up to make little cups out of themselves to conserve water. Isn't that cool? See that acacia? When herbivores are feeding on it, it releases ethylene gas. Any acacia within fifty feet of it downwind turns tannic. That's why giraffes feed up wind. Did you know that, Syddo? Did you?" He is so busy telling me giraffes have tongues twenty inches long and grinning at the pure joy of being back on the land, that it seems he couldn't care less if Matuse knows his way back out of this place or if he does not.

After several minutes of me trying to see what it is that has him grinning like the idea of bugs in his teeth hasn't occurred to him, the radio crackles and a deep voice alerts Matuse that there's been lion kill.

Under a ledge, near the Baobab, not the big one clawing the sky, but the small one: that's where the lion is. Matuse bounces the vehicle off the unpaved road and onto a smaller dirt path.

Jake lights right up. Over the clanking of the safari truck, he yells beginner's luck. I smile back at him, thinking I really had no idea how much it would bother me that Matuse doesn't seem to know where he is going.

Perhaps he has no need of landmarks, I tell myself. Perhaps having spent every day of his adult life driving nervous tourists from one herd of animals to another his eye is more discerning than mine and, for him, a red-colored rise in the dirt is directional beacon enough. Whatever it is, he never slows to get his bearings. Churning up clouds of rust colored dust, he rockets us through clumps of tall, dry grass, careens past a stand of yellowish-green fever trees, zooms past a flock of birds we send chattering and protesting into flight and then swings wide to avoid a series of towering terra cotta-colored anthills that, Jake yells proudly into my ear, are probably older than he is, and so energy efficient that architects copy them. Imagine termites spitting that much dirt, he says as we brace our forearms against the rolled bar of the seats ahead of us, keeping a firm grip on our binoculars so they don't bounce painfully hard against our chests.

After fifteen or more dusty minutes, Matuse suddenly brakes. The spotter parts the bushes with his snake stick and peers into the distance. Nothing.

Matuse then creeps us forward until the spotter again indicates he should roll to a quiet stop. After several minutes of this tense driving dance, stopping, peeking then moving stealthily on, not one of us daring to speak a word, the spotter waves a hand behind his back.

Matuse stops the vehicle dead.

"Those," Jake whispers, waving his hand to a pile of granite boulders stacked one on top of another looking nearly as precarious and as likely to fall as the Tower of Pisa, "are *kopjes*."

I relax. This is fine, I think. It's fine that we are near such beautiful, if unstable, scenery. It's fine that we are so far from the ocean, from Starbucks and Nordstrom and all those other perks of living in California I cherish. It's fine. Rocks are fine.

What's decidedly not fine, I discover when Jake nudges me, is the view from the other side of the vehicle. Just there, under the wide canopy of a huge, flat-topped tree with leaves the pinks and reds of vital bodily fluids—a *msasa,* as Jake says lowly—is a lion. A lion. Full grown and scarred, his khaki face dripping with blood.

I don't think it hears me gasp, but through a haze of flies the beast raises his head. Slowly, slowly, he turns his unblinking yellow gaze on us. *Ten feet away,* he seems to be estimating. *Twenty. Maybe thirty.* One bound, anyway, is all it would take.

Jake's hand covers mine and squeezes. Left unsaid are the words, *don't move.* But Jake needn't have bothered warning me because I'm trapped in the lion's stare. I'm paralyzed. Even if Jake yelled, *Jump!* I couldn't.

I read somewhere, in the pounds and pounds of Africa literature I poured through when Jake and I first started checking each other for fleas, that you should try blinking at a lion, and the lion will blink back at you. Then, you should try lowering your head very slowly, and the lion will cozy up and fall asleep: The article said that too. It was something I thought was worth remembering. But now that I'm in a position to put such helpful hints to the test, I'm too scared to try any such thing.

I could never blink lazily, not while the lion's giant tongue is smearing the gelatinous mess further toward his eyes—eyes that I swear do not blink. Not even when he gives a sucking sort of grunt; not even as he dips his head; not even after he returns to the task of dragging the glistening, purplish entrails from the stomach of an impala—a doe, whose face can't really look as shocked as I think it does—not even then could I deliberately make eye-contact with a killer that whose first act, even before he disemboweled her, was to dig the soft, brown eyes from the doe and swallow them.

For a moment, the sweet little female's empty stare stops bobbles with every bite. Then the killer takes a moment to growl, deep and low, his tingly rumble pounding to the depths of my stomach. He's warning us, we humans. And too, he's warning the vultures in the trees and the hyenas over there—see them? See how they're watching from a safe distance?—Or so the guide's low voice explains. We must all stand back.

It's unusual, Matuse adds, smiling at me knowingly. It's unusual to find a male lion making a kill. Normally, it is the females who do all the work, who hunt and who raise the cubs. Normally, the mighty male muscles in to steal the food from his mate. It's the same as humans, right, he says: females prepare. Men consume. "Right?" he says, sliding his eyes toward Jake.

While the spotter flicks his stick against the bushes like he's heard this very same speech hundreds of times before, Matuse directs his kind smile straight at me. I would smile back but my forehead is beginning to sweat and I am barely registering his dreamy voice—even if his is a voice that somehow manages to distance him from our vehicle and even though it somehow manages to place him squarely in the mind of the lion.

Our lion is an old guy, Matuse says thoughtfully, while I spread my fingers across my stomach and try not to stare at the hundreds of flies already buzzing in the sightless sockets. According to Matuse, we, unlike the doe's infant who is surely going starve, are seeing something special; we stumbled upon one of those fortunate, exiled males who are lucky to have been evicted from his prides without experiencing any life-threatening wound. That is a rare sight indeed, Matuse muses aloud as the lion chomps down on something hard and his paws get into the act.

The sound of his teeth grinding is all I can hear until a sudden gust of wind blows the stench of lion kill right into our faces.

Jake digs his fingers into my shoulder. "Remember, no running in Africa."

Ω

The Edible and the Beauteous and the Dead

by Anneliese Schultz

No no, it is not a problem. Example: he is chaperoning the dog, who has a spinning head-tilting version of vertigo, through the shared backyards. Still obstinate, Bella pokes and pulls, wanting to get at something in the middle of the hedge. He parts cedar, sees what it is, edges her away.

As they wobble-walk along the fence, the closest neighbor sinks onto a patio chair, a few minutes' respite from her kids. He looks away, then decides to update her on the staggering dog. "She's better. But she keeps trying to get in the cedar hedge. Some of the big kids threw uh something in there. Their sandwich…" He pauses for the word. "Uh—the edges of sandwiches, the—what do you call them again?"

"Crusts, Frank." The neighbor smiles.

"Crusts, yes. Thank you." And he and Bella continue the halting trek through pocket yards, past the eternal-BBQ neighbors, down the middle walkway, finally back, up the makeshift ramp, home.

Bella will be fine. It looks much worse than it is. It will pass. Settling her, settling himself, he nods, satisfied. Crusts. Excellent. These words that are beginning to hide from him, that fail, are simply opportunities to let the people in his life give back. (Or just give. More likely he has never given them a thing.)

Who doesn't like a good fill-in-the-blank? They *do*. They whip the word back to him, proud as punch, or else pretend to search their minds, giving him a further chance or two, before supplying it. Yacht. Or GMO. Or miracle.

Only a few refuse, overthinking things, deciding that if they bail him out on 'persimmon' or 'Justin Bieber,' before you know it, he will be reduced to speaking Caveman. "Dog good. Want eat. Me too." Not anytime soon.

Overall, it is a win-win, everyone gifting him with lovely words, gifted themselves by the chance to give. Long story short: Errant words? No problem.

As a matter of fact, precise and gratified, he is making a list.

WORD   **DONOR**   **DATE**

Not that many words so far, but there will be. Perfectly-filled pages. Raw material. A kind of gold. Maybe when they start adding up, he will get on the computer and alphabetize them. Maybe write thank-you notes to all the kind donors. Create a crossword? Or bundle them up in blister-pack word-packages of twelve and sell them at the farmers' market. The possibihoolities, as Uncle Noah used to say, are endless.

Well, all right, there is one person who could well have quite a problem with this. His daughter, one of the overthinkers. Of course. Not from *him* did she get the fussing and the impossibility of decisions, the fear. He who keeps it simple and positive and clear. From where, then? He does not remember her mother.

But back to the list. It was the lawn-mowing guy who restored 'azalea' to him, the single dad of three who came up with 'runner beans.' Hey. Maybe he should be organizing them into categories, bundling all the vegetation, the things of daily life, the famous—the edible and the beauteous and the dead.

Well, now there's an idea: elegant strips of bamboo with the word engraved in cursive. Each half dozen cinched with a raffia bow. Tagged as to subject and stratum. Prices may vary.

"Dad!" She has caught him wandering again between words; she does not understand that the pathways are fertile, sweet-smelling and good. Hers is fear.

He lays a hand on her shoulder. "Lucinda. What is it?"

Her head turns almost imperceptible the other way. To hide her eyes?

"What can I do for you, my dear?"

He can actually feel the tension, hear the worrying in her muscle and bone … what do I do, tell him that he was losing focus again? if I keep pointing it out, will that make it worse? it isn't something to be ignored. they say once it starts … we have to *do* something about this before it gets any worse … A great shuddering, and then something in her relaxes. "Just talk to me, Dad."

Well, that's easy. He tells her about the pair of hawks in the big oak this morning; magnificent coloring, their cry like a squeaky-toy. About Bella's startled encounter at the vet's with her double in the waiting room mirror. About the postcard from his old buddy Josh. About—no, *not* about the vocabulary garage sale idea. "I had a nice lunch."

Which reminds him of crusts.

WORD	DONOR	DATE
Crusts	Charlene	July 24th
Doormat		
Intractable		
Carbon tax		
Eldorado		
Rock salt		
Impetigo		
Jane Austen		
Wi-Fi		

Frank sees now how important it is to get the donor down right away, to record the date. Surely it was not his daughter who gave him (in a manner of speaking) 'Impetigo,' not the three-year-olds world-building daily with chalk in his empty carport who supplied 'Intractable.'

July 24th, 28th, 31st. Should he add the day of the week? Maybe he will find that certain types of words will hide on Saturdays, others preferring mid-week; that verbs like to hibernate on Friday; that on Monday mornings, all but food and beverage have disappeared. Who knows…

But back to Rebecca, or no, he means Lucinda. Rebecca might have been her mother. That could be. A blank, this, that shall be left unfilled. Lucinda who frets and puzzles and can't just be. A week later, and here they are at the same old question.

"What, Dad? *What* did you have for lunch?"

Ah ha. A test. Spaghetti? Blackened rock cod? Mead? Let's say a tuna sandwich, carrot sticks, iced tea. "*And* I took my vitamins."

She nods, satisfied, and begins a crossword. Good. It tethers her. Leaves him free to study his own horizontals and verticals, whip this list into shape. Who *did* give him 'carbon tax' and 'Jane Austen?' Come on now, do this properly—complete data right from the get-go.

Unfortunately, it seems to be too late for the first batch. So now what—erase them? Or he could always fudge it.

WORD	DONOR	DATE
Doormat	Greenpeace canvasser	
Carbon tax	Uncle Sam	
Rock salt	Mr. Morton	
Jane Austen	Emma	

Ha ha. Maybe just start over. But we need some words, and in order for there to be words—the preceding blanks. He looks over at Lucinda, chewing her tongue, staring into space. But of course. Pretend that he too is struggling with strange clues and unmatching vowels. Holding meaning in his hand, seeking answers. Aren't we all?

"God of the sun," he says, businesslike. Cradles his chin.

"Helios." She doesn't even blink.

"Too long. Is there another one?"

"Ra."

"Ra?"

"R. A. Ra." Raising her eyebrows. "Does that fit?"

Shielding the page, Frank puts it at the top of the list. "Perfectly."

"He's the Egyptian one." And she hunches again over her trellis of letters.

This is good. This is nice. Before long, he has:

WORD	DONOR	DATE
Ra	Lucinda	July 31st
Adamant	"	"
Hibiscus	"	"
Serpentine	"	"
Messenger pigeon	"	"

Two things, though. He does not like the repeating "; we need variety. And there is something awful about the word Donor. How can you have a gift drawer, a treasure trove of words headed by the wrong one?

Giver. Benefactor. Contributor. Bestower. Savior?

"Dad!?"

He jumps. The word 'Tithe' becomes unintelligible, perhaps somewhat improper. "What is it?"

"Oh, just how late it is. We kind of forgot all about dinner."

Not that he is ever hungry, but: Idea. "Why don't we go to that nice new Italian restaurant? My treat."

"But you never—"

"It's all right. I feel like it." Feel like finding some new benefactors, like stirring some exotic flavors into the mix.

"Well…" It is clear she can't quite tease out what is wrong with this picture. "Well, okay. I guess."

As they enter Maurizio's, it is all he can do to refrain from collaring the maître d', asking what the buffalo cheese is really called, the name for that pasta shaped like small doughy butterflies, or their too-sweet wrap-y kind of Sicilian dessert. Patience.

Pazienza. He savors the menu, asks his multitudinous questions of the also patient waiter, blindly scribbles words into his notebook under the table, looks up to face his food. Mamma mia. Perhaps he took this a little too far.

Lucinda gasps but then is back to her eggplant *parmigiana*, her *insalata*.

So. Start from the left, Frank thinks. Like writing. But first, eat. Here we go.

WORD	BENEFACTOR	DATE
Bocconcini	waiter	July 31st
Minestrone	"	"
Basil		

Wait! Does it count if he doesn't have to ask, if he knows the word? No, it does *not*. Who would be giving it to him—his brain, ancient memory, the Akashic Records? That would be called cheating.

Suddenly anxious, he tries to savor the basil, slurps a spoonful of minestrone, burns his tongue. All right, slow down. But now, despite himself, he is motioning for the waiter again, whispering, "How do you say uh Slow down, Relax in Italian?"

Blank stare. Apparently, despite the boy's patience, all he speaks is menu. Oh. Wait. He is gesturing to a fellow waiter, going over and asking him. The guy looks dumbfounded, but, hey, now there's a third party. No. Now they all look confused. Until the third one snaps his fingers, checks around for supervisors, then heads toward Frank. "I got it. I can call my *nonna!*"

This is so exciting, Frank almost forgets to keep at the soup and start on the pasta.

"Nonna, no, it's not that big game show; no, it's not any big game show. It's just—a man." He rolls his eyes. "No no no, not money. That's right, no money. Well, just because he's a nice guy and he just wanted to know the word."

As Nonna's voice rises, breaks up, then builds again, Lucinda doesn't even look up from her half-clean plate. The waiter exhales loudly, stamps his foot, flings out an arm, barely missing a passing tray of drinks. Maybe this was not the best idea Frank has ever had.

"Nonna! What?! Why are you yelling at *me* to relax—Oh. Oh, okay—that's the **word**. I didn't get that that was the word. Sorry, Nonna. No, I'm sorry. I said I'm sorry! *Ti amo* too. Really, I'm sorry. *Si`, ti amo anch'io*. Really! K, bye." He puffs, wipes his forehead, slides the phone into his pocket and leans in close. "*Calma.*"

Frank nods solemnly. "*Calma.*"

Then they both try it. "*Calma!*"

Lucinda blinks as if trying to fast-forward an unintelligible scene, cautiously asks to see the dessert menu.

The third waiter straightens up, stares at her. "Oh, I'll uh go get your waiter."

As he leaves, Lucinda leans toward her father. "So, who is *he*?"

"Hold on a sec," Frank tells her. "Wait!" he calls. "What's her name?"

The waiter turns. Complete confusion. "Name? Whose?"

Frank is starting to feel a bit dizzy. Maybe it is the *balsamico*. "Your *nonna*."

"Right. Rebecca Luciana Federica."

Oh. Awkward. Well, Rebecca (possibly mother of Lucinda) was definitely not Italian. That much he is sure of.

WORD	BENEFACTOR	DATE
Calma	Nonna	"
~~Rebecca~~ Luciana	~~2nd~~ 3rd waiter	"

Over coffee, he spares the waiters, uses the menu as Contributor. A red, white and green antipasto—insalata caprese! A first-course legume? A regional dessert… By the time they head for Lucinda's car, he has enough for a whole monthly meal plan for the city of Siena jotted on page and napkin and left hand. Crostini and Bruschetta (note: that is with a 'k' sound!) overlap at the top of the page, Fagioli something something fades into Calamari, which scrawls over something manzo, the line below entirely illegible due to olive oil and a splash of sugo. In the palm of his hand, Panforte.

They're home. Ah. It would be nice if Lucinda didn't have to leave now. Never mind.

"Dad." She stops as if there wasn't really a question to follow this. "Dad, why don't we ever talk about anything, like—anything?"

Well. That would certainly be the billion-dollar question, wouldn't it? And he doesn't know. The great flights of expression in his mind. In hers as well? The 'Hi. How are you?' reality. He is suddenly unbearably sad.

"Dad?" Softer now. "I'm so tired. From all the…" She searches her mind. "All the food, I guess. I think I'll just stay here tonight."

"You do that." He pats her hand. "Yes. All that food." Food of Italy, food for the imagination. Food of love. And then he needs pen and paper again.

WORD	BESTOWER	DATE
Lucinda	Rebecca	

His daughter looks over his shoulder. He keeps writing.

WORD	BESTOWER	DATE
Lucinda	Rebecca	That beauteous day.

"Oh!" She bends closer. Maybe she is seeing things. "What is this? Dad, what do you mean?"

He puts the pen down and reaches an arm around her. "Why don't we talk about it in the morning?"

No need to write it down. No, he'll remember.

Ω

"The Edible and the Beauteous and the Dead" originally appeared in *Literary Imagination*.

We're Standing on a Shallow Sea

by Sheila Thorne

For my seventieth birthday the kids and their spouses threw a party. They gave me a $250 gift certificate for a facial, massage, manicure and pedicure package at a local spa. My god, who do they think I am? After all these years, they don't know me better than this? But they meant well so I smiled and acted as if I loved it, because I'm polite, always polite, when really, sometimes the world calls for not being polite at all.

*

Helmet Man is back pacing the neighborhood. I haven't seen him for months, almost a year it seems. He disappears and then reappears, like one of my perennials.

I remember the first time I saw him, shortly after Bernie and I moved into this house, I was in our front yard on hands and knees planting a California lilac, *ceanothus,* and he stopped on the sidewalk as he ambled by and said, "Oh lovely, that's very lovely." He had a freckled face and a gentle smile. He wore a round helmet like a motorcycle helmet, out of which poked some stray brown curls. I assumed his motorcycle was parked up or down the street somewhere. But then I kept seeing him walking along other streets, or sitting on a bench in front of the corner coffee shop, drinking a coffee, always alone, and still wearing the helmet, so I began to think the helmet was not for a motorcycle but because of some kind of head injury.

One day I saw him shaking his helmeted head back and forth, muttering to himself on the bench. I approached and asked, "Are you all right?" He looked around from side to side as if trying to locate me. "Mmmmm. Mmmmmm. They're coming. They're trying to dissolve me into space but I won't let them. STAND BACK! Uh huh. It's dangerous out there. Here's some trees. I can float on them. I WON'T LET YOU! NO!"

Then I understood.

Over the years he's gotten thinner and shaggier until his jeans hang low and the plaid shirt he always wears flaps loosely, and he's lost some teeth which has made his face crumple sadly, like my wilting petunias, and he slouches along more and more slowly, still wearing the helmet. I see him all over the north side of town. He still stops in front of my house and admires the ceonothus, which is now full grown to ten feet by eight feet. He still says, "Oh, lovely, lovely."

*

I pulled out sour grass from my garden. Their roots make a little juicy pop when the tiny round bulbs at their ends come up, which is very satisfying. You have to pull just right—very gently—and the soil has to have just the right amount of moisture—a little but not too much. As always, whenever I weed, I lost myself for hours, lifted from the sadness of life.

Molly called and asked if I'd gone to the spa yet. I told her I was going to wait until I felt more beat up.

*

The apple tree is blossoming, and the dogwood and hawthorn are about to. The roses, wisteria, azaleas, California poppies, purple toadflax, and coral bells streak the yard with color. I've pruned and shaped everything to fit my vision of paradise. How I love the orange and the purple next to each other, even though some think it clashes, and the blend of different colors on the Champagne roses. "Glory be to God for dappled things," as Gerard Manley Hopkins writes.

*

I went this morning to fetch the newspaper and there was a slip of blue paper with this poem on it, neatly typed, tucked into the mailbox:

> *Thanks for your lovely garden space.*
> *Where I lay you'll see no trace*
> *And morning dew will find no waste*
> *For I have taken care to bag it*
> *Leaving nothing for a maggot.*
> *I carefully removed my boots*
> *And did not trample tender shoots.*
> *May prosper all your floral roots!*

From the word "lovely" I was sure it had to be from Helmet Man. I didn't mind.

*

I'm rereading *Madame Bovary* for the book club. Sarah is after me to "go on a cruise, or something," the last thing on earth I'd ever want to do. Bless the kids, they've been so worried about my mental state since Bernie died. It's been a whole year now. As much as I've missed him, sometimes little spritzes of "ah-hah, free-at-last" feelings bubble up from deep in my soul.

I don't know what to do with them but I know it's certainly not to go on a cruise.

About once a week I find Helmet Man's blue calling card. At night Bernie's absence still pervades the house, and it's kind of comforting to think there might be another soul close by in these dark hours. I wonder where he's sleeping the other nights? I've begun to listen for the creak of my warped wooden gate to the backyard, just to know whether he's there or not.

*

Now after the first incandescence of bloom the roses have been hit with a blight of black spot disease and a plague of aphids. Out of curiosity I took a magnifying glass to the aphids and got a close-up of their tooth-and-clawed ferocity, sharpened jaws plunged into the leaves with the rapacity of sharks in a feeding frenzy. I wouldn't want to meet them in a dark alley! I sprayed them off with a jet of water that will probably make the black spots worse. Oh well.

*

Last night the nearly full moon shone through my window so brightly it woke me up, and next I heard the unmistakable creak of the garden gate. Without thinking I got up, put on my robe and slippers, and tiptoed down the stairs to the back door. Don't know why I tiptoed except for some reason I felt stealthy. I went out into the yard taking care to open and close the door quietly, and then stood for a while, wondering why I had done this and what to do next.

A strange new silvery wilderness confronted me. Dark masses and long shadows cast by the moon formed shapes I never see during the day. The pittosporum trees along the southwest fence, ordinary suburban yard trees, suddenly appeared immense, their black branches sweeping the sky and leaves rippling in the silky fur of night. It reminded me of the mountains, when Bernie and I would go camping and shortly before dusk the wind would come up with a slightly scary, premonitory sough. A shiver of excitement ran through me.

I set off wandering through the garden, across the small moonlit patch of lawn, and spotted the shiny white helmet against the trunk of the deodor cedar in the southwest corner. When I approached he didn't act surprised. He was roosting under the sheltering branches with a sleeping bag spread beside him.

"Hello," I said.

"Such a lovely night," he said.

"Yes, it certainly is." I gazed up at the moon. "I do love the moon."

"Would you like to sit here a while and watch it?" he asked.

"Well, okay." I lowered myself onto the soft needle duff a few feet from him. This was just the place I, too, would have chosen to sleep if I'd been homeless. For several minutes we sat in silence, heads upturned to the moon. A few houses away a dog barked and then a door thumped closed. The wind shushed. An underground train passed a few miles away with a low whirring hum.

I asked him if he slept here often.

He answered, "You have a lovely garden."

"Thank you," I said. "I like working in it."

"That's good. That's good," he said.

Then more silence. I sat there enjoying the night with him, long enough to be startled out of a dreamlike state when he suddenly said, "Do you know there's a creek over there?"

"Over where?" I asked, and he pointed to the other side of the yard.

"Really?" I said politely.

"I'll show you," he said.

He clambered up with a huff and a grunt, gave a hand to me, which I took, and taking care not to trample shrubs and flower beds in his way—he clearly knew my garden well—led me to the southeast side of the yard and pointed at a shadowy cluster of ferny-like reeds that emerge here every year in late spring, though I never planted them.

"Oh these. Horsetails," I said.

"Equisetum," he said, surprising me with the Latin name.

"I like them when they're fluffy and green like this," I said.

"Do you notice they grow in a line along here?" He swept his hand along the fence where my roses grow. "Equisetum. From the Carboniferous Era three hundred million years ago. We're standing now on a shallow sea. When the tide comes in we'll have banana trees."

"I see. But where's the creek you mentioned?"

"This is the creek. It's underground. It wants to get out. Up there in the streets division they're trying to poison it, probably when the houses were built."

I didn't know what to say. I stared down at the horsetails. I love the little black rings around their joints and the delicacy of the whorls on top even though they're invasive, popping up in the well-mannered spaces of my garden like a troupe of mimes.

"I'm a creekwalker. I keep my ear to the ground," he said.

"Yes, well, that's very interesting," I said, and then I said goodnight and returned to the house.

But I was too stirred up to fall asleep. I'd forgotten how exciting the night could be, with everything transformed by moon and shadow into strangeness and the hint of danger. I thought about how, as a teenager, I'd climbed onto the roof over the front porch, lowered myself down the trellis, and run to the waiting open convertible to drive away with friends into the darkness and stars. Like through a tunnel into another world. The smoking, drinking, and sex were part of the excitement, but most of all it was the wide open space of night, a far-flung new land. As a small child, I sometimes woke up afraid in the middle of the night and I'd get up and walk out into the field behind our house, barefoot and wearing only a nightie, and skirt the scary woods at the edge of the field, daring the witch to come and get me. To prove to myself there was no witch. The danger affirming my own existence.

I realize now I've fallen into a rut. No wonder the kids gave me that stupid spa treatment. Once upon a time I led an exciting life, doing rowdy, illegal things to oppose the war in Vietnam, for instance, but then I let myself become a school marm. Why haven't I changed my life around more since retiring, and since Bernie died?

*

Last night I listened for the squeaky gate, and when I didn't hear it I went out anyway to make sure I hadn't missed it. I hadn't, but I stayed out there prowling around and squatting under the same deodor cedar where I found him before, enjoying the moon and stars again.

*

I've started going out every night and strolling around the neighborhood. Some people forget to pull their curtains or their curtains are so flimsy I can peak in when the lights are on and see little slices of their lives. I feel sly and subversive.

*

I had coffee with my friend Helen and went to the book club in the evening. Later I heard the squeaky gate, went outside, and hung out with Helmet Man until almost three in the morning. I told him he could stay in my yard as often as he liked.

*

Helmet Man has been taking me on night tours of other people's yards, showing me where he's sometimes slept. I carry a flashlight to help with my footing, but my eyes are growing so used to the dark I hardly have to use it. I'm surprised by the variety of hidden landscapes behind all the neat, boring, rectangular front lawns. A Pleistocene tableau of giant cacti and huge spidery Australian plants. A labyrinth of hedges leading to a concrete question mark. Fountains, gazebos, flower beds in all shapes, beehives: secret, florid dreams of Eden just like my own yard. Owls hoot from high branches, and raccoons scramble about. Where there's no fence, deer come down from the hills above and nibble on the roses. It's almost like hiking in the wilderness. We came across one backyard overgrown with bramble and thickets so impenetrable we couldn't enter. A few days later, happening to walk by the same house I heard a clamor of chirping and turned to see a cloud of little birds rising and sifting and dropping back down into the yard like puffs of smoke.

Sometimes a dog barks and then a light switches on and we have to run, and a few times we've been chased. Helmet Man, like Superman or Spiderman, is speedier and more surefooted than you'd expect from seeing him shambling along the sidewalks during the day, but he gets agitated when this happens and afterwards has episodes of hallucinating. Then I have to talk to him insistently, so he'll hear my voice, to bring him back to the real things around him. "This is me, Freya. There's no giant birds. You're just imagining them. You're not dissolving. You're right beside me and I can see you're not dis-

231

solving," I say. Etcetera. Eventually I can get him to calm down.

Sarah called Tuesday morning and woke me because I'd been out late with Helmet Man and was still sleeping, and now she's all concerned. "This isn't like you. Are you all right?" she insisted. I lied to her that I'd stayed up reading, but she called again on Wednesday to check up on me. It's nice she's concerned but it's also invasive.

*

This is what Helmet Man has told me so far: His real name is Jack Hartman, though he likes being called Helmet Man. He thinks the helmet protects him from being dissolved into space as well as from voices he doesn't want to listen to. He was born in Chile because his father "was doing something there," he said with a conspiratorial whisper and covering his mouth with his hand. He wouldn't say what. His mother was a biology teacher. She died of cancer when he was fifteen. The first time a voice came to him was at her funeral. It told him to jump into the grave after the coffin was lowered, but he was able to hush it up. Voices have returned to him ever since, mean voices, urging him to do terrible things. "Such as what?" I asked. He moaned and shook his head and repeated, "Oh terrible, terrible. I can't say." When he tried to go to college the voices drowned out the professors' lectures and he had to drop out.

Over the years he's managed to hold a few jobs, house painting, landscape work, newspaper delivery; jobs where he could work alone so he could concentrate on not dissolving. He probably tolerates my company because I don't try to talk too much except when he's hallucinating. I enjoy the long silences we share, the companionship without any affect, like an

232

old married couple almost, a couple on holiday as we go roaming about every night.

*

It's the Fourth of July and I went with Sarah and Molly and their families out to the coast for a picnic at the beach. I loved taking the little ones into the water, how they shrieked and yelled, "Hold me, hold me, Grandma!" I swam more than anybody. We all had a good time together but something kept nagging me, this feeling that my daughters were keeping their eyes on me as if I were one of the children, as if I were supposed to *behave a certain way,* like a little old grandma or something. There was nothing specific I could put my finger on but there it was, I could feel it.

When I came home, quite late, Helmet Man was not in the yard as usual. Perhaps he's gone somewhere to watch the fireworks? But I think they might upset him.

*

Helmet Man has disappeared, it's been ten days now. I worry because I know there are incidents of violence among the homeless and against the homeless. I've checked the jail and local shelters, but nothing.

I'm so used to the nightlife now it's hard for me to sleep. My attention wanders when I try to read. The only thing that soothes my anxiety is weeding and trimming the garden. Today a crow lit onto a branch of the deodor cedar and silently watched me work. As I pulled diseased leaves off the roses I was pricked, and thought of how Rainer Maria Rilke died of a rose thorn prick, and hoped I wouldn't die.

*

I finally located him in a mental institution over in Walnut Creek. They promised that if no kin came forward they would notify me when he was ready to be released.

I picked up Helmet Man at the hospital. He has a new prescription for meds which I will make sure he takes. He looks healthier, rosier. He's consented now to let me feed him and to take showers in the house, but he still insists on sleeping outdoors, under the cedar, and to tramp the streets much of the day. I've begun to walk along with him, which I think is very good for my health. I feel my old bones hardening. We barely talk, we just walk along together, and not talking, I see more of the concealed world—a translucent spider web in the bushes, a tiny bronze flea beetle on a blade of grass.

I've stopped going to book club meetings. Sarah says she can never reach me and I should have a cell phone. "At your age, you need to be in contact," she said, which is the last thing I want, to be tracked down every minute.

A few nights ago we explored a street high up the hill and heard the echo of splashing and gurgling from some deep chamber below. Helmet Man looked around excitedly and after finding the storm drain, hurried onward—I struggling to keep up—and turned into the street above, where he found another drain also resounding with the rush of water. "You see? It runs through here, and it comes from there, and then it'll go there, and there," he said, waving his arms around and pointing out elaborate patterns like a bee dancing its message. We followed streets and storm drains up the hill until we came at last to a large, darkened house and behind it, a lawn that sloped down to a tiny creek gleaming in the obscurity as it reflected the starlight. It came out of a pipe at one end of the yard and went back into a pipe at the other. A redwood tree grew beside it, reeds were planted along the banks. We sat down and watched the water rippling and burbling past. I thought about the mountains again, and about Bernie. He used to fly fish in streams that ran through alpine meadows while I would sit on the banks and gaze at the tiny minnows, the walking-stick bugs and the dragonflies, gaze into the glassy, transparent, flowing water and feel as if there must be another watery world, separate from this world, and I wanted to—tried to—enter it. But I never quite could.

"Isn't this lovely," I said at last.

"You have a creek too," Helmet Man said.

*

I went to City Hall and the County Courthouse and looked at old maps that trace where creeks rise from springs in the hills and fan out like a delta. A study said the springs were created a million years ago when fracturing along a fault line thrust a mass of Plio-Pleistocene sedimentary complex upward to create our hills. The maps show dotted lines where the creeks were culverted and covered by the square grid of streets when the city was built. Helmet Man is right, one of those culverts runs under my rose bushes! And all this time I've been watering them. No wonder they get so many diseases, they're getting too much water. I've decided to pull them out and daylight that creek.

*

We've been digging. The dirt is cold and sodden and feels like death, it sucks at our feet and slurps, it hardens on our fingers. We've uncovered a burrowing child of earth with a huge humanoid head and striped body; burnished pieces of brown and green glass; some faded shards of broken pottery; tiny bones of birds and squirrels; and stones, round, smooth river stones.

*

We uncovered a very large femur. Is it animal—a grizzly, an elk? Or human—indigenous burial? murdered settler? We've surmised all kinds of things. We finally hit the ceramic pipe, which is cracked and leaks water, and have started shoveling along its course.

The cedar has become a magnet for crow parties. They're fun, chattering and hopping about, but they've chased away the song birds.

*

Molly paid a surprise visit; usually she calls first. I wonder if the neighbors have been spying on us from their upstairs windows and telephoned her. She looked at the trench and the long high mound of dirt alongside it covered with burlap mesh and the piles of dirt throughout the yard, and said, "I can't believe this, Mom! You're destroying your beautiful garden! What do you think you're doing?" I replied, "You have to break an egg to make an omelet." My jeans were caked with mud. She told me I was going to ruin my health, working in the cold like this. Helmet Man kept working. I told her he's my handyman. Thank god he wasn't muttering to himself just then. I made her coffee and noticed her furtively inspecting the house, but Helmet Man leaves no trace even though on these rainy nights of winter he's consented to bringing his sleeping bag inside.

*

Yesterday evening we completed the channel. Today we broke up the pipe between the two ends, where it enters my yard and where it exits, and the rain-swollen water gushed in. We sat on the bank for an hour watching it slither along, shimmering like a snake newly burst out of its old skin.

*

We've lined the stream bed with the stones we dug up and I bought more, plus some gravel, planted arroyo willow, sedges, and buttonbrush along the banks, bunch grasses on the re-

236

maining piles of dirt, and scattered native flower seeds around. I expect the equisetum to come up of its own accord.

The water burbles and chuckles as it flows over the stones—loud and soft, with pauses, like talking. Helmet Man spends many hours sitting beside it, nodding and laughing quietly to himself. "Ho, this creek has a lot to say," he said. Maybe it drowns out the bad voices for him. He's moved his sleeping bag over to its bank, which is not grown over yet and still quite muddy, so he and his bag are filthy. He won't come in to take a shower anymore, wants to bathe in the creek instead.

I listen to it out my window when I go to bed. Most of the time its rippling lulls me, reminding me of high alpine meadows cut by winding streams, but sometimes, when I wake in the middle of the night and hear the incessant gurgling, it begins to sound nonsensical, and I think of its inexorable, mostly underground passage out to the bay, to the sea, and a vague fear sweeps over me. I have second thoughts about it then— maybe I shouldn't have daylighted it. But in the morning I'm glad again I did.

*

Last night Helmet Man and I hunkered behind the arroyo willow and waited. Heavy fog had rolled in from the ocean muffling the moon and stars, but I've bought an infrared flashlight. Finally we heard a scuffle of leaves, such a whisper it might have been the breeze, and a stag with a big rack stepped lightly and cautiously into the circle of red light, lifting each leg high and placing it down carefully, looking around, sniffing, ears cocked. The stag approached the water and sipped as delicately as a society lady drinking her tea with a raised pinkie, then he turned and started to come our way, but must have sensed our presence at last because he wheeled suddenly and trotted back to where he came from, through the torn-down gate at the side of the house.

Soon afterwards we heard the raccoons squealing and grunting as they dug for grubs and worms in the piles of dirt. I've gotten little to grow there thanks to them—as soon as I plant anything, they overturn it. Caterwauling with delight, and with no fear of us humans, they plopped themselves into the water to drink and wash their paws. As they passed by us they bared their teeth and hissed. Later a possum waddled into our field of vision, took a drink, and mosied away. Holding our breath, we waited for the mountain lion we saw from the window last night. But it didn't come.

*

With the summer dryness the creek is down to a trickle, but the banks have stabilized. We've seen a salamander and are waiting for the appearance of the red-legged frog.

Helmet Man is restless and I am too. All the work of digging and planting made us so used to heavy exercise that now my muscles feel jumpy and want to engage.

*

Molly and Sarah came over together and it ended in a big fight. They'd called beforehand so I told Helmet Man to go for a long walk while they were there.

They said I'd ruined the yard. I defended the new landscape. "Yes, there's more weeds," I said, "but many of them are edible—dandelion greens and wild radish and lamb's quarters."

Then Helmet Man returned too soon and stood in the kitchen talking and gesticulating. He'd sensed my anxiety about the kids' visit. "The C.I.A. is out there. Hiding in the banana trees. Do you want to die happy? You've got to survive the dinosaur. Be a turtle and crawl the first year. CAN YOU DO THAT? NO? Don't touch anything." And so on.

"He's a little bit crazy, but he's harmless, he's a very good person. You just have to wait him out," I said to Molly and Sarah, hoping he'd stay in the kitchen and gradually calm down.

"He's not really your handyman, is he. He's living with you, isn't he," Sarah said. So I explained that I was seeing to his meds and giving him shelter. "Then why did you tell us in the first place he was your handyman?" they demanded. "Well, I thought you wouldn't understand," I said. Which they clearly didn't. I felt like a little child caught out in a lie and being disciplined. They were flashing eye signals at each other. "You're not a social worker and you shouldn't be doing this," Molly said. "You shouldn't be telling me how to live my life," I said. "Just go away and leave me alone." All this while Helmet Man was raving in the kitchen. "We don't want to leave you here alone with that crazy man," they said. I told them he'd calm down as soon as they left and the tension in the house was dispelled. They didn't believe me and finally I had to chase them out with a folded umbrella.

Afterwards I took Helmet Man down to the creek, which always seems to calm him. We sat there and I responded to his crazy talk, interjecting my own voice, until he came back to reality.

*

It's the dog days of summer. The plants look haggard and lean, as if a shroud has been cast over them. The water's barely running.

"The creek is asking a lot of questions but it doesn't have any answers now," Helmet Man said.

*

I'm leaving these pages as an explanation. Please know that I love you all, especially the dear grandkids, though I wish you knew me better by now than you seem to.

I finally got the spa treatment. Thank you for the gift and the thought, frivolous as it was. So it is with an exfoliated face and painted toe nails that I'm setting off, with my friend Helmet Man, into the wilderness of hidden landscapes and buried creeks. To affirm my existence. You won't find us: we know how to disappear without dissolving.

Ω

"We're Standing on a Shallow Sea" originally appeared in *Natural Bridge*.

The Cartographers

by Alexander Weinstein

Publically, we sold memories under Quimbly, Barrett & Woods, but when it was just the three of us, working late into the night, we thought of ourselves as mapmakers. There was something nautical about the loft we'd rented: the massive oak beams and triangular plate glass window that stood like a sail at the end of the room. In the day it showed us the tar-papered roofs of neighboring apartment buildings, and at night it revealed the illuminated Brooklyn Bridge and Manhattan's skyline. We called it The Crow's Nest, and we were the captains, lording over the memories of the world as we drew our maps into our programs. Here was the ocean, here the ships, here the hotel, here the path that led to town, here the street vendors, here the memories of children we never had and parents much better than the ones we did. And far out there was the edge of the world.

What happens when you get to the edge?

You fall off, we joked.

Early on there were many edges. They existed within our restaurants and hotels as well as the borders of our cities. Most of our hotel rooms were well-charted—open the drawer and you'd find a Bible, take the paintings down and there'd be more wall—but behind the closed doors of neighboring rooms there was nothing but white light. There are of course, the Japanese maximalists, like the legendary Shimazaki, who design every carpet fiber of every hotel room to avoid any edges, but what Quimbly, Barrett, and I found was that most people trusted memories like they trusted films. You beam a movie between your eyes and remember the plot in vivid detail; you don't wonder where a sidekick's parents live. When you beam a vacation, you remember swimming at the beach and caipirinhas in coconut shells, not the unexplored outskirts of town. Granted, if a tourist tried to remember swimming far enough, say past the ships, had they gone further than the edge of town, up a highway, stepped onto the dirt roads at the edge of the map, they'd see that place where the ground ended and the white light began, but people were happy with their memories. What they wanted was a family trip that went well. They wanted the feeling of skydiving to tingle their bones. They don't care about the rivets and bolts of the plane they jump from; they merely want to remember that the pilot's name was Chip, that he patted them on the back, that he said *nice jump.*

What the populace wanted, what they still want, what they'll always want, is pulp cybernetics. Perhaps not as cheap as the corner-store memories China's producing—$8.99 porn thrills, so poorly constructed you can see the patches of light where the hardware burns through the girls' skin—but give them palm trees, a restaurant with an attractive server, coral reefs and sand dollars for the kids, and you have a package that retails for $79.99.

*

242

It was shortly after *Circuitry* did the article on us that Quimbly began experimenting with bad memories. It was a natural progression for him. He specialized in emotional recollections: childhoods, marriages, and adolescence. He'd always cringed from anything Hallmarky—the happy marriages and quint-essential childhoods—puppies and kittens as he called them. His first generation of memories all contained some element of sadness within them: grandchildren for the childless elderly, losses of virginity to lonely men who'd never known love. But there was something truly sinister to Quimbly's second batch. He sold heroin addictions to artists wanting darker aesthetics, affairs to couples who'd never cheated on one another, gunfights to rappers, and suicide attempts to Goth kids.

It was to get away from the dark energies Quimbly was manufacturing that I ended up meeting Cynthia. She was sitting in the coffee shop across from the office where I'd go to get my coffee, clear my head, and work on constructing my own happier memories. There was no computer or phone in front of her, only an open journal which she leaned over in concentration. I was fascinated. I hadn't seen anyone using a pen since college, and even then it was mostly older professors who'd used them. She was in her thirties, with long brown hair and flushed cheeks, and every now and again she rested the pen against her bottom lip as she tapped her sandaled foot against the table. If her pen hadn't run dry, she probably never would have seen me.

"Hey," she said.

"Me?" I asked stupidly; there was no one else around.

"Yeah, you. Do you have a pen?" She held hers in the air. "This one's done for."

"Sorry," I said, and looked back at my laptop, wishing I wasn't such an idiot around women. Say something, I told myself, and so I looked back up and said "Hey." She raised her eyes. "I'll go ask if the barista has one."

It turned out he didn't. I walked back to her table. Sorry," I said, "no luck."

"Doesn't surprise me." She closed her journal.

"What are you writing?"

"Memories," she said and pointed her pen at my laptop. "What about you?"

"Pretty much the same. It's my work; I make memories. Maybe you've heard of us? Quimbly, Barrett & Woods?" She shook her head. "We're in a lot of blogs right now."

"I don't read blogs," she said. "I try to stay disconnected."

"You've heard of beamed memories though, right?" She shook her head again. "Well, I'm Adam," I said and extended my hand.

"Cynthia," she said.

"I could show you what I do, if you'd like. Our workshop's just across the street. I'm sure there's a pen there."

She put her journal in her bag. "Sure," she said. "Show me your memories."

*

Cynthia kept me out of the office that weekend. It'd been a long time since I'd been with anyone, and never with someone like Cynthia. When we lay in bed together, I could feel the loneliness of my previous life, filled with computer programming and take-out containers, giving way to the happiness of a future together. In short, I was falling in love.

I called in sick Monday and stayed in bed with her, afraid that if I left she'd disappear. It was the first time in months that I didn't work on constructing memories. Instead, I let my mind fill with details of her: what her lips felt like, the timbre of her voice when she said my name, the way morning spread across the bedroom, how I'd forgotten what happiness felt like.

When I finally returned to work on Tuesday and told the guys, I got ribbed by Quimbly. "So that's what happens when you get laid?" I shrugged and blushed. "Thought you'd both left me," he said. "Barrett's lost in the Bible."

Barrett was sitting by his computer with his head down, the golden-rimmed pages of a King James on his desk. He'd found his niche with religious experiences. "What are you doing?" I asked him.

"Shhh…" he said darkly and didn't look up.

"He's writing Sunday sermons now," Quimbly said. "Turns out folks are just as happy thinking they've been to church than actually going. Barrett, put that fucking Bible down, we've got something serious to talk about." Barrett raised a bloodshot glare from the book before marking the page and rising.

We'd gotten our first complaint. A tech-savvy grad student had intentionally gone seeking the edge. He'd tried to remember driving to the border of the Mexican town we'd created for Spring Break and had run into the white light. His blog posts were already circulating the Internet.

"We haven't been designing tight enough memories," Quimbly said.

"The kid went searching," I said defensively; it'd been my memory. "We can't control where our users go."

"Maybe not, but we can test each other's memories," Quimbly said. "From now on, before we release anything for sale, you go into Barrett's memories, he goes into yours, and both of you go into mine. You test out the edges. Search every alleyway, open every door, drive as far as you can. You find the edge of a memory, you fix it. Go ahead and test at home if you want, just make sure you log every beam."

"And what are you going to do?" I asked.

"I'm the control group," Quimbly said. He promised to watch over us and hold our memories straight. "Don't worry," he said, "I'll keep your brains from getting fried."

*

The problem with testing memories was that after enough blasts it became impossible to recognize the difference between authentic memories and beamed ones. Had I really fought in Afghanistan? Cynthia was lying next to me in bed, reading a book. It was one of her things—she read actual books. Where she found them, I have no idea. But there she'd be, pillows propped behind her head, reading a novel word by word, page after page, taking endless hours when she could've had the thing memorized in minutes.

"Was I ever in Afghanistan?" I asked.

"You weren't born yet," she said dryly.

"How about Bermuda?"

She lowered her book onto her knees and shook her head. "The last place you actually went to was your parents' house for Thanksgiving." It was February. I tried to remember back to November, the dinner with my parents; but it seemed less real than my memories of the tropics. "Are you sure?" I asked.

She raised her book. "Yeah, I'm positive. You've got to stop beaming."

Cynthia was vegan and almost entirely anti-tech. She was devoted to causes like buying back land for Native Americans and safeguarding water rights for third world countries. Though I supported her causes, I resented that she never praised my work. "You know that indigenous tribes are buying our memories, right?"

She let out a heavy sigh. "I'm not trying to put down your work," she said. "But you're spending more time trying to figure out memories you never had than making real memories with me. You're getting addicted."

This wasn't entirely true. In those first months together, I'd go to the Crow's Nest and work on memories during the day, then take nights off with her. A bistro had opened near my place, and we'd go there on the weekends for breakfast. Nights we'd order in Chinese, lie in bed, and make love. But Cynthia was right. There were many times when she'd catch me staring out the window, trying to find the edge of Quimbly's latest memory.

At work, Quimbly, Barrett, and I focused on making our memories last longer. The key was to package memories together. A vacation to Europe couldn't simply be the Eifel Tower and the Louvre, it needed to involve the airplane ride, the week at work before, the mundane details which helped make the memories stick.

"All good memories have boredom buried in them," Quimbly told us one night.

"You should write children's books," I said.

Barrett was unusually quiet. He'd grown more silent ever since he'd begun designing past-life memories, and we mistook his silence for Zen satori rather than the madness that was slowly taking his mind.

"Look, if we make perfect memories we're not going to have customers left," Quimbly said and leaned over the coffee table. "The key to our success is to give people ninety-nine percent perfect experiences. Make them *almost* happy and they'll keep buying. Trust me on this." Then he gave us the next batch of memories to test.

*

Cynthia hated Quimbly from the first time they met. I'd invited Quimbly for dinner in hopes they'd get along, but by the time we sat down to eat, it was a mess. Cynthia was working on a clean water project for African children and, in typical Quimbly fashion, he started an argument. "Look, I get you, it's good to give them water, but let's be honest, water isn't going to change their history. Give them memory sticks and at least they'll have happy memories before they die."

"That's really sick," Cynthia said.

"You're telling me if you could give them a happy childhood, you'd deny them?"

"It's not a happy childhood; it's forgetting their actual past."

"I think you *want* them to suffer," Quimbly said. "Somehow their pain makes things real for you."

I tried to sooth the tension, suggested we do both, send them water *and* memories. Getting the kids water made sense, I said, it was the right thing to do, but I didn't see any harm in giving kids good memories as well.

"Fuck that," Cynthia said. "What you're talking about is making a bunch of beam-heads who won't ever work for social change."

"That's not true," I said. "We're designing parents for inner city kids with horrible upbringings; we've donated memories to the poor."

"That's not social change," Cynthia said, and got up from the table, leaving her dinner unfinished. "I hope you know the work you guys are doing is evil."

Quimbly took a sip of wine and gave me a smile after she left the room. "You sure she's the one?" he asked. "You might want to take a closer look there, buddy." He stayed long enough to finish his dinner and fix himself another drink, and then, when I said it was probably best I see him tomorrow, he left. I cleared the dishes from the table and went into the bedroom, where Cynthia sat reading.

"I can't believe you work with that asshole."

"You guys didn't get off to the best start," I admitted. "He's actually a good guy; he just likes to push people's buttons. He's a brilliant designer."

"That kind of brilliance I can do without." She looked at me for the first time since I'd entered the room. "His fetish is getting inside people's heads. That's why he likes being, what did you call it, *the control group*? Control freak is more like it. He loves that he controls your memories—you're his guinea pigs."

In retrospect, I can see that this was precisely what Quimbly was doing. I'd thought of him as a friend—and maybe Barrett and I were as close to friends as Quimbly would ever be capable of—but, deep down, we were just social experiments to him. I couldn't see it then however, and was angry at Cynthia for calling our work evil and me a guinea pig.

"It's no different than what you do," I said before I could stop myself. "You only want *real* memories, memories you get to hold onto and no one else. You talk about our future and all the memories we'll have. You plan for a farmhouse that doesn't exist." I sounded exactly like Quimbly. "You like controlling my memories as much as he does."

She looked at me for a moment before turning back to her book. "You don't have a fucking clue what you're talking about."

"Right," I said. "That's why I have a company worth millions, and you're just reading a book."

"Here," she said, tossing me a pillow. "How about we sleep apart tonight."

249

And so I went back into the living room and lay on the couch, late into the night, wondering why I'd defended Quimbly against the woman who loved me. Perhaps this proved everything Cynthia was trying to tell me—that he'd already gotten so deeply into my head that I'd willingly hurt anyone who reminded me, not out of control but out of love, that I'd never been to Russia or had a brother. It was this thought that brought me back to the bedroom, to climb beneath the sheets, and to hold her, telling her I was sorry, and that I wanted to make memories together.

*

It was hard to shake the memory of our first real fight. In the months that followed, Cynthia and I avoided that night with Quimbly, and I made an effort to be more present. We went for walks, ate at our favorite bistro, and we'd return to my apartment and make love. But there was a growing distance between us, and when she'd fall asleep, I'd edge my way out of bed to beam memories in the darkness of the bathroom. It was, I realize now, a time when I had everything: a woman who loved me, a company worth millions, and bidders waiting in line to buy us out. Quimbly was calling us the history-makers. It was a time when I believed we would become the masters of the world. Then we destroyed it all.

"We'll make a fortune," Quimbly said, putting his palms together.

"What exactly are you suggesting?" I asked.

"Simple ad placement. We layer one into your Cuba memory. Show sweat beading along a glass of Coke, carbonation fizzing. We're talking big money for a single placement."

Barrett was deadly silent. Over the past weeks he'd become increasingly taciturn, but this was something different. His lips were working back and forth against each other as though he was grinding his teeth.

"We're selling out?" I asked.

"Just being practical. They're lining up at our door. We could own the world."

"*Enough!*" Barrett ordered, his voice echoing in the beams.

"Hold on," Quimbly said, "You haven't heard me out."

"*You dare argue with me?*" Barrett boomed, his fingers clenching. "Do you know who I am? I am the Lord of lords and the King of kings; I am the alpha and omega. I am the Lord Supreme." He rose from his seat, stepping onto the couch and lifting his hands into the air as though holding a staff. "You, who sow discontent, shall be crucified! Your hands and feet shall be cut off—"

"Barrett, chill," Quimbly said.

"In my presence the mountains quake! The hills melt, the earth trembles, its people are destroyed! The day of judgment has come!" Then Barrett jumped from the couch and seized Quimbly around the neck so hard it left bruises for weeks after. It was when I saw Quimbly's face turning blue that I took my beer bottle and broke it over Barrett's head. We tied his legs and arms together and called 911.

That was the end of Barrett. He was sent upstate, where he ranted at the walls and played God to anyone willing to listen. When we cleaned out his apartment, we discovered the memories he'd never told us about. He'd begun a personal log which detailed beaming thousands of his own created memories; the notebook deteriorated into pages of an indecipherable alphabet.

Still, Barrett had tried, in his own way, to warn us. Come May, less than a week after our first memory ads launched, the word spread that we'd sold out. A blogger posted a scathing piece that went viral. Memory startups took the bait and began selling their memories as "100% ad free."

"Who'd have guessed they'd resent having their brain space tweaked, they never seemed to mind before," Quimbly joked. But he, too, was shaken. Within the month, sales fell and our inboxes were full of hate mail. We were no longer the masters of the universe, just owners of a failing company.

*

Quimbly ended up taking a job for another company that manufactured thought-ads. He told me the news as we cleared the Crow's Nest of our belongings, and I listened vaguely as I cleaned out my desk, realizing the life we'd created together was now only a memory. Barrett was gone, Quimbly was moving on, and I had nothing but my dwindling savings and Cynthia.

"People resist thought ads, but soon enough they'll be as commonplace as napkins," he said. "I can get you in, but first clean yourself up."

I looked up from the floorboards where I'd been staring, thinking about the years I'd spent in the war. "What do you mean *clean myself up*?"

"How many memories are you beaming a day?"

"Not that many," I lied. Like Barrett, I was designing my own memories and downloading them when I couldn't sleep. I still logged the memories I tested, but not my late night binges or the hundreds of high-end Shimazaki memories I'd spent my bank account on. "Maybe a few a day," I said.

"Uh-huh. Look, I'm not telling you what to do with your life, but you're starting to act like Barrett. Go visit him. Refresh your memory of what happens when you lose track."

"I'm fine," I said.

"No, you're not," Quimbly said. "You probably don't even remember the time we went skiing."

"Of course, I do: Breckenridge; three days of fresh powder."

Quimbly shook his head. "That was one of mine," he said. "Listen, I know you won't stop beaming because I tell you to, but if you're going to keep beaming, at least use this one next." Quimbly pulled a memory stick from his pocket. "It's a going-away present."

"Thanks," I said, and though I knew he and Cynthia were right, and that the best thing for me would be never to touch another memory again, I couldn't help myself from reaching out and taking the gift.

When I got back to the apartment, I left the boxes from the office in the hallway and sat down on the couch. I placed the tip of Quimbly's memory stick against my forehead and pressed the button. I was halfway into the beam when Cynthia walked in.

"You've got to be fucking kidding me," she said.

"What?" I opened my eyes.

"You just went bankrupt because of those things and you're—" Then she stopped. "No, you know what—go ahead and enjoy yourself, beam all night if you want, I'm out of here." She raised her two fingers into a peace sign then turned her back on me and left the room.

"Hey!" I said. "Just wait a minute, I'm almost done." I finished Quimbly's gift and got up to find her, but she wasn't anywhere. Not in the bedroom, the kitchen, or the bathroom. The only trace of her was a note taped to the mirror. *I'm done. Goodbye, Adam. Thanks for the memories. Sorry you liked yours better.*

For the next two weeks I binged on memories to keep from letting the pain sink in. I went to the Himalayas and gambled in Vegas, I slept with porn stars and got wasted with celebrities, I drove in stretch limos through Hollywood and sat on the beaches of the world watching sunrise after tropical sunrise, beaming one after another memory, until one morning I found myself in the early light, dehydrated, shaking and sweaty, without a clue of who I was.

Did I have parents? Were they both still alive?

In one memory I recalled attending their funeral. In another I pictured them tanned and happy in L.A. And in yet another I remembered our childhood home in Tibet. I scrolled though my phone, my grip sweaty and slippery, until I found a number listed as *Home.*

A woman picked up on the third ring.

"Hello?" she said, her voice distant and unfamiliar.

"Mom?" I asked. "Can I come home?"

*

My life since leaving the memory business has mostly been recovery and learning to forgive Quimbly. I work to get my memories straight. I'll recall my parents' death, envision myself as an angry teenager, smoking cigarettes in the Rockies after their funeral. Then I'll hear the floor squeak above me, hear my mother in the kitchen, listen to my father cough before he lets the door slam, and I'll remember that I never lived in Colorado but grew up here in Brooklyn. I live in my parents' basement again, like when I was a teenager, and I never smoked cigarettes, merely spent my daylight hours in this subterranean darkness programming computers.

I got a job at a coffee shop in the neighborhood where I help curate the art on the walls and brew lattes for the kids who are settling this outpost of New York City. And I work on my letter to Cynthia. I sit, pen in hand, trying to remember what love felt like. *I miss you,* I write. *I'm better now. I want to make real memories together.*

Quimbly saved me, there's no doubt about that. Had I never fallen in love with Cynthia, she never could've left me; had she never left me, I never would've stopped beaming. Typical though, that even Quimbly's acts of kindness were sadistic. It was when I'd finished my letter that I understood his real gift had been motivation, not merely memories. Sealing my pages into the envelope, I picked up my pen to write Cynthia's address, and realized I had no clue where she lived. Every memory I had of her involved my apartment, the bistro, or walking the streets in winter. Hadn't I ever seen her apartment, I wondered. And then, before I could stop myself, I understood that I'd found the edge. Light poured through the cracks where stories of her family should've been. It came streaming in from the hallway of my old apartment, which had never been clean, but was a dark, curtained cave, filled with take-out containers and an unmade bed. The bistro where we ate never had a name; the Chinese take-out never had fortune cookies. And yet, all the other details had been masterfully placed, every memory bunched together to form a life that had never happened. I sat there in the coffee shop, the light fluttering behind my eyelids, feeling my heart sail off the edge of the world.

Love scars memories, even if it was never real. When I walk the streets I think: we walked here together, she used to touch my arm like this, and the pain of white emptiness sets in. You can't get rid of memories; you can only try to ignore them. I've been weeding through my old notebooks, finding the edge of the world in one after another memory. I was never in France or Tokyo, have never seen the California

Redwoods or swam in the Caribbean, and I've never made love with Cynthia. All the same, I keep working on my letters to her. I tell her I can still remember her skin against mine as we slept, the light in her eyes when I'd open my apartment door for her, and the sound of her voice, telling me, over and over, just how much she loved me.

Ω

"The Cartographers" originally appeared in *Chattahoochee Review*.

Sefeed

by Mathew Javidi

If I could go back,
I would have clutched my tongue,
not let it pirouette into
the soft, dim spotlight of
　　your living room.

I reassured your parents
"Don't worry. I'm not a Muslim,"
and tried to win them over with
a heartless,
　　tasteless,
　　　　hopelessly ignorant quip about
how Islam is the *Spider-man 3* of religion—
　　in that the first two installments were better
　　it doesn't represent its creators best work
　　and everyone involved just looks silly.

In hindsight, it was not worth
your mother's chortle, or your father's muddy
grunt, and it was not worth
the look on my father's face
when I told him he would never meet your parents,

because Iranian men are shrapnel
in the souls of nice Jewish girls.

I would go back and hold that comment
I didn't need it to prove
    that I am hardly a member of my own race
that I don't even qualify for a plastic
    participation trophy
        in the scrimmage between Persians and Jews
that I know just enough Farsi
to tell people I don't speak it,

but now I stand victorious,
    holding your heart above the ashes
of those who trusted me
    to carry their blood with pride.

Ω

User

by Heather Altfeld

I told myself last Friday I needed some new words
before I left town, which might be why
I spent the evening slipped down
along the vinyl seat of his Ford F-150,
jamming my sandals against the crescent blade
of an unplugged sliver saw, listening
to a monologue about tile.
Mitering, backsplashes, hardibacker,
long lines of grout traversing

the thin rivulets of his skin
and I pretended he was speaking of literature,
tried to bathe in the glow of it,
quarter round, mortar, set lines,
his hip rounding a quarter turn
toward me, offering the want
of Nin and Neruda.
He pulled out a pouch of Bali, told me
the price of cigarettes lately makes
my butthole pucker,

and while contemplating whether
I could let a man who shares this grim detail

lay scratch in my driveway
and climb beneath my sateen sheets,

a lime green Kawasaki
rode past our little parked nook. *Did you see
the way that bike chewed through that corner?
That was sick!* he said, shifting gears,
moving on to the vitals of the V-8 engine,
carburetors and gaskets,

how *I wouldn't be caught dead
on a creeper under the rear end of a 67' Camero,*
all the while rolling the thick pads
of his fingertips on the back of my neck,
his tongue-pierce rapid-firing *fuel lines, traction, water pumps*

against the fat line of dentures
meth had given him; the sweet high
wrenching his real teeth, leaving steepled brown crags
and mouth rot; nothing but a gumless stare
and the long ache of enamel
until they pulled the last of them in Chino
just before he cracked parole.
*Man, the ass on that Buick! I'd jack that thing up
so fast,* he exclaimed, reaching behind my shoulders

to pull me closer, downshifting me into his scent;
the chalky concrete he'd poured
in my bathroom that morning,
Red Bull, tobacco, his arm rippling beneath my scapulae

in something I could only call tenderness.
I didn't need him to go all iambic
on me, or purse his brow trying to think of a line
he once read by Keats;
here was a man who'd begun
the small workings of his lips on my neck,
here was a man whose heart was thunking
against the nest of my blouse,
reminding me to cut my internal professor voice-over,
intake, felonies, probation, deep tread of scars
that wheel the mind—I could slide under
the chassis of this, find something here,
I could like it.

Ω

God Bless
by C. Wade Bentley

While waiting at the light I reach you a dollar
out my window—for bus fare, so says your sign,
and I have no reason to doubt you, and am,
in fact, long after pulling through the intersection,
imagining that happy reunion walk up the dusty
driveway to the family home in Kearney, Nebraska—
or Mishawaka, Indiana or Big Piney, Wyoming,
could be—and mom hugging you all the way in
to the kitchen table where there are biscuits and gravy
waiting, and dad coming in from the field, not asking
what the hell happened to the $300 dollars
they'd kept in the Clabber Girl can or why you smell
like warm roadkill. Only the dog circles you skeptically
and thinks you used all the dollars for cheap vodka
in Elko, Nevada and never made it home at all
but are in fact still standing by that on-ramp, smiling
shitfaced at all the cars, hoping you remind us
of something or someone we had meant to forget.

Ω

"God Bless" originally appeared in *A Narrow Fellow*.

Manifest
by Kierstin Bridger

I am a child of HUD houses,
the cardiac arrest of the Rockies.
I am a child of sage and tumbleweed,
of living a sandstone's throw from the cemetery—
a frozen crust and moonboot trudge,
the dusty bike ride to the rodeo grounds,
the dare to walk across vast wooden beams
above splintered stadium seats.

I am a child of the 80's, of television, turning the silver knob
on the squat console, no '84 Olympics; the smashed
black-and-white against the drywall's corner bead.
I am a child of a Vietnam vet and a beauty school queen.
I am the grandchild of an Indian man,
whose mother skinned more than knees on the Trail of Tears,
who sold her heritage for two beets and a warm chicken egg.

I am the mutt of Black Ireland,
dark veins and snake-handling Sundays,
of winding Kentucky hollers
and panthers who scream in the night—
moonshine feuds and bottles broken for scarring.
Folks who lived deep in the ivy of Appalachian mountains,
of mustard poultices, and honeycomb on the table for biscuits.

I am sanity's child who fled by rutted frontage roads
stained by black lung and bad luck,
who reached out to a man I didn't have to save because,
though I am the product of generations of teenage lust
and long highways of losing him in the rearview,
I am also the daughter of women who work,
of deep grease in the folds of corporate uniforms.

I am a child of stocked pantries, aluminum canisters
of powdered milk and blocks of government cheese.
I am public education, taxed on the back of a mother
who cut hair for years, who fed countless strands
through two fingers under the florescent light
of a beat-up, post-war shack.
I am a child of cottonwood and aspen,
who hand fished in the Arkansas.
My voice, crack and lightning strike
in the heart of piñon pine.

Ω

"Manifest" originally appeared in *Fruita Pulp*.

Viewing *Guernica* in Madrid

by Susan Cohen

Their kindergarten teacher could be telling them
this imaginary horse
was not in Picasso's early drawings.
In the Spanish I cannot understand,
maybe he says once upon a market day in Guernica
the world collapsed around whole families
whose luck ran out, or did not,

from a burning building.
Maybe he mentions German pilots
high above the town, who were imagining
what would happen in that instant
when their dropped bombs stopped whistling,
while down below, a horse
was incapable of imagining

how to gallop out from under
the sky's sudden piercing rain.
When the teacher points to the wall behind him,
his class rapt, surely he explains they're lucky
to sit cross-legged before a masterpiece,
a painting people come from far away to see.
And I, who am one of those people,

look past the heads of tiny children to the painting
that takes the whole wall, and see it's not
Picasso's wailing woman trailing into ghostliness,
infant slack and cooling in her arms,
and not the bull with its bayonet horns
that makes this an object of devotion,
but the horse's gaping terror,

the horse's tongue razored sharp by pain,
the horse's leg severed and strewn,
and most of all, its dumb dying scream
still open to us decades later and so pure
in black and white—
as animal terror can be pure—
because a horse could never understand

the human imagination, no matter how long
you talked to it, how clear your diction
and enthusiastic your voice,
how careful and small your words.
I wonder if their teacher's telling them
Guernica started out in color,
but color would have added nothing.

Ω

"Viewing *Guernica* in Madrid" originally appeared in *Atlanta Review*.

My Father Asks for One Last Thing

by James Crews

Bending over rows of four o' clocks
now wet with evening, he picks off
dead blooms, tipping their seeds
into an envelope for next year,
though he knows he won't be here.
Through the screen door, I smell
cut grass, wild onion, gasoline.
Under his T-shirt stained green,
his skin's already begun to yellow
like a window shade finally ruined
by too much smoke and sun.
Gloaming is not the word for how
night shows up, draping the city sky
whose trapped sulfur and junk-light
fight off true dark. He looks up
from cleaning the mower blades,
knows I'm checking on him again.
I open the pantry, pretend to be
absorbed by the jars of tomatoes
he canned last summer, heirlooms
floating soft in the murk of time.

And when he calls my name, asking
for a massage, having asked too much
of his body today, his face is blank
and gray like the sky just before rain.

Ω

Hermes in Hades

by Elizabeth Crowell

When my uncle Hades heard
the news of the old neighborhood,
the frozen earth, Demeter's rage,
he whipped his black hair,
flashed a smoke-stained grin,
pulled on a red velvet robe,
and told me how great business was
now that everyone was dying.

Persephone lay behind him
on a bed of soft dead leaves.
Yellow flowers still stuck in her hair.
"Your mother misses you," I said.
She looked down at her flesh,
white as the clean bones
floating down the dark river.
"What does my mother know?"

From the pocket of his robe,
Hades tossed a flight of seeds,
quick as starlings in the sky,
She caught one and ate it fast,
as if she couldn't think or look.
A yellow honey,

the hue of late autumn,
split from her purple lips.

There was the crack-dry sound
of the wasted pomegranate seeds
falling off the bed
onto the warm ash of the ground.
We did not know that was the sound
seasons made when they split.
I led her to the chariot.
Hades kissed the honey off her lips.

As we rose in fire and air,
the horses leering steadily towards home,
I told her how when I stole the cattle,
my father could have hated me instead,
for all the trouble that I caused.
She liked the story a lot.
All the way back, we spoke of
what children do to their parents.

Ω

Chetwynd Morning
by Jesse Mavro Diamond

The spring your twins were born
I found upon our stone steps
the shell of a robin's egg perfectly formed.
I held it in the shadows of my palm:

Not a single crack! I stood there parsing
the secret a symbol keeps. Soon after,
we awoke to shrill peeps of baby birds
nestled in our bedroom's eaves.

For some reason, I imagined the mother who grieves
her lost embryo as she feeds the newly born.
Here on Chetwynd the steps of homes are worn
by those who lost eggs and those lucky enough to find one.

All the eaves on all the houses hold shadow as well as sun.
But then I thought, Oh, to be plucked from dusk's dark palm
lengthening on the stoop. To be found as I was
by your own mother, as mothers can be by children,

as children often are by one another.
Best of all perhaps, to tender the lost, empty shell,
to imagine, to believe, to foretell one's lifeline
becoming a living filament.

To weave from mud and dry, broken sticks
a holy cradle. And with the heat of one's hope
to devotedly sit, to wait for as long as it takes
until the cry of hunger brings us, once again, awake.

Ω

What I Mean by Beauty
by Doris Ferleger

What I mean by beauty is not the strange red sky
you say belongs only to me or the regular blue sky
with white clouds you claim as your own
because you believe, you say, only what you see.

What I mean by beauty is how you trust me,
let my words wash over you though you have
no idea what I am talking about when I say
the sky's fire-red feet rake across our bodies.

What I mean by beauty is not the brilliant broach
of white moon against the eloquent deep blue,
the kind of blue that enunciates and disrobes
in the parking lot at the Home Depot.

I mean how the heavyset couple walks out
of the store side by side, how each then drifts,
one in front of the other, how they look happy,
unadorned, with white PVC piping poking out

of the super-sized orange cart, how they indulge
me when I point to the sliver of moon the way
a child might. How the woman with a blond-streaked
wig stops her jalopy beside me, her front seat filled

with marked-down shiny fat-leafed rubber plants,
how she says, *I see you got some too*! Though
I got coreopsis with spidery leaves, pale yellow flowers,
tiny stars, I agree with her since she just wants to say

from One came many and how we need each other.
What I mean by beauty is when I point to the moon,
the woman with the bright abundant wig laughs
and says, *Ya gotta love that*! How she doesn't turn her head

to look back at the white crescent. She is sure of love
as she drives off with her rubber plants. What I mean
by beauty is freedom; when I say freedom I mean how
the moon lifts us, seats us into the deep curve of her hip.

Ω

Line of Scrimmage
by Alexis Finc

Nearly thirty and I'm learning the game of football
by a man and a TV, both loud and aglow, hued blue
with light. I never attended a game during those high
school years when football is food to teenage boys
and glory exists in the space between two poles
held up in the night sky like a tuning fork.

This man, once one of those boys, took three steps
back and kicked the ball straight through November.
I was states away, in an old Moose lodge at a punk show
handing out buttons with images of bibles lit with flame,
happiness mean struggle just like these men on the TV

now, a muscled pile-up. All we can see: numbers—
2, 37, 15—crush of limbs, they begin to pull apart,
separate, take their places again. Then touchdown.
I know what that means even if I don't know the point
value. The men are happy, so is this man and I'm happy
for him, our frequencies aligned this year, this night.

The mascots dance. Someone is a tree. And even
the silly tree is happy, performing for the crowd.
But that is not the magical part of this whole orchestration,

no, the magical part exists in a single phrase "imaginary
line of scrimmage." I don't understand it, I just know
it sounds beautiful, like the man who is sitting next to me

trying to explain, as beautiful as him. That in this world
of bright lights and heavy bodies there exists a place
where this struggle, this clash can exist in the imagination.
I know that's not really right, but it doesn't matter.
Just the notion is enough. Throughout the night I repeatedly
ask, where is it now? And he never gets tired of pointing

to the imaginary line drawn on the TV screen.
The game continues,
the line moves up and down the field. And then it is over,
one team a trophy, another none. This man clicks off the TV,
thoughts on the next game, other teams and stadiums
and I'm thinking of how once our worlds
barely orbited one another,
when we were different. A near miss—
and didn't we get lucky?

Ω

They call all experience of the senses mystic,
when the experience is considered
—D. H. Lawrence
by Kim Garcia

All the great lovers are brown, like thrushes
or wrens, with their eager uplifted tails
their small, hidden nests, eggs warmed
in shit and straw, settled in the hollow
their own breasts have made, with singing.

                    Give me a stone
when I ask for bread. Give me a snake
when I say fish. Give me the senses
when I say God, and God when I call
for light—*first light, last light. Light.*

This is a catbird's song. Sounds like thrush, like
wren. Like a lover, not so great, not so God, small brown
mystic, a hidden stone snaking, my eager fish.
All sense uplifted. Shit uplifted. Straw uplifted.

277

Why call for light? There's plenty of light.
Why call for God? There's plenty of God.

Ω

"They call all experience of the senses mystic" originally appeared in *Madonna Magdalene*, published by Turning Point Books.

one sentence on the old house

by Megan Gilmore

We left you beside a dip in the
road near Buffalo Ridge,
curled into a corner of trees
forgot to bring you, too
because you had no arms,
no legs to stand,
no voice left to call to us,
your mouth aghast,
the breath knocked out of your every
window; but I am older now
and you are strange, old house,
that runs to me in dreams, somehow alive again,
and Max runs alongside too, his tongue
hanging out, tail wagging patiently,
as if he never got hit that day
on the road—
as if we were all still
what we were.

Ω

Karaoke Night at the Asylum
by Jennifer Givhan

When I was eleven, Mama sang karaoke
at the asylum. For family night, she'd chosen

Billie Holiday, and while she sang,
my brother, a fretted possum, clung

to me near the punch bowl. I remember
her then, already coffin-legged—

mustard grease on her plain dress,
the cattails of her hair thwapping along

with the beat. The balding headstones
of the others—quarantined

from their own mothers and sisters and daughters—
I wondered if they, like us, were strange

alloys of sadness and forgetting
the words to the songs. I was a grave-

digger then. A rat fleeing ship. Mama,
who hadn't sang to me since I was a baby and

never would again, was the lynchpin—
I'm still turning and turning the screw.

Ω

"Karaoke Night at the Asylum" originally appeared in *Indiana Review*.

Boarding Up
by Alex Greenberg

We drilled holes
in the kitchen light bulbs
and scraped their fluorescence
into grandpa's steel urn
tossed his cremation into
the fire pit and tried
to rekindle the ashes
reattach them like the burned
pieces of a love letter.
The chins of the curtains
toppled in on each other
and we started finding things
we'd lost that winter;
Ring, tooth, vinyl
I found my soul
lodged in the back door's
broken lock
like a useless key.

Ω

Crisis Hotline
by Christina Hammerton

In the tiny room where we answered calls,
big binders full of instructions lined the shelves.
Lists of numbers for support groups, meeting times
scratched out and never rewritten. I loved people
in a very simple way at 22, listening with wide eyes,
pizza getting cold. A man called with AIDS.
A woman was beaten and had her child taken away.
The rain slid down the dark windows for them
as I crawled in through the holes of the heavy phone,
armed with attention and raw trust.

If you ever try it you should know
that most people expect not to cry when they call,
and it's the shame they feel from this that needs
pulling out like a poison, then washed down
with a voice warm as tea. Some kind of space opens,
if you're lucky, that you sit in together.
It blocks out everything else and locks doors
until you open them. When the work is done for now
you will know. It's time for a makeshift gauze
on the wound, a plan for a hot bath or a walk.

The strangest thing is going out to the Sunday night street,
dark and wet, the empty cars. Making the connection
that just happened impossible.
How quickly you forget how to do it again.

Ω

The Maximum Effective Range
by Matt Hohner

for the victims at Virginia Tech, April 16, 2007

The diameter of the bullet is .22 inches
and the distance of its maximum effective range
is thirty yards, but further when fired by anger
fueled with paranoia, curving with the earth,
falling in a graceful, parabolic arc, unlike these
thirty-two dead, one suicide, twenty-six wounded.
The muzzle flash of a Walther P22 discharging
one hundred rounds is orange; the results maroon,
spilling out into a hallway from under a dorm room door.
In an expanding color wheel of panic and space:
thirty hungry ambulances, three hundred terrified parents,
a shocked nation of three hundred million.
But the old man who holds the door closed against the fury,
inches and moments from death, sixty-two years removed
from the six million dead of Auschwitz, of Buchenwald,
reduces the maximum effective range in a classroom
considerably, while the echoes of the shots
and the moans of the dying
carried by the howling winds of that day

reach distant shores far across an ocean named for peace,
and the maximum effective range of the sounds
somehow amplified and heard by heaven,
washes over the ears of an unrelenting God.

Ω

"The Maximum Effective Range" originally appeared in *Lily*.

Living Room

by Andrea Hollander

In the cave of memory my father
crawls now, his small carbide light
fixed to his forehead, his kneepads
so worn from the journey they're barely
useful, but he adjusts them
again and again. Sometimes
he arches up, stands, reaches, measures
himself against the wayward height
of the ceiling, which in this part of the cave
is at best uneven. He often hits his head.
Other times he suddenly
stoops, winces, calls out a name,
sometimes the pet name he had
for my long-dead mother
or the name he called his own.

That's when my stepmother tries
to call him back. *Honeyman*, she says,
one hand on his cheek, the other
his shoulder, settling him
into the one chair he sometimes stays in.

There are days she discovers him
curled beneath the baby grand,

and she's learned to lie down with him.
 I am here, she says, her body caved
against this man who every day
deserts her. *Bats,* he says, or maybe,
field glasses. Perhaps he's back
in France, 1944, she doesn't know.
But soon he's up again on his knees,
shushing her, checking his headlamp,
adjusting his kneepads, and she rises
to her own knees, she doesn't know
what else to do, the two of them
explorers, one whose thinning
pin of light leads them, making
their slow way through this room
named for the living.

Ω

You Are Not Here
by David Jauss

It started as a joke:
stuck on the world
map behind my desk,
a Post-it note with the words
You Are Not Here.
Each morning I move it
someplace—anyplace—
but Little Rock, Arkansas,
where I'm writing this.
Managua, Katmandu,
Beijing, Port-au-Prince,
Athens, Jakarta, Gdansk,
Ypsilanti—my students laugh
when they see where we're not
but I stopped laughing years ago.
Still, each morning,
I move that note again.

All these years
and I still haven't exhausted
all the places I'm not
and never will be,
though I've exhausted myself
from trying. It's too much

like life, all this traveling
toward absence. A long slow
unraveling of here into there
and there into nowhere . . .

Osaka, Rio de Janeiro,
Seoul, Melbourne, Havana,
Cairo, Saskatoon—
each morning I ask myself
where I won't be today
or ever. The list
is almost infinite, but maybe,
if I keep practicing the art
of not being somewhere,
when I die I'll be able
to cross that border with joy,
like a refugee at long last
returning to the old country.

Ω

The Drift

by Abriana Jetté

Four o'clock in the not
yet evening and I am thinking
of fixing a drink. Sound of ice
against the bottom of the glass

and I wonder what Dad
was thinking. Some mornings
the white throated sparrow's child
masters her mother's song.

They sing. I listen, sip,
search for nests between leaves.
Their whistling stirs the breeze.
He said if you say you're happy

you're happy. Mom says I
have too much man in me,
meaning I'm too much
like him. And anyway, I fight it

or tell her in college everyone I knew
carried a water bottle filled with vodka
in their purse to class, say there is
nothing wrong with wine

before dinner. She worries. Watches.
Searches for anything she can find.
But there is nothing to worry over,
I've already told you about the ice.

Ω

The Traveling Voice
by Jeffrey Kingman

Give me a shout if you need to warn me
that I'm about to crash.
Or if you're leaning on the ship's railing and I'm on the quay.

Or if the cat has run out of the house.

Or our son is backward on the soccer field or you just found
out you've won a prize or there's a yellow jacket.

Or we're in a noisy bar and you need to tell me
what kind of drink you'd like.

Maybe you're frustrated there's a poor signal.

The ocean waves are very loud and maybe
you've about had it.

An old man left his wallet behind and
the dead mouse in the hallway turns out to be

not quite dead after all.
Are you mad at me?

When a rate of four apologies per second is reached
my voice still won't arrive within the hour,
never mind the facts.

I don't know how this works.

$$\Omega$$

By the River Bank's Edge
by Carol Munn

I rest my bones, your picture
of a misspent life. Catfish prowl
the shallow mud scooping up beer
can tabs, buttons, cigarette butts,
fattening for someone's idea
of supper. Hot summer sun stirs
up cicadas in the mesquite trees,
the wind mixes juniper and clover,
copperheads sleep in the shade.

If it weren't for sorrow, this day
would be almost perfect. You left
as soon as you got your license,
mail me art cards on Mother's Day—
The world is bigger than Texas
you greet me, still roaming
to find where that is.
The dark eyes stare
back at me, black hair coursing
around her pale skin. You see
a Dutch masterpiece, I see
a naked girl earning her way.
In your eyes I gave up to settle

for a plot of tumbleweeds
higher than my head.

I once wanted more than this
latticed double-wide anchored
by the Brazos, painting scenes
all day in this field forgetting
to make meals, to haul in the wash
before storms. The River Seine flowed
through my veins promising hope
even for a long shot like me.
Mother's money kept us
kicking until you left for the life
I bred into you the day I roared away
from her white pillars and long brick drive.

On the rocks of this river I still feel
you asleep in my arms while I read
you all my books, sing French lullabies.
At sixteen you pronounced me
too Southern to leave, simply content
to spend the rest of my life
painting what I see, sweating
in the land of my dreams.

Ω

The Night Before

by Barry North

my heart surgery
I treated myself to a hot bath,
after months of in-and-out showers,
amidst a busy life.
The bath was soothing,
but the reason for it
came into the room with me,
and wouldn't leave.
I thought of my father,
on the day of his surgery,
calling my brother and me in to tell us
how much he had enjoyed us as children.
I lay in the warm water
trying to absorb the fact that
my time had come so soon, thinking,
surely, there must be some mistake.
The years were not supposed
to run off of me
like rain off a pitched roof.
Why, only yesterday,
I was making my first communion
at St. Anthony of Padua church,
worrying about being struck by lightning
if I let the wafer hit my teeth.

My mother, my father, and my brother
were all there watching me.

I swallowed it whole,
and was spared.

Ω

"The Night Before" originally appeared in *Green Hills Literary Lantern.*

Living Too Long
by David Sloan

Some nights I feel I've lived too long,
when the moon's a squint-eyed mute,

oak branches turn into fish bones,
and the wind's a whimper.

I hobble out to the shed, our old chicken
coop. How you'd loved those hens,

made the mistake of naming them—
Blackie, Maude, the rest. We never figured

out how the owl got in, but we learned
the cost of attachment. The path I cleared

through the woods is overgrown now,
so I lean against the maple in the yard.

How many more tattered moons
will seek me out? You embrace this waning,

but I can't find a way to love the less.
You said, *Yes, we lose leaves, but we gain sky.*

I say, *Give me back my legs.* Let me
scale this tree, turn panther, pounce

on an owl under a hatching moon,
pillow the night with a fury of feathers.

Ω

"Living Too Long" first appeared in *The Irresistible In-Between*,
Deerbrook Editions, 2013.

Each Photograph That You Take of Me
by Colby Cedar Smith

makes me look
more beautiful than I am

smudged in the dark
halo of light
cars whizzing by
leaving red and green stripes

standing next to a crumbling
ancient wall
at the market
stalls filled with spices
in every shade
cerise and chestnut
russet and vermillion

and here,
on the bench
next to the pink azaleas
at the opening of the city
I point to a place
where you should
rest your bike
on your way to class

or at the restaurant
where we ate
sardines in romesco sauce
where I look proud
of the empty bottle of wine
and the ocean
in front of us

where my eyes
love you always
beauty filled with beauty among beauty

Even at the hospital
when I hand you
our infant saying

look,
you are a father
we have begun something
we can never undo

your eyes say
keep silent keep strong
keep very still

Ω

The Dreams of Daughters
by Elizabeth Harmon Threatt

I have had dreams where you are alive again
as if you were never dead in the first place,
dreams where you are alive but I dream-know
that you will be dead again when I wake up,
dreams where I see you in the grocery store
because you have faked your death and run away,
dreams where you cheat on my father with lots of men,
dreams where you eat ice cream and watermelon
on the 4th of July in a red-striped shirt,
dreams where you shave your head and arms
to learn how to sweat, dreams where your smell becomes
the whole dream—of tampons and
baby powder in a blue space
with my head lying next to your stomach,
dreams where you are still my mother but
younger than me and Japanese with a white face
and purple flowers in your black hair, dreams where I
can remember what your voice sounds like again,
dreams where you touch my shoulders shyly
and your hands become small birds brushing against my skin,
dreams where we both know that I am dreaming,
and so you are nothing more than you,
and many, many dreams where all of your dream-lives
exist together, but
I have never had a dream where I ask you why
you have been dead, why you are still dead,

why you are dead in the first place,
or why the memory of you is always like
sticking my tongue in a vastness of sand
instead of the simple taste of honeysuckle
I grew up believing it would be.

Ω

Superman

by Emile DeWeaver

A mother-of-pearl mirror-stand, rolled rugs from Damascus, and other brick-a-brac from when I went through my I'm-gay-but-proud-to-be-Syrian bullshit fill the shadows in my garage. Tossed among the clutter, boxes that once held photographs spill their 5×7 guts all over the concrete floor. I throw and twist and rip the best shots, yelling as I obliterate. The remains look like ash piles surrounding my wheelchair.

The award-winning photo of a boulder that in the blue dusk-light could pass for a contemplating superhero—ripped; mallards shaking the wetlands off their wings as they take flight—ripped; a self-portrait of me in my chair—ripped; there's Hannah Lowman, my one and only girlfriend—ripped. She called me a camel-fucking faggot when I told her the truth.

One picture I have yet to destroy. The sun has slid its warm hand over my shaking shoulder to touch the glass frame. There, my father holds me over his head, one large hand under my chest, the other gripping the blue pajama legs around my knees. Arms stretched like the Superman action figure at my father's feet, I pose as if I'm about to fly out of the camera shot. I'm laughing, and my father's teeth shine up at me through his beard.

I search the picture for a kind truth. I can only think of my father, smelling like dirty dishrags on his hospital bed, that fucking word exploding like a suicide-bomber from his lips.

Abomination. He had exactly enough breath to blow out the word before he passed out in his nest of tubes and wires. With one word, my father forbade my mother from signing the papers for the transplant.

I've spent my life struggling to belong again, but white lions have no place in brown deserts, and homosexuals don't belong under God's sun.

The picture frame clatters on the floor and falls quiet next to the open fuel can. The photo follows one piece at a time. Fumes fill the garage. That pinching smell is the stink of terror beneath sleeping flame. It's the smell of shame, of my mother begging my father not to burn me alive after he caught me with a boy.

I pick up the can and upend it over my head. Cold streams spread greedily as my clothes grow heavy. I lean my head over the back of my chair, craning my neck to ease the knots in my chest. The splatter of gas against the floor slows to a drip. The green Bic I slide from my jeans is warm and weighty.

The sting in my eyes forces them shut. In the dark of my mind, a memory waits—me soaring in my father's hands, my caped hero lying at his feet.

I idolized Superman. What wasn't to admire? Speeding bullets, burning rockets, and getaway cars bounced right off him; a whole DC universe loved him.

The day I lost my action figure, Superman saved the world nine times, riding beneath the creases of my palm. As I flew him on his last adventure, I zoomed outside to put the sky above us. We vanquished butterflies from hedges while Hannah Lowman and her friends played freeze-tag in the street.

Sirens wailed on a distant block and swelled until there wasn't room left in the neighborhood for playing children. A rust-colored car, sleek and low, squealed around the corner. Hannah's friends scattered for curbs and porches, but she just covered her mouth and trembled.

I ran toward her.

Muscular steel sped toward us; its sounds tore at me through the asphalt. Its growl pressed against my cheek as gas and hot rubber burned inside my nose.

I shoved Hannah; Superman tumbled after her.

The collision that followed feels like it never stopped. I remember teeth snapping together as the bumper crashed into my hip. Both legs bent toward the sky. My arm swept like a clock-hand across the hood, its hot paint setting me on fire as I burned. I screamed without breath. I flew. Not the powerful flight of my hero, but the tail-spinning collision course of a flaming jet.

Below, the street grew small. The car jumped the curb into my mother's rose garden, spraying dirt and bricks.

I continued flipping upward, the clouds and my screaming mother on a tilt-a-whirl.

My father later told my nurses, "Take care of my son. He's a hero."

I float, no longer tumbling wildly. Wind flaps my ripped shirt like a cape. The flames go cold. I'm Superman. And everybody loves me.

Ω

Down in the Station

by Seth Sawyers

She was sure it was our sixth date but I said, no, it was only our fifth as we took the steps down into the 28th Street station. Even the screeching of the train cars sounded like it was music just for us, singing: nothing can go wrong, not now, not as long as your ears are hearing this. We were on our way to a museum, one of the small ones, a strange one, and I can't, no matter how hard I try, remember which. The trip to New York was my idea. She had red-blond hair and I had wanted to see how it would look against her black wool coat with all those buildings in the background. When I said I'd found a cheap, clean hotel in the twenties, I thought she'd chipped my front teeth the way she jumped on me and kissed me so hard. She had pale cheeks that I had hoped would turn red in the cold up there, and they did.

In the station a black woman with thick braids played the cello. I thought she was good, but I don't know if she really was good, because what do I know about the cello? I pointedly did not say anything about the cello player to prove to myself, and to the girl with the pale cheeks, that I was so used to the subway that the cello-playing woman hadn't affected me. I was trying to play it cool. Laura was the girl's name.

I was in the middle of noticing but at the same time not commenting on the cello when the screeching from the train approaching the 28th Street station grew. We had heard it before, if only a few times. I suppose it was another of the many little things that happen in New York which is familiar if you live there but not if you're just visiting. Laura grabbed my arm and pulled herself close. That sudden warmth made me think: oh, this is something. I wanted to fall down that endless warm passageway for which I've yearned so long but the screeching turned into a sound I had not heard before and the feeling of her hand on my arm went away.

It happened fast, as they say these things do. There was a quick shout, and then silence and a bright-blue blur. The man was wearing a jacket, a bright-blue jacket you'd wear to go running, or maybe it was a raincoat, though it hadn't been raining. That blue color was flying, and then, through the screeching, there was a hollow thump. And though I've thought about it so many times since, and I can't figure out why, the cello kept going.

*

It's tough, trying to remember, like remembering what it was like before you got the flu when you're aching and hot all over. It had been either our sixth date or our fifth and after we got off the bus in New York we sat on a bench and ate slices of pizza and then drank wine in a dark basement place. I never drink wine, but this girl made drinking wine seem like something I might eventually like. Back in the tiny hotel room that had been made to look like the inside of an English pub, there had been no discussion. We simply took off each other's clothes. There was laughing. And slowness, and then it got faster and faster still and she told me to slow down and when I did I saw that of course she was right and we did that for a long time, for as long as we could, for as long as I could. Afterwards, I noticed her cheeks had flushed. Just before I went in to kiss her forehead, she closed her eyes, and her eyelids reminded me of milky, spotless moons.

She wriggled free of my arms and legs and put on some of her clothes and some of my clothes and left our room for the bathroom down the hall. I lay on my back, staring up at the ceiling. I waited. I would have done anything she wanted, for I was only a vessel, a thing, benevolent, I think, empty but willing. That's what I thought, at the time. I mean, I was still able to think that of myself.

She slid in beside me. She was smiling. I always forget that, how much she smiled. She slid in and said, "Want to know something?" I nodded and then she said, "It's not that I love you or anything, but I will say that I have moderate feelings for you." She tapped her finger on her breastbone. "In here."

I don't remember what I said next, probably because it couldn't have been as good, but I remember our weird little room, the light that went from white-blue to blue-white, an electric, humming blue that, since then, I picture when I think of New York. We fell asleep but I woke up when I felt her leaving the bed again. After she finished pulling on her high boots, she said, "Let's fucking eat," and we ate expensive hot dogs standing up in a corner place and after that we walked down the steps into the 28th Street Station, on our way to that small museum whose name has escaped me. It was just the next thing we were going to do together in a series of things that had no end.

The man's body sort of curled around the far corner of the train's flat front. The train kept going. It didn't seem to be stopping. There was a moment where nothing at all seemed to be happening anywhere in the universe and then, suddenly, everything turned sharp and bright and jangly, as if the air had been dosed with an extra-large helping of bitter sugar. I wasn't feeling anything yet, not really. It was still too soon. But it was coming. Everything suddenly had edges that you could trace with the tip of your finger. Everything pulsed.

By the time I remembered her, she had moved several steps away and was sitting still as if she'd always been there, had been born crouching down in that station, perched on her heels, her coat enveloping her small body. I hugged her from the side, but she wasn't hugging back. Instead she was focused on clasping, over and over, each of the fingers on her left hand, pulling, as if to crack the big knuckle at the base. She kept doing this, four, five cycles of it. I couldn't believe how long she went on like that. The fingers on her left hand were turning red. I kept trying to hug her but that wasn't working. Finally, I took hold of her hands. By then, the subway workers in the bright-yellow jackets had arrived and were telling everyone to leave.

"Hey," I said to her. "Hey."

She had been far away. It's so clear to me now, so simple, and expected. "Oh my god," she said. She seemed to notice me for the first time.

"Hey," I said. "Are you all right?"

I had let go of her hands and again she took one of her fingers and pulled on it before quickly moving to the next. I watched her: index finger, middle, ring, pinkie, thumb, and back around. As she started on a third time, I wrapped my hands, not gently, around hers. "Hey," I said. "Stop that now."

She turned to me, her whole body rigid, as if some important string within her had been pulled, and then she was straightening herself, standing. "You stop it," she said. "You stop it now. You stop it. You stop it."

I didn't want to repeat myself but I couldn't help it. I was trying to be comforting but I had no other words. "Hey," I said. "Come here." I wanted to hug her. I hoped that would fix things, reset things.

She looked at me then as if I were someone she did not know but suspected she would dislike. When I tried to kiss her cheek, she stiffened and turned her head away and my lips met nothing soft and giving but instead only the flat, final dryness of her hair.

The way she was looking at me was different from how she had looked at me in the hotel room. I knew, even back then, that some tender part of me, just in that terrible moment, was hardening and would maybe never be supple again.

*

And all of this happened some years ago and I think of her often enough, and too often when I've had some beers at the cheap places where I meet my friends now. This past Thanksgiving, we met at a diner in the suburbs, near where she grew up. She was already in a booth, waiting, drinking hot tea. Her hair was different. She had a tan. She had gotten some work doing commercials, out in California. One was for a company that sells home-security systems. She played a scared housewife. We ate whatever we ate and talked plenty and then I walked her out to her rental car, which was for some reason a Corvette. She got into the Corvette and rolled down her window and when she did I asked if I could kiss her. We kissed for

312

a long time. Then I walked around and got into the passenger-side seat and we kept going but it wasn't the same as when I was standing outside. After a minute, she said she had to get home, to her family. I'd met them twice, back before. I liked them. They were kind people.

"Do you ever think about that time in New York?" I asked.

"Oh, yes," she said.

I realized that I'd made a mistake, bringing it up. Her face turned. I kept going and maybe I kept going because I needed to.

"It wasn't the same after that," I said.

"No."

I should have stopped, but I didn't. "I wish I could go back and stop that man from doing what he did. Do you ever feel that way?"

Her eyes softened. "Do you really not remember?" she asked.

It was beginning to come back. I was making it come back.

"After, out on the street," she said. "You must remember."

I stared at the dashboard. It was true. I did remember.

"I wish I could just forget what you said. The way you said, you know, 'How about the cello player.'"

My stomach shrunk. Of course I remembered. But she wasn't quite right. What I'd said, and I'd said it after we'd walked ten or maybe fifteen blocks, was, "At least the cello player was good." I was trying to be funny, or cute, or coy. After that, the rest of the weekend in New York was quiet and soon it was over. And I remember holding her hand, both of us in shock for the first few blocks, and then after a few minutes it came pouring out of us, which felt natural and good. And at some point we hugged and I felt close to her again. But then she kept talking and talking about it and I can still remember that rising thing inside of me, like an electric charge in my belly slowly turned up, that urge to go back to the way it had been, and I said what I said.

Sitting in the rental car, I looked up at her. "But before that, it was nice, right?"

She smiled. I'd forgotten, again, how much I'd liked her smile. "It was," she said.

I leaned in. This time, she really kissed back, really pressed herself against me as much as she was able, took my hand and placed it on her warm waist, the wonderful soft spot between her ribs and her hip bone, that soft warm place which I had once known. That's the part that's going to stay with me. Her taking my hand like that and placing it on that spot. I just know it.

I opened that Corvette's door and stepped out. It had begun raining and had turned cold. I could see my breath. I hunched over, and looked in through the passenger-side window. She wanted to go home. I could see that. She was cold, and tired. She'd always gotten sleepy earlier than I did. She rolled down the window. She was looking at me. I opened my mouth, but I had nothing, and so I just said, "A pleasure." That's what I said. Maybe one day I'll say something that's so true and pure, but not on that day.

She smiled a little smile. "It was nice seeing you, too," she said, and drove off across the parking lot, the Corvette's big clouds of exhaust white and milky. She eased out into the road. There were no other cars around. It was only the Corvette's metallic shininess, its bright and sleek newness. I kept waiting for her to push it, to open it up on this rental car she'd probably never drive again, to fly away from me in some kind of final roar, but instead she only drove away slowly, even using her blinker before moving over a lane. And still, there she goes, moving farther away, and farther away, that shiny car inching away from me down that empty road, and I can still see her.

Ω

Dark Rum & Tonic
by Molly Fisk

Sometimes what you need is a road
house, blast of laughter and warm air pouring
out the door, where the waitresses know

your name but the customers don't, shrill
on the third martini or fifth Blue Ribbon,
steaks searing on a huge propane-fired grill.

Two birthday parties in full swing—
mylar balloons leashed to a chair-back slowly
turning—tonight you're a few years shy

the median age, at your back-wall table drinking
iced tea because you don't spend time with
the person you turn into after a frosted glass:

chardonnay, dark rum & tonic, you remember
her well, that girl, that woman, with great
compassion: her loneliness behind the amber

liquid disappeared, or seemed to, she got funny
and affectionate, softer, sexually daring but
not a *femme fatale*, always more honey

than darling, her courage long-gone by morning,
that terrible waking into a stranger's sheets.
You don't miss any of it. Headaches, longing

that's miles easier to bear when sober,
wishing a friend would come along and love you,
even though you're just getting older.

Some nights you need a road house, boisterous
laughter and warm air pouring through open
doors, the kind of place where your choice

is simple: well-done, bloody, or medium rare,
and no one gives a shit that you're by yourself,
writing in a notebook. Nobody turns to stare.

Ω

How to Pay Respects to a Serial Killer
by Robert S. King

A funeral director must have
a way with words that sound
more like silence.
Undertaking is an art form
that shaves the blood-stained beard
of the honored beast
so that the eulogist may outline
his good points to explain why God
allowed a monster among us.

Remember, both mourners and celebrants
would rather be home with martinis.
Don't frown, but a sympathetic smile
will ensure repeat business.
Today, especially,
keep the service short.

Follow the script and the scripture.
Even the biography of the damned
is told with sobbing compassion.
In the case of a killer, stretch the tales
of good deeds as far as possible,
whispering priest and rabbi jokes as filler.
Deliver his death with rose petals,

sweeter scented than any twisted
life whose sins are left unspoken
on this his only day of tribute.

Know your audience.
Though so many pour out,
no one dare say
that these are tears of joy.

Ω

"How to Pay Respects to a Serial Killer" originally appeared in *Developing a Photograph of God*, Glass Lyre Press, 2014.

Sunday

by Lee Martin

A porch swing sways, and the chains in the eyehooks screwed into the rafters let out their lazy creaks as if this is a day of rest for them, too. Or nearly so. They still have to support the weight of the neighbor who pushes ever so lightly with her foot and feels the breeze on her face and listens through the window screen to the radio playing dance music in her living room. The faint sounds of big band tunes: "Moonglow," "In the Mood," "Begin the Beguine."

Somewhere down the street, a screen door taps against the frame. This is one of those afternoons when the air is so still that sounds travel. Someone is listening to a Cardinals' game on the radio; someone else is turning the pages of the *Evansville Courier*, or the *Vincennes Sun-Commercial*, or maybe last week's *Sumner Press* that they've finally found enough time to read. The pages rattle just a bit, but not in an unpleasant way, more the way a soft brush sounds when swept through a girl's long hair.

And maybe it's that girl who sighs, daydreaming about the boy she loves.

Uptown, a ceiling fan turns slow circles in the sundries store where the girl's mother sits behind the counter using a file on her fingernails and watching the hand on the Bubble Up clock click off another minute.

Across the street, in front of the TV Repair Shop, a boy and girl sit on the hood of his Impala and watch the color set that's always on in the window even though they can't hear the sound. The boy has a Pall Mall between his lips, but he hasn't lit it. He keeps flicking the lid of his Zippo open and then, after long intervals, closed, and the woman in the sundries store closes her eyes and remembers her husband when she first fell in love with him and how he was never in a hurry, how she thought they had all the time in the world.

"Baby," the boy on the Impala says, and he draws out that long "a" sound as if it's the sweetest taste he can ever imagine, and he wants to hold onto it as long as he can.

Eventually, the Impala inches away from the curb. The woman in the sundries store switches off the ceiling fan and turns the deadbolt lock on the door. Her daughter writes her boyfriend's name over and over on a piece of notebook paper, her handwriting all loops and tails. The baseball game ends and the radio goes off, its hot tubes ticking as they cool. The newspaper slips to the floor as the reader dozes. The porch swing, empty now, sways a time or two and then is still.

Call it a sleepy town. Call it a dead town. My hometown where once upon a time on summer Sundays there was time, if we wanted it, to listen. I hear the porch swing creak, the radio play, the baseball announcer murmur, the girl sigh, the newspaper pages rustle, the ceiling fan turn, the clock hand click, the Zippo open and close, the boy say, "Baaa-by. Oh, Baaa-by."

I hear it all, and my listening tells me this: when it comes to our writing and our living, nothing is too small a thing.

The lock turns at the sundries store. The woman's sensible heels make gentle tapping noises on the sidewalk as she starts toward home, taking her time as she strolls past the houses where baseball games and newspapers and porch swings and lovesick girls have gone silent. So slow and dreamy her pace until she climbs the steps to her house, takes the doorknob in her hand. Just before she turns it, she whispers to herself, *Baa-by, Baa-by*. That word. Just before she goes inside, she sighs.

Ω

Things I Did Not Learn From Dead White Male Authors

by Jennifer Zobair

I have loved books by white, male authors. I have stayed up all night with them, avoided studying for the bar exam with them, sought refuge from broken hearts or unrealized dreams with them. Once, I called in sick for them. Still, you can have your lists, your "best of" this or that, you're *New Yorker* table of contents with predominantly male contributors. There are things, I believe, you cannot learn from reading the work of white men. *There are things*, and you must go where you can find them.

*

Like most second year law students, I interviewed for a summer associate position. This involved scheduled twenty-minute audiences with partners and senior associates, often conducted at hotels, where we sat around a small table and pretended there was not a bed two feet away.

In the middle of my search, I found myself on the threshold of one such hotel room, standing before an African American partner from a prestigious Chicago law firm. It was her last interview of the day, and she looked weary. She motioned for me to sit, and then did the same before glancing at my resume. She sighed. I did not take her protracted exhaling as a good sign, but was in no way prepared for what came next.

"I expected you to be black," she said bluntly.

I was so caught off guard that I said nothing.

"Okay," she said, folding her arms. "Tell me why a white girl gets a concentration in African American Studies."

I'm not sure until that very minute I had thought about why I'd taken so many African American Studies classes at Smith. I just *did*. But she asked, and I told her the truth.

"It's a story of survival," I said. "It's a lot of other things, too. But African American history is absolutely a story of survival."

She nodded and we were quiet for a minute, sitting in the company of things that must be survived. And then we proceeded to talk for more than an hour, despite the twenty minutes we'd been allotted. When we finished, she told me she was calling me back to her firm for further interviews. She never asked me what I'd had to survive. There were things, she seemed to know, and that was enough.

*

It started with *The Color Purple*. The book, pinkish-hued, with the simple house on the cover, sat on my mother's bedside table. I picked it up and was consumed by Celie's voice, so raw and wounded, so unable to see her own worth. I watched her go from making herself "wood" to withstand her abuse—from saying she didn't know how to fight, just how to stay alive—to

324

finding a voice, to believing she had the right to use it, to soaring in her own ways by the end of the novel.

I was hooked.

In college, I moved on, ravenous, to the description-defying sequel, *The Temple of my Familiar*. I was certain I had never read such a brilliant book. I was certain I would never read a more brilliant book if I lived to be a thousand years old. It is a frenzy of plot and theme, spanning centuries of racism and struggle, and making the agonizingly obvious and so-often-unheeded argument that it matters whose recollections—whose *stories*—inform our collective spiritual and political narratives.

Next, I devoured the heart-wrenching *Possessing the Secret of Joy* about the horrors—plural, so catastrophically *plural*—of female genital mutilation. I read Walker's essays and became a vegetarian in one fell swoop sitting outside of a McDonald's on a pre-law-school road trip. I learned about multiple points of view, about how backstory is done deftly and for maximum effect, about unreliable narrators—unreliable because of wounds, because of suffering, because of the urgent, soiling need to survive.

But there is always a first love, and for me, it was *The Color Purple*. There are things that have the power to erase us. Celie knows it, and we know it, too. In some ways, *The Color Purple*'s epistolary form teaches us what we know in our hearts: We can write our way back.

With a voice, we can *be*.

*

I was a relatively new Muslim on 9/11. I had been married for four years. I had an adopted three-year-old son and a one-year old daughter. I watched on the news, holding my baby, distracting my toddler, as two planes crashed into the World

Trade Center. I wept in the bathroom where my children couldn't see me. I called friends and family. I worried that more attacks were coming. I didn't sleep, spending long nights staring at my children and wondering if I could take them in public, or on a plane to see their great-grandparents. I opened the mail outside, with arms stretched in front of me, in case of anthrax. I was frightened, angry, devastated.

I was also now the same religion as the people who did this.

I was not prepared for the ways I would need to prove my loyalty to my country. I was not prepared for how, even though I felt part of the collective America that had been attacked and victimized, I would be lumped in, by some, with the enemy "other."

I purchased a giant American flag and hung it outside our house, like proof.

*

In the tragedy, I lost my ability to criticize the policies of my government. I knew I would be given no benefit of the doubt. I was also aware that simply identifying as a Muslim would be seen as seditious by certain people. I felt my way along this new path of trying to assimilate into the country in which I was born and raised, where I had been a Catholic for 27 years.

This feeling lingered for two years, five, ten. It swam below my surface when I read Mohsin Hamid's *The Reluctant Fundamentalist*. I finished the book in one sitting. It is a quick, compelling read, but it is more than that. Hamid dares to create a Pakistani Muslim protagonist, Changez, who, after achieving the American dream, questions its material underpinnings and the global oppression it seems to require.

Whether you agree or disagree with Hamid's protagonist—who either returns to Pakistan to lecture about the dan-

326

gers of colonialism, or to foment anti-American sentiment and terror, depending on whether you are a thoughtful reader or the unnamed person to whom Changez tells his story—it is hard to ignore that it was an act of courage for Hamid to write about such a character, to tell such a story, as a young Muslim man in a post-9/11 world.

There are lessons here about speaking out even when people stand ready to make a monster out of you, when entire industries, including "news" organizations, have sprung up to make monsters out of people like you.

I purchased a tee shirt with an identifying slogan—*This is what a Muslim feminist looks like*—and wore it in public, like proof.

*

The counterpart to losing my ability to be critical of my country as a Muslim after 9/11 was feeling unable to be critical of my new faith. I struggled with "telling secrets" about the Muslim community, already so weary and maligned.

I did not want to pile on.

But there are boxes for women. They can vary by culture or religion or class, but there are always boxes, and I have felt pressed into them. Before I converted, there was the relentless wrath of the western beauty myth and the ways women are bullied into tolerating inappropriate male behavior and society's notion that being aggressive in the classroom or the boardroom makes a man admired and a woman a bitch. After I converted, there were new boxes previously absent from my radar. I was told, sometimes by people who barely knew me, what I was supposed to wear (nothing showing my arms or legs), where I could pray (behind the men or in a separate room with noisy children), even where I could eat at a party (with the women, in a different room). When my husband

and I were first married, we navigated social gatherings by lingering in kitchens, the architectural neutral zones between where the men and the women ate in separate spaces, until we were shooed back like straying children. I played along more than I'd like to admit.

When I didn't play along, when I said to someone, for example, that it was possible Islam does not condemn homosexuality and referenced the work of Emory Professor Scott Kugle, she did not speak to me for days.

Still, I wrote the complaints. I told the secrets. I wrote other things, the beautiful things, the affirming things, the ways the women in my community are strong and educated and kind and capable, the ways most Muslim men have not made me feel unsafe, but I didn't flinch from writing about the parts that are anti-woman or anti-gay or have made me feel marginalized or small or unseen. I wrote a novel about all of these things. I showed it to a fellow Muslim, long before I had an agent, back when I didn't necessarily believe I would have an agent. She didn't look so happy upon finishing. "It's like you're telling secrets," she said. Her words wrapped around me until I thought maybe I was doing more harm than good. I thought maybe I should put the book away. I considered that maybe I should return to the practice of law.

I said this to my best friend during a long walk in an old cemetery. I was melodramatic enough to wallow in the symbolism of our setting. She tried to gently shake the courageous parts of me. "I understand the woman's point," she said. "But you can't give up on this novel." And then with more conviction, she repeated it.

"You are not going to give up on this novel."

*

I read Chimamanda Ngozi Adichie's *Purple Hibiscus*, and watched her TED talk, "The Danger of a Single Story." Simply put, Adichie makes the most eloquent case I've ever heard that who gets to tell stories matters, that underrepresented voices need to be heard. But she also speaks to something else: When a member of a stereotyped community tells her "complaints," some people will extrapolate from the specific to the whole and assume that, say, an abusive Nigerian father is *all* Nigerian fathers. Similarly, *The Color Purple* also tells secrets. It depicts violence by black men against black women even though so many white people are already inclined to see such men as violent and culpable, when the risk of piling on is astronomical.

In some ways, Adichie and Walker show us, we must trust the reader to know better, to *discern*, but even when the reader cannot be trusted, even when the reader will let our words stoke the xenophobic, subtle or not-so-subtle racism in the secret or not-so-secret parts of their hearts, we cannot be limited by those who will use our work for their own purposes, who read their own agendas into our narratives. We must still tell the stories of our experiences, in all of their complicated complexity. Good fiction requires truth, even—or especially—when people do not want it told.

I did not give up on my novel.

*

The actual color purple, of course, runs thorough Alice Walker's Pulitzer Prize winning novel. It is the color of Celie's abuse, a longed-for dress, her sexual organs, her pain. But it is also royalty. It is also beauty. It is also her finding her voice and knowing it is no small thing.

I find this incarnation of the color purple in multicultural fiction, in the bold, beautiful storytelling of writers like Walker and Hamid and Adichie. I spread their words before me, like pieces of a makeshift map. I trace along their courageous paths, understanding, at last, that lessons about writing are so often lessons about life—not just to process what has been, but to navigate what will come.

Ω

Contributors

Heather Altfeld has an MFA in Poetry as well as undergraduate degrees in Anthropology and Writing from Columbia University. She is a member of the Squaw Valley Community of Writers and is finishing her second book of poetry. Her recent and forthcoming publications include poetry in *Narrative Magazine, Pleiades, Poetry Northwest,* ZYZZYVA, TLR, *Cimarron Review, Miramar Poetry Journal,* and others.

Michelle Collins Anderson received her MFA from Warren Wilson College. Her stories have been published in *Midwestern Gothic, Literary Mama, The Green Hills Literary Lantern, The Sulphur River Literary Review,* and others. She currently teaches creative writing to a group of cool fifth graders at Franklin Elementary School and serves on the board of *The Missouri Review.*

Wade Bentley's poems have appeared or are forthcoming in *Green Mountains Review, Cimarron Review, Best New Poets, New Ohio Review, Western Humanities Review, Rattle, Chicago Quarterly Review, Raleigh Review, Reunion: The Dallas Review, Pembroke Magazine,* and *New Orleans Review,* among others. A full-length collection of his poems, *What Is Mine,* was published by Aldrich Press in early 2015.

Kierstin Bridger earned her MFA at Pacific University and her Bachelor of Arts Degree in English at University of Washington. Her short fiction and poetry have appeared in publications such as *Prime Number, Memoir, Thrush Poetry Anthology, Mason's Road, Pilgrimage, Stripped, The Best of Split Infinitive,* and elsewhere. Bridger is co-curator for the Open Bard Poetry Series in Ridgway and "Editor-in-Sheaf" of Ridgway Alley Poems. She teaches creative writing classes through Weehawken Creative Arts, Ah Haa School For The Arts, and through private workshops and consultations. Bridger is a recipient of an Anne LaBastille 2014 Writers Residence and the Mark Fischer Poetry Prize. She is a contributing writer at *Telluride Inside and Out.* A chapbook, Demimonde, is forthcoming from Lithic Press.

Janna Brooke Cohen's short fiction has been published in *upstreet, The Alembic, PMS PoemMemoirStory,* and *SNReview.* She is currently finishing her first novel.

Susan Cohen is the author of *Throat Singing* and recent poems in *Atlanta Review, Poet Lore, Salamander, Sou'wester,* and the *Bloomsbury Anthology of Contemporary Jewish American Poetry,* among others. Her honors include the 2013 Kessler Poetry Award from *Harpur Palate.* She has an MFA from Pacific University.

Chris Connolly's work has been broadcast on RTE Radio and has appeared in such publications as *Boston Literary Magazine, Carve, The New Guard Review, Galway Review, South-*

word, and *Wordlegs*. His first collection of stories, *Every Day I Atrophy*, was published by Sidecartel in 2012. His website is www.chrisconnollywriter.com.

James Crews is the author of *One Hundred Small Yellow Envelopes*, *What Has Not Yet Left*, and *The Book of What Stays*, winner of the Prairie Schooner Book Prize for Poetry. Recent work appears in *The New Republic*, *Ploughshares*, and *The (London) Times Literary Supplement*.

Elizabeth Crowell has an MFA in poetry from Columbia University. Her work has been published in *The Worcester Review*, *Sheepshead Review*, and *The Healing Muse*. Her essay "The Tag" was the *Bellevue Literary Review* winner of the Burns Archive Prize for Nonfiction.

Emile DeWeaver is a columnist for Easy Street. His work has appeared or is forthcoming at The Doctor T. J. Eckleburg Review, Nth Degree, Drunk Monkeys, and Frigg. He lives and writes in Northern California.

Jesse Mavro Diamond's book of poems *Swimming The Hellespont* was published by Wilderness House Press in 2014. "Chetwynd Morning" was featured in *Scout Somerville's* April issue celebrating National Poetry Month. She teaches high school English at Boston Latin School.

Jennifer Dupree's short stories have appeared in *The Master's Review*, *Swimming*, and *Front Porch Review*, among others. She lives and writes in Maine.

Jen Fawkes's work has appeared in *One Story*, *Crazyhorse*, *The Iowa Review*, Amazon's *Day One*, *Shenandoah*, *Michigan Quarterly Review*, and elsewhere. Her stories have won prizes from *Washington Square Review*, Writers @ Work, *Blue Earth Review*, and *Salamander*. She holds an MFA from Hollins University and a BA from Columbia University.

Doris Ferleger, winner of the New Letters Poetry Prize, Robert Fraser Poetry Prize, and the AROHO Creative Non Fiction Prize, is the author of three volumes of poetry, *Big Silences in a Year of Rain* (finalist for the Alice James Books Beatrice Hawley Award), *As the Moon Has Breath*, *When You Become Snow*, and *Leavened*. Her work has appeared in *Cimarron Review*, *L.A. Review*, *South Carolina Review*, and elsewhere. She holds an MFA in Poetry and a Ph.D. in psychology and maintains a mindfulness based therapy practice in Wyncote PA.

Alexis Finc received her MFA from the University of North Carolina, Wilmington. She currently lives in Los Angeles.

Molly Fisk is the author of The More Difficult Beauty, Listening to Winter, and a volume of radio essays, Blow-Drying a Chicken: Observations from a Working Poet. Her honors include fellowships from the National Endowment for the Arts, the Marin Arts Council, and the California Arts Council, as well as a Robinson Jeffers Tor House Prize in Poetry, a Dogwood Prize, a Billee Murray Denny Prize, a National Writer's Union Prize, and a grant from the Corporation for Public Broadcasting. She has taught at the UC Davis Extension and with the California Poets in the Schools program, and presently runs the online workshop Poetry Boot Camp. Fisk's radio commentary is heard weekly on the News Hour of KVMR-FM, Nevada City, CA.

Kim Garcia is the author of *The Brighter House*, winner of the 2015 White Pine Press Poetry Prize, *DRONE*, winner of the 2015 Backwaters Prize, and *Madonna Magdalene*, released by Turning Point Books in 2006. Her chapbook *Tales of the Sisters* won the 2015 Sow's Ear Poetry Review Chapbook Contest. Her poems have appeared in such journals as *Crab Orchard Review*, *Crazyhorse*, *Mississippi Review*, *Nimrod* and *Subtropics*, and her work has been featured on *The Writer's Almanac*. Recipient of the 2014 Lynda Hull Memorial Prize, an AWP Intro Writing Award, a Hambidge Fellowship and an Oregon Individual Artist Grant, Garcia teaches creative writing at Boston College.

A recent graduate of Minnesota State University, Mankato, Megan Gilmore is now living in the Chicago area. Besides words and poetry, she has a passion for theatre, music, antiques, and cooking pasta.

A PEN Emerging Voices Fellow, Jennifer Givhan currently attends the MFA program at Warren Wilson College. Her work has appeared in over sixty literary journals and anthologies, including *Best New Poets 2013*.

Perry Glasser is the author of *Riverton Noir*, recipient of the Gival Press Novel Award; *Metamemoirs*; and three short fiction collections: *Dangerous Places*; winner of the G.S. Sharat Chandra Prize; *Singing on the Titanic*; and *Suspicious Origins*. He has been a fellow at the Massachusetts Cultural Council, the Norman Mailer House, and The Virginia Center for the

Creative Arts. Presently he is a contributing editor at the *North American Review.*

Alex Greenberg's work has appeared or is forthcoming in *The Cortland Review, The Florida Review, Grist, decomP,* and *Spinning Jenny,* among others. He is a four-time runner up in the Cape Farewell Poetry Competition, recipient of the 2014 Critical Pass Review Junior Poets Prize, and winner of the *The Adirondack Review's* 2014 46er prize. He is 16 years old.

Tina Hammerton's work has appeared in *Tipton Poetry Journal, Orange Room Review,* and *Rufous City Review.* She has taught creative writing to kids in India using a virtual classroom and to kids in Phoenix in a live classroom.

Matt Hohner holds an M.F.A. in Writing and Poetics from Naropa University in Boulder, Colorado. His work has been a finalist for the Ballymaloe International Poetry Prize, and taken both third and first prizes in the Maryland Writers Association Poetry Prize. His work has appeared in *The Moth, The Irish Times, Oberon Poetry Review,* and *The Sow's Ear.* His chapbook, *States,* was published by Third Ear Books.

Andrea Hollander is the author of four full-length poetry collections: *Landscape with Female Figure: New & Selected Poems, 1982 – 2012,* a finalist for the 2014 Oregon Book Award; *Woman in the Painting; The Other Life;* and *House Without a Dreamer,* which won the Nicholas Roerich Poetry Prize. Other honors include a 2013 Oregon Literary Fellowship, two Pushcart Prizes (for poetry and prose memoir), the D. H. Lawrence Fellowship, the Runes Poetry Prize, two poetry fellowships from the National Endowment for the Arts, and two from the

Arkansas Arts Council. For twenty-two years Hollander served as the Writer-in-Residence at Lyon College, where she was awarded the Lamar Williamson Prize for Excellence in Teaching. In 2011 she moved to Portland, Oregon, where she teaches writing workshops at the Attic Institute and Mountain Writers Series.

Lesley Howard is a co-founder of the New River Land Trust (community land conservation) and New River Valley Voices (community prose and poetry). She offers writing workshops at joyfulquill.com and blogs at artofpractice.com.

David Jauss is the author of two poetry collections, *Improvising Rivers* and *You Are Not Here*, three short story collections, including *Glossolalia: New & Selected Stories*, and the essay collection *On Writing Fiction*. He has also edited three anthologies, including *Strong Measures: Contemporary American Poetry in Traditional Forms*. His poems have appeared in numerous magazines and anthologies, including *The Georgia Review, The Missouri Review, The Nation, The Paris Review, Ploughshares,* and *Poetry*. His awards include a National Endowment for the Arts Fellowship, the Fleur-de-Lis Poetry Prize, the AWP Award for Short Fiction, a James A. Michener Fellowship, and fellowships from the Arkansas Arts Council and the Minnesota State Arts Board. A professor emeritus at the University of Arkansas at Little Rock, he teaches in the low-residency MFA in Writing Program at Vermont College of Fine Arts.

Mathew Javidi is a graduate of the University of California Santa Barbara with a degree in literature. He founded his university's first ongoing humor publication and is currently pursuing a career in comedy.

Abriana Jetté earned an MFA in Poetry from Boston University, where she was a Robert Pinsky Global Fellow, and an MA in Creative Writing and English Literature from Hofstra University, where she graduated with distinction. Her work has appeared in the *Iron Horse Literary Review*, *Poetry Quarterly*, *The Moth*, and elsewhere. She is currently a doctoral candidate in English at St. John's University. She teaches for the City University of New York and the nonprofit organization Sponsors for Educational Opportunity.

Robert S. King's poems have appeared in California Quarterly, Chariton Review, Kenyon Review, and hundreds of other magazines. He has published four chapbooks: When Stars Fall Down as Snow, Dream of the Electric Eel, The Traveller's Tale, and Diary of the Last Person on Earth. His full-length collections are The Hunted River, The Gravedigger's Roots, One Man's Profit, and most recently Developing a Photograph of God.

Jeffrey Kingman is the winner of the 2012 Revolution House Flash Fiction Contest, a semifinalist in the 2013 Frost Place Chapbook Fellowship, and a finalist in the 2012 Midwest Writing Center contest. His novel *Moto Girl* was a semifinalist in the 2009 Dana Awards. His poetry has appeared in PANK, *lo-ball*, *Squaw Valley Review*, *Off Channel*, and the *Crack the Spine 2014* print anthology.

Judith Lavinsky's work has appeared in the *North American Review*, *Florida Review*, *RE:AL*, *The MacGuffin*, *Eclipse*, *String-*

town, Oasis, and elsewhere. Her story collection, *I'm Dating Your Husband,* was a finalist for the Flannery O'Connor Prize.

R. Daniel Lester is the author of three books, including the novel *Die, Famous!* His short work has appeared in *Geist, Shotgun Honey, The Big Adios, 365 Tomorrows, Broken Pencil,* and *Pulp Literature.*

Jenna Loceff is a Northern California-based journalist and photographer.

Louise Marburg is a graduate of the MFA program in fiction at Columbia University's School of the Arts. Her stories have been published in *Prime Number, Labletter, Reed, Corium, Day One, Necessary Fiction,* and others, and forthcoming in *The Louisville Review.* She has been a contributor at the Sewanee Writers Conference, and a member of the community of writers at Squaw Valley.

Lee Martin is the Pulitzer Prize Finalist author of The Bright Forever and other works of fiction and nonfiction. His stories and essays have appeared in Harper's, Ms., Creative Nonfiction, The Georgia Review, The Kenyon Review, and elsewhere. He is the winner of the Mary McCarthy Prize in Short Fiction and fellowships from the National Endowment for the Arts and the Ohio Arts Council. He teaches in the MFA Program at The Ohio State University, where he was the winner of the 2006 Alumni Award for Distinguished Teaching.

Karen McIntyre lives in New York City with her husband and daughter.

Carol Louise Munn lives in Houston where she teaches English at Awty International School and Creative Writing at the Women's Institute of Houston. Her poems have appeared in *Poetry, The GSU Review, So to Speak, Ilya's Honey, Fugue, WomenArts Quarterly Journal, Poetry Quarterly, Ampersand Review, StringPoet Journal, 10X3 plus,* and *The Midwest Quarterly Review.* Her poems have been anthologized in *Stories from Where We Live: The Gulf Coast,* Houston Poetry Fest Anthologies, and in *Bird in the Hand: Risk and Flight.*

Barry W. North's work has appeared or is forthcoming in *The Paterson Literary Review, Slipstream, The Dos Passos Review, Hawaii Pacific Review, Green Hills Literary Lantern, Amoskeag,* and others. His published chapbooks are *Along the Highway, Terminally Human,* and *In the Maze.* He is a recipient of the 2010 A. E. Coppard Prize for Fiction.

Jason Pollard is an undergraduate student at the University of North Texas. He has had multiple screenplays produced by the North Texas Television network.

Karen Recht holds a degree in English from Stanford University. She was a contributor at Bread Loaf and a resident at Vermont Studio Center.

Seth Sawyers's writing has appeared in *The Rumpus, The Millions, Salon, Sports Illustrated, The Morning News,* and elsewhere. He teaches writing at the University of Maryland Baltimore County and serves as an editor at *The Baltimore Review.*

Anneliese Schultz has an MFA in Creative Writing from the University of British Columbia. Winner of the 2013 ALSCW Meringoff Fiction Award and the Enizagam Literary Award in Fiction, she has been published in *Enizagam, The Toronto Star,* and *Literary Imagination,* among others. The first title in her YA climate fiction series, *Distant Dream,* reached the second round in the 2012 Amazon Breakthrough YA Novel Awards and won the 2013 Good Read Novel Competition at *A Woman's Write.*

A graduate of the University of Southern Maine's Stonecoast MFA Poetry Program, David Sloan teaches in Maine's only Waldorf high school. He is the author of two books on teaching. His debut poetry collection *The Irresistible In-Between* was published by Deerbrook Editions in 2013. His poetry has appeared in *The Broome Review, The Café Review, Innisfree, The Naugatuck River Review, New Millenium Writings, Poetry Quarterly,* and *Passager,* among others.

Colby Cedar Smith holds degrees from Colorado College and Harvard University. She is the author of two chapbooks: *Seven Seeds of the Pomegranate* (The Penny Press, 2006) and *Transplanted* (Bokbinderigatan Press, 2013). Her poems have appeared in *Bellevue Literary Review, Harper Palate, Memorious, Potomac Review, Saranac Review,* and *The Iowa Review.* She critiques poetry and fiction for *ForeWord Reviews* and teaches creative writing in Princeton, NJ.

Sheila Thorne's work has appeared in *Nimrod, Stand Magazine, Literal Latte, Green Hills Literary Lantern, Louisiana Literature, Prick of the Spindle, Clockhouse Review, Saranac Re-*

view, and elsewhere. Her stories are also included in the anthologies *Texas Told'em* and *Prairie Gold*.

Elizabeth Harmon Threatt is a lecturer of English Composition, literature, and creative writing at the University of West Alabama, where she also serves as faculty editor of *The Sucarnochee Review*. She holds a PhD from the University of Cincinnati, as well as certificates in Women's, Gender, and Sexuality Studies and Deaf Studies. Her poems have appeared in *Mississippi Review*, *Cold Mountain Review*, *Big Muddy*, *Poet Lore*, *Reunion*, *Rattle*, and others.

Alexander Weinstein is the Director of The Martha's Vineyard Institute of Creative Writing (www.mvicw.com). He is the author of the forthcoming collection *Children of the New World* (Picador 2016) and his short stories and translations have appeared in *Cream City Review*, *Pleiades*, *PRISM International*, *Sou'Wester*, *World Literature Today*, and other journals. He is the recipient of a Sustainable Arts Award, along with the Gail Crump Prize in fiction. "The Cartographers" first appeared in *Chattahoochee Review*, where it received the Lamar York Prize for fiction.

Jennifer Zobair's debut novel, *Painted Hands*, was published by St. Martin's Press in June, 2013. Her essays have appeared in *The Rumpus*, *The Huffington Post*, and elsewhere.

28126317R00224

Made in the USA
Middletown, DE
03 January 2016